SOMEONE LIKE YOU

OTHER BOOKS BY XAVIER BOSCH

What the Light Touches

SOMEONE LIKE YOU

a novel

XAVIER BOSCH

TRANSLATED BY SAMANTHA MATEO

AMAZON CROSSING

This is a work of fiction. Names, characters, organizations, places, events, and incidents are either products of the author's imagination or are used fictitiously. Any resemblance to actual persons, living or dead, or actual events is purely coincidental.

Previously published as *Algú com tu* by Planeta in Spain in 2015. Translated from Catalan by Samantha Mateo. First published in English by Amazon Crossing in 2026.

Published by Amazon Crossing, Seattle

www.apub.com

EU product safety contact:
Amazon Media EU S. à r.l.
38, avenue John F. Kennedy, L-1855 Luxembourg
amazonpublishing-gpsr@amazon.com

ISBN-13: 9781662537721 (paperback)
ISBN-13: 9781662537714 (digital)

Cover design by Eileen Carey
Cover image: © Cristian Todea / ArcAngel Images; © Dennis Hallinan / Getty Images

Printed in the United States of America

To my parents, Jordi and Maria Rosa. Even if they don't read it, I owed them one.

Love is born from memory, lives on intelligence, and dies in oblivion. —Ramon Llull

"Tell me about my mother!" —Don José to Micaëla (*Carmen*, Bizet, Act 1)

Contents

I ask only one thing: Don't turn our story into a novel. It has to be for the two of us. —Paulina

1

A Mysterious Person

I'll never forget the first time I noticed you.

"I'll bet you anything that she won't come to class tomorrow," he murmured.

"What do you know?" I responded in an even lower voice.

Maybe I wouldn't have seen you, watched you leave before it was time to, if Axel hadn't come up with that bet.

"From the way they're leading her away, Gina isn't coming back." We watched through the window, and seeing how you held hands with that man with the serene walk, he added, "Not at least until Monday."

"You two, in the back . . . Do me a favor and quiet down."

The school librarian wasn't in the mood for excuses. He was the philosophy teacher for the older kids, and even though he had to warn us over and over again, we were lucky that he still hadn't learned our names. In fact, the nine-year-old kids only had permission to enter the literary paradise one day out of the week, Wednesdays after lunch. Some wise pedagogue had thought that, if we viewed it as a forbidden place, we'd be even more excited to go hold the books and poke through all those volumes and series of fantasies until we found a story that captivated us, the capital *B* book—everyone had their own—that awakened us to the pleasure of reading. But for Axel and me, the library had become the perfect place to mess around. No doubt that at the back of the library, from floor to ceiling, from one end to the other, there were shelves and shelves of books, organized, lined up with the spines facing out, and classified by Ayuso's rules, which must have been precise, but we preferred sitting right on the other side, next to the bay window. We would place an open book, any would do, on the table, and we'd spend an hour whispering and watching the courtyard with the three pine trees while Ayuso, sitting at the head table and helped by small glasses that rested upon the tip of his nose, archived his collection of ancient Barcelona postcards.

Axel and I had discovered that the library window was the most strategic position to watch over the whole school. The view spanned the whole length, from the door that led to the gym and lockers for boys and girls to the school's main inner door, which, if you stretched your neck, let you see a slice of Bellesguard Street, a cul-de-sac where the teachers and early bird professors could park their cars diagonally. On the other side of the enormous library window was the art classroom and, next to some bougainvillea that were having trouble sprouting, was the secretary's office, which by chance of a scrape or a headache, also became an infirmary, a refuge, or a place of consolation.

On Wednesdays, from three to four, the three pine trees experienced a moment of rest. They no longer functioned as goalposts or as a place to tie a jump rope. Practically no one walked through the courtyard once the students were all in class. After washing the plates and pans, the lunch ladies left, trudging wearily. The lunchroom monitors, more desperate to enjoy the evening and life itself, climbed up on their bikes and shot straight down Bellesguard. Sometimes, on some Wednesdays from three to four, while students in the C third-grade class were in the library, we'd see some parents arrive to discover directly from their teacher whether their child was guilty. That swampy Wednesday, a day in May that made our uniforms more annoying than usual, at the hour when the wind and calm passed through the courtyard, we watched a mysterious person arrive.

A taxi braked in the very front of the entrance of the school, and immediately, a man who looked to be our fathers' age but didn't look like any of the fathers at the school stepped out. He was wearing a tie. A dark suit and a tie. Those types of guys who wore ties rarely entered our school.

"Look, Biel."

Axel pointed him out to me, but I wasn't sure what I was supposed to look at.

"The taxi isn't leaving."

How I loved the yellow-and-black taxis of Barcelona, an eyesore of a color combination that gave them a lot of personality for a car. You look at a taxi like that and you think . . . surely even in Buenos Aires the taxis are yellow and black.

The man with the tie had a black tuft of bristling hair; he climbed up the stairs from the street to the library without too much work. The school principal walked out from the secretary's door to receive him with a grave expression. Axel pointed out that it couldn't be just any prearranged visit. The head honcho, Mrs. Ramos, only appeared, reluctantly, on serious occasions. They shook hands, entered the office, and for a few minutes we lost sight of the action. It must have been short, because the head honcho came out alone, and with a stiff walk and a tense posture—whether from a pinched disc or from putting on airs like a stubborn ballerina—she limped to the art classroom. While those of us in the C third-grade class had to go to the library every Wednesday after recess, the B third-grade class had drawing or art class. That week we had to copy Joan Miró's farmhouse in Mont-roig that Mr. Torío had hung up on the board. No small feat: copying a Miró in an hour. And with paints that were so dry that by the time we had softened them by mixing them with water, we had to turn in the illustration to Mr. Torío.

He was a cool guy, Mr. Torío. Maybe it comes with the territory of being an art teacher. That Wednesday, however, when he walked out of the classroom with the head honcho, he also looked serious. And they went back in, and soon Axel, who was better positioned, said: "Look, Biel, look. They're leaving with Gina."

And Mr. Torío stood there, with the design classroom door open, and you and the principal walked toward the secretary, and I thought that was weird.

"What do you think she did?" I asked Axel.

You still hadn't reached the secretary's office when the mysterious man and your teacher, whose name I can't remember, came out, and she slipped your backpack onto your shoulders, and maternally, if I'm allowed to say so, she gave you two kisses. And the head honcho, who had never given anyone two kisses, limited herself to touching your tiny face, in a rather cold way. And the man firmly took your hand, and slowly led you toward the street. As you passed by the art classroom, Mr. Torío waved goodbye with a paintbrush, and from what I could tell from afar while craning my neck, smiled at you.

"Do you think she's been expelled?"

"Gina?"

"I mean, why else would they take her?"

"That man isn't her dad . . ."

"Then who is he?"

"Her dad has a mustache, and I've never seen that man before."

And from that moment onward, while Ayuso was distracted by some delinquent returning Italo Calvino's *The Baron in the Trees* late, Axel and I speculated over why you might have been expelled.

"She stole money," one of us asserted.

"Money from where?"

"From the class," we speculated, for example.

"Or she entered the boys' locker room," and we started to want to laugh.

"Yeah, she entered and got naked and showed all the boys in B third grade her vagina."

Ayuso, from the doorway, yelled at us. We pretended to read as if nothing had happened, and in super low voices, we continued to weigh different options. In that moment, you and the taciturn man who had come to take you left the school and got into the taxi. The driver, waiting with the counter running, had taken advantage of the moment to make a U-turn to come out of the alley and head down Bellesguard again.

"Maybe her parents died . . ."

"You must mean her grandparents. How could her parents have died?"

In that exact moment, on a hot day in May, around four in the afternoon, in front of the window of the library, with a view of the courtyard from the three pines of a school with the name of some saint, and with Ayuso turning into a phantasmagoric character who didn't stop grumbling in the background, my world came tumbling down. I realized that moms and dads could also die. No one had told me that before. I had never thought about it. And suddenly, everything I had thought was true blurred. A new threat had appeared in my life. A new one, unknown and deep.

"Are you sure, Axel, that if we're kids, our parents can die?"

He told me how it had happened to his cousin. And he confirmed that it wasn't true that parents only died when they were old. Not strictly, anyway. I was hesitant to believe it, and when my parents picked me up, as soon as I got into the R5 and asked my mom if it was true that . . . I pushed the thought out of my head, hoping that it was one of Axel's jokes. And I don't remember the exact response, but I learned that anyone could kick the bucket at any age and at any moment. Like the three goldfish that we had at home who kept dying, may they rest in peace, in the fishbowl, without our knowing the cause. Do you know what a debacle that was for me for several months? That's why I told you I'd never forget the first time I noticed you. Until then, I knew who you were, of course. Gina, the girl in the same grade but in another class, who was maybe the best when it came time to do somersaults in gym but whose last name I didn't know.

The next day, in school, our teacher, Núria, in C third grade told us about it. Standing up in front of the blackboard, she told us that in what was left of the school year, we had to help Georgina Castro, if we saw she was sad, because her mother had died. Never had a classroom of boys and girls listened to Miss Núria so attentively. Never, in her thirteen years of teaching, had Núria seen little faces so receptive to the story she was telling. Around me, I saw more than one pale face of someone who, like me, had just learned of a fate never before contemplated. And someone even sobbed. It must have been one of your friends. And we felt so bad for you. Axel, who might have been on the verge of signing up for journalism school, asked Miss Núria if your mother had died suddenly or if she had already been sick.

"It was a stroke," Gina responded, who, holding back her nostalgia, had listened to Biel's cathartic monologue.

"They didn't explain it to us quite like that. They told us that she had felt sick and had died suddenly. Since then, every time my parents felt sick, or they looked a little sickly, I never told anyone, but I suffered silently and hoped that a doctor would come to the house to check on them. And listened to see if they were breathing normally. And if . . ."

"Biel, can I tell you something?" Gina had started getting cold.

"Of course . . ." Biel, at her side, with his eyes glued to some spot on the ceiling, caressed the hair on her arms. "I would only hope . . ."

"You discovered the dangers of life. And I'm so sorry. Your innocence snatched away. But I was the one who suffered. My mother died. At thirty-one. From one day to the next, it was goodbye forever."

"Hey, I . . ."

"She takes you to school in the morning, and your uncle comes to pick you up in the afternoon and takes you to his house in a taxi, and while he gives you a glass of milk for your evening snack, he tells you why."

"Come on, Gina . . . I didn't mean to . . . I said all of that because Axel would have won the bet. He could've saved his neck . . . If that happened on a Wednesday, it's true you didn't come back until Monday."

"I don't remember. I don't remember anything about those days. It's like it never happened. In fact, you know what the worst part is? That I don't remember my mother. Not her voice, her scent, nothing at all. How can that be when I was nine years old? If it were my choice"—she smiled to make Biel feel better—"I would have preferred to have shown all the boys in third grade my vagina."

2

A Lover in Your Arms

There was only one person who hadn't put on the 3D glasses. In the whole audience, out of those two hundred people (or maybe more) who watched the screen pop out of the frame, there was only one boy who wore his own glasses and must have watched the whole movie in a strange blur without seeing very well. It was a photograph of the cover of the magazine *Life*. "J. R. Eyerman, November 26, 1952." That was all the information contained in the caption. A black-and-white snapshot taken in the US during the premiere of the first 3D movie. Gina had the poster hanging in her room. It made her laugh to see all those people in their Sunday best, the women all dressed up, the men in ties, and everyone, aside from the boy, with the white paper-framed glasses covering their eyes. And all of them had pride on their faces, knowing they were participating in something new, an event that had never happened before in the centuries of human history. Those invited to the premiere didn't know, however, that because of a photo they weren't even aware was being taken, they'd be immortalized with that permanent grimace. Gina loved photos of crowds in which everyone was now dead. She needed there to be many people, many faces in different angles, and of course, in black and white. They could be soccer fans in the grandstands from the days gone by, soldiers in a Nazi parade, or citizens simply out on a grand walk of Las Ramblas in the era in which men used to wear flat caps. She looked at their faces, imagined their lives, and always thought the same thing: *They're all dead.* It was her way of alleviating the terrible and persistent feeling of impermanence that, whoever we might be, follows us all, no matter how much we try to hide it.

Gina, who never wore makeup, curled her eyelashes. Her hair pulled up, she stepped into a dress she had on the floor. She put her legs into the dress, and in one fell swoop, she slipped it over her body. She buttoned the three buttons at her waist; she looked at the mirror next to the poster; she opened her bedroom window to ventilate the room; she stretched out her patterned comforter; she grabbed her school folders and her Walkman headphones, and left quickly to get to the university. From the hallway, she could hear the snores.

"I'm leaving." Her father, completely immobile, hadn't heard her. Not even the end theme of the news channel stirred him. She approached him and spoke a little louder. "I said I'm leaving."

Like a log. His daily evening nap in the armchair, the one she'd always seen in the dining room of the house. She realized that in the photos of her grandparents' apartment, that armchair always appeared. At its worst, in order to survive the passing of time, they had refilled the cushions and reupholstered it with a darker, more durable velvet so that it looked new. She shook him by his shoulder to wake him up.

"It's like you're seventy years old."

"What?"

"You keep passing out in front of the TV."

"I'm exhausted," he responded, hardly opening his mouth and his eyes.

"I'm leaving. I'll see you tomorrow."

"Where are you going?"

"To class, Dad." *Where else would I be going?* she thought.

"'I'll see you tomorrow'?"

Gina had no intention of explaining further, and pretending she hadn't heard, she walked toward the hallway, motorcycle helmet in hand and Gloria Gaynor's music blasting in her ears, due to the small, cushioned round headphones.

"I asked you where you were going." Her father was waking up and starting to act like himself.

"To class."

"You said 'See you tomorrow.'"

"Aren't you going to Bilbao?"

"So? I wanna know where you're going when I'm not home."

"We'll see where I end up after class." It wasn't the first time Gina asserted the right to keep secrets.

"May I know what your plans are?"

"First of all, I'm not sure, Dad. I'm not sure where I'll go, who I'll see, and when I'll come back once class lets out. Second of all, I'm eighteen years old, and I do whatever I want."

"The hell you do." She had managed to fully wake him up. "As if you were twenty-eight. While you live under my roof, you tell me where you're going and what you're doing."

"And what about you?"

"What about me?"

"You won't explain anything to me? We're two strangers living here, it feels . . ."

"What's next?"

"Who are you going to Bilbao with?"

Her father, the shape of his butt imprinted on the armchair, couldn't muster the energy to tell her he was going alone, that he was just taking the last flight of the day between Barcelona and Bilbao, and that in the morning he'd be meeting with a lawyer for a company that made rods for windshield wipers in Galdakao, and that he couldn't stand landing in the Sondika airport because there was always a gust of wind that shook the wings back and forth so it seemed like they would touch the ground before the wheels even could. He had accumulated a lot of bad memories at that exact airport. Let's be honest, Manuel Castro did not like planes, and he only took them when he had no other choice. And when he couldn't avoid it, he spent the whole flight with a knot in his throat, silently murmuring one Our Father after the other, his lips never moving, until the seat belt light was turned off. Instead of mentioning any of that—Manuel had spent years keeping things close to his chest—he looked Gina up and down.

"Will they let you into the university with a dead woman's clothes?"

"You always do that. You . . ."

She hated how her father said "a dead woman's clothes" with an emphasis on the *d* and a contempt that irked her. She couldn't stand it when he criticized the way she dressed and lived her life. And laughed. And thought and ate (in small, healthy portions). She grabbed the keys to the motorcycle that hung from the Tintin rocket on the front dresser; she opened the door, stepped out, and without saying a word, closed it less angrily than she would have liked.

Once she got back home at 8:45, there was no one home. Isabel had left at six after ironing and preparing dinner.

"Come in. You've never been over before?"

"When would I have come over?"

Biel guessed that, based on the kiss Gina had given him in the elevator, this evening might be one he'd never forget.

"I don't know. When we went to school together, did you come over to play at some point?"

"No."

"Or for some birthday party . . ."

"We were never really friends . . ."

"But we could have been. What do I know?"

"Is this your room?"

"Does it look like my dad's, dork?" Gina walked to the window. "It faces the back courtyard. A garage with asbestos isn't the prettiest of views."

"It's nice. It looks like a guy's room." He tried to clarify. "I mean it's not a girly color or too cheesy . . ."

"Right, right."

Biel's eyes fell directly on the poster on the wardrobe.

"That's a sick picture . . ."

"Only one person isn't wearing 3D glasses. Let's see if you can find him."

Biel positioned himself inches away from the poster. He decided to filter down each row. Never without a strategy. He fixed his eyes on the lower right-hand corner of the photo and raised his gaze, in a zigzag, row after row, person after person.

"Are you sure one of them isn't wearing glasses?"

"Are you giving up?"

"Never."

"Just a hint." Gina wrapped her arms around him and rested her chin on his shoulder. "It's a little boy."

Biel, pretending he hadn't heard, continued scrutinizing the audience from right to left and up and down.

"Found him. Here." He pointed. "It's a little boy."

"I told you. Do you think he's still alive?"

"Oh man . . ."

"Oh woman . . ."

"He must have been ten or twelve years old? Of course he might still be alive. He would be—how old? In his middle age?"

"And the rest?"

"If this is from 1952 . . . Do you know what they were watching?"

"I looked it up, yes." She thought hard. "*Bwana Devil,* the first 3D movie."

During her first year of college, Gina had distracted herself by learning about the poster hanging in her room, on the door of her winter clothing wardrobe. There'd been a screenwriter for Metro-Goldwyn-Mayer, Milton Gunzburg, who had an ophthalmologist brother. Between the two of them, Milton and Julian had invented a type of cinema called "Natural Vision." No one paid any attention, not to them or to their invention. Not until a producer and radio personality, Arch Oboler, realized the enormous business opportunities offered by the kinds of projections where the audience felt like they were part of the story, falling off a cliff like the main characters or dodging as the murderers throw themselves into the crowd. It premiered on November 26, 1952, at the Paramount Theatre in Hollywood in Los Angeles, and J. R. Eyerman took a photo that was turned into the front cover of *Life*, a long time before Gina Homs hung it up in her bedroom. For her, as a first-year student of art history at the University of Barcelona, the best part of it all was finding the posters that announced the first 3D movie. The slogan cried "A *lion* in your lap! A *lover* in your arms!"

"A lover in your arms." Gina hugged Biel.

"I really like your room," he responded, just inches away from her.

"What I like most is the bed." Gina let go of him and jumped onto the mattress with a leap revealing it wasn't her first time. It was so gentle that the wool blanket warmly received her without letting her bounce back. "Come here."

Gina unbuttoned her dress and let it slide down onto the room's rug. *A dead woman's clothes,* she thought, *to hell with that.* She let Biel take care of her bra and panties, which didn't even pretend to match. With the delight of a child who gets to play outside, the boy took pains to do so. He knew not much was expected from him, but that if his guitarist's fingers were used to their utmost talents, with a finger inside her and the other on her nipple, he could make Gina climax before he finished performing the Concierto de Aranjuez. He knew by the first arpeggios that he had been able to surprise Gina, that she was living the experience in 3D with her eyes closed. Fifty gasps later, and with a cushion pressed to her face so that the neighbors wouldn't hear her scream, she let herself go.

Once finished, he, having undressed on his own, quickly climbed on top of her. He was also quick in his thrusts. And finally, too quick so he could catch up with her. As if it were written in the handbook on misunderstandings that sex was a game that always ended without winners or losers.

He had just pulled away, his breathing still ragged, when Biel asked a question. One he shouldn't have.

"How was it?"

Even as a young woman, Gina couldn't stand the damn obsession men had, at all ages, to be graded at every hookup. Like everything could be boiled down to a statistic. Like every man thought they deserved an outstanding score or higher. To avoid grading him, to avoid turning the night into a forum of sexual debate that she didn't like, she changed the subject.

"Who would have thought that I'd hook up with the ugliest guy in class?"

"Oh man . . ."

"Oh woman . . ."

"But I got better, right?"

"Don't get your hopes up. We're not getting married."

They laughed. Biel finished drying himself off with the hand towel that Gina had passed him at the exact moment so he wouldn't stain the sheets. He threw it on the floor next to his shoes. He took a deep breath and lay on his back, staring up at the ceiling. He gently caressed the hair on Gina's forearm. For a couple of minutes, as they recovered their breath, they were silent. Relaxed and empty, the boy with the crooked nose and thick oversized eyebrows became chatty.

"I'll never forget the first time I noticed you."

Biel was thankful and euphoric, because he had conquered an old schoolmate he never thought he would. He whispered everything like sleepaway camp friends, who make confessions in the dark between bunk beds.

He told her about the bet he made with Alex in the library, some Wednesday in the afternoon when they realized that a man they had never seen before was coming to the school through the courtyard with three pines. The man spoke to one person after another with a grave expression until they brought out Gina Castro from the arts classroom. Gina, who at that time still went by Georgina Castro, left her Miró painting halfway done, and the cool guy Torío was waving goodbye with the brush in his hand, while the school principal watched tensely from the secretary's door. The mysterious man and their third-grade classmate wearing her backpack got into the taxi and entered into civilization.

Gina listened to the story, like it was alien to her, like it hadn't been the most impactful day of her life. She didn't understand how, being one of the most grave hours, she didn't remember anything, and how everything Biel revealed, she seemed, at most, to have lived in a foggy and brief dream. She also had never thought about how her classmates had found out about the death of her mother. She hadn't ever thought, not even for an instant, about what they said about her in the moment she became the center of attention without knowing it. Or what her classmates thought about her when they saw her in the courtyard, in the lunchroom, or in class as an orphan girl left without a mother at nine years old, just like that, in a flash, without warning. She didn't understand what strange oxytocin had made her forget that whole afternoon at school, like none of it had ever happened.

"Actually, do you know what the worst part is? I'm eighteen, and I don't remember my mother. Not her voice or smell or anything at all. What can you expect of a nine-year-old? If it was my choice, I'd have rather shown my vagina to all the boys in the third grade."

They laughed again. In the silence, Biel picked up on a sharp noise. Like a closing door.

"What's that?"

"Nothing. Just the elevator."

"It's not in here?"

"Chill out, my dad's on a trip."

"I hear it in here."

"It must be the neighbors." Gina wasn't worried. "They have six kids."

But suddenly she recognized the jingle of her dad's keys. Everyone, due to routine, slides their key into the lock in a unique way.

"Shit, it's my dad."

And that exact sound, she had heard many times every day for so long.

"Gina, what the hell are you saying?"

"Get under the bed."

Biel jumped over Gina, and in the same leap ducked under the mattress. He had traced a perfect parabola in the air, just like the one of his nose. She gathered all his clothes, and like a winning bowling strike, she threw them behind the bed.

"Hello, honey," her dad called out from the entrance before closing the door.

"My shoes, my shoes," Biel whispered.

"What happened to Bilbao?" Gina called out as she quickly pulled on her pajamas.

"My shoes," Biel repeated nervously, so low that Gina didn't hear him.

"Storm at the airport." Her dad's thundering voice sounded closer and closer each moment. "They didn't let us take off."

"Just a second, Dad, I'm changing."

"They said there was a downpour up north, for Christ's ache. I mean, for Christ's sake . . ."

Based on the footsteps, Biel could hear that he was already there.

"Don't come in," said Gina, putting her hands to her head.

"You know I can't stand locked doors."

And then Manuel Castro, widowed in his first marriage, to Paulina Homs, opened the door.

3

It Was Not a Good Day

It was not a good day, was what Isabel had said. Gina's grandmother had shown up at her house with a sense of urgency and without even a hello. She barged into her granddaughter's room to confirm. Her son had told her the news, and she could hardly believe it. She couldn't swallow that Gina, after an argument with her father—the motive of which Manuel had failed to mention—had cleared out her room. Gina had only left behind her childhood stuffies, a box full of school notebooks, a Rubik's Cube with the green side entirely solved, and the poster of the men and women wearing 3D glasses in Los Angeles. Her grandmother did not like that end-of-the-world poster. Grumpily holding on to a cane that walked faster than she did, she went back into the kitchen and asked Isabel in every way possible if she knew why her granddaughter had left the house, if she knew why she had moved into that student apartment, if she knew where that run-down apartment was, if she knew who the hell she lived with, if they were boys and girls, how many of them there were cooped up in that cave, if she had her own room, and more than anything, she asked if Gina planned to go to her house, Grandma Lourdes's house, at some point. She was her only grandmother.

Isabel had all the answers, but didn't say anything. Without looking up from the marble kitchen counter, she limited herself to saying "It wasn't a good day."

"How long have you worked here? It must be around twenty . . ." Grandma Lourdes wasn't giving up.

"Not yet. I started a little after the mister and madam got married."

"You've been like a mother to Gina since Paulina's death. You know it all . . ." She thumped the cap of her elegant cane on the floor. "Tell me what happened."

Isabel, who had learned through trial and error that the best way to handle conflict in that family was to act as if she were deaf, of course loved Gina. She had watched her grow into a woman and encounter the fears and emotions of everyday life. But she didn't think that washing Gina's underwear or cleaning her hair out of the drain or wiping down her toilet or making her bed or putting together her countless salads, no onions, every week was enough to make her her mother. It was honest work. Well paid, depending on how you looked at it. And it was true that she knew all of Gina's secrets. She had turned into her confidante and life adviser. But it was a job like any other, and she didn't want to be burned by that fight between father and daughter. Even though Isabel, with her black mane and wrinkled nose, looked like she had been carved out of stone, she worried that, now that he was alone, Mr. Castro could finally do away with her services or decide that he didn't need a cleaning lady the whole workday every day of the week, every week of the year. Maybe he could get by with less. Or he wouldn't need her to come by for as many hours, with all that would signify for payment at the end of the month. And Isabel, in her lair in Masquefa, had a good-for-nothing husband on the couch and two sons who could eat enough for four people. A couple of bums who she was actually the mother of.

"It wasn't a good day."

"For Christ's ache, Isabel."

"You know how your son gets when he's mad." She didn't know if she should continue, without stopping from julienning celery, but she added, "And your granddaughter is just like you, ma'am. The Bonjoc pride."

"Gina isn't a Bonjoc."

But it's the damned inheritance you've left her in this life, she thought. Prideful and temperamental, just like her. *Cut from the same cloth,* but she didn't say that part out loud. Isabel knew how everything had gone down. At the very least she knew Gina's version, mad at her father like she'd never seen her before.

Manuel had dragged Biel out from under the bed. He'd thrown his clothes at him and warned him to get the hell out and never even try to see Gina again.

"Do you understand me?"

"Yes, sir."

"And you, Gina, do you understand me?"

Out of breath and enraged, Gina had managed to put on her underwear and bra and threw the Rubik's Cube at her father's belly. "I told you not to come in." She locked herself in the bathroom and cried silently. She didn't want her father, now in a rage like she'd never seen before, to hear her from the other side of the door.

"We'll talk about it tomorrow. I can't stand to even look at you right now."

Counsel Castro knew that the case would never get solved in the heat of the moment.

Biel had never gotten dressed so quickly, almost like there had been a fire. He passed by Gina's father, and in a thin voice, he dared say:

"We are adults."

"So why were you hiding under the bed?"

"It's definitely crazy, but . . ."

He shrugged his shoulders without stopping moving.

"Get out!"

The yell was just as sharp as the door slamming behind Biel, who disappeared from Gina's life for twenty years.

The next day was not a good day.

Isabel, who worked from eight to six with an hour to eat and catch up on her soap opera, had made them breakfast: two grapefruit juices, hand squeezed and strained; a latte; a slice of toast with peach jam for Mr. Manuel and a measly cheese roll for Gina. Just like every morning, she had set the kitchen table for them with the colorful tablecloth Paulina had bought in Bergen the last time she was in Norway. Isabel had washed and ironed it so many times that those blue and red drawings and Christmas-like trees had started to look rather faded. But that was the only tablecloth Manuel and Gina wanted. They wouldn't accept anything else for breakfast.

Manuel, showered and sprayed with 1916 cologne, was the first to sit down at the table. He didn't open the newspaper, not even to look at the front page. He didn't even take off his blazer and hang it on the back of his seat like he did every morning, not even caring if it wrinkled. He wasn't vain. He had three dark suits, two blue blazers, and without paying too close attention, combined the outfits with his sizable collection of wide ties. He didn't care if the skinnier ones were in style. He, who always bragged that he had never ever stopped in front of a storefront window, always marched to the beat of his own drum. That morning Isabel noticed he seemed downcast. Mr. Manuel had only said "Stop" and "Thank you" to let her know his exact measure of milk in his coffee.

Gina, scrawny and bony like her mother, as everyone made sure to tell her, didn't waste time in coming into the kitchen. Her hair was still wet, worn loosely. Sometimes, a drop of water would trickle down and die on her blouse. She felt confident in that shirt. It was new, beige, with yellowish buttons, deliberately frayed at the very tip.

"Good morning," she said politely.

"Good morning," he said without much vigor.

They didn't look at each other. Isabel left them alone. She knew that it was the meal that father and daughter shared. That's what Mr. Manuel had wanted since Isabel had started working in the house.

"Do you want to say anything about yesterday?"

"Nope."

"You don't think we should talk?"

"What do you want me to say?" She sighed so her father could see that she wasn't in the mood for the conversation, that she would rather act as if nothing had happened. "Pathetic."

"What is?"

Only silence.

"Tell me. Talk to me calmly. What's pathetic?"

"No. You talk first."

"Fine." Her father finished the grapefruit juice in two gulps. "I don't want this house to turn into a brothel every time I leave on a trip."

"Are you calling me . . . a whore?"

"I didn't say that."

"You called me a whore. You're starting off strong."

She backed up her chair in one strong push as if she were about to get up.

"I said, and don't try to twist my words, that I don't want my house to turn into a love shack. And I want you to be careful who you hang out with. You can't just bring any guy you meet on the street home."

"Biel is not just any guy. He's my friend from school."

"I don't care who he is." Manuel, who hadn't been able to sleep, thinking about how the conversation might go, spoke without raising his voice. "In all these years, I've never brought anyone home."

"Just what we'd need."

"Out of respect for you."

"Of course."

"And out of respect for your mother."

"Ha, we really owe you for that one."

If the ceiling hadn't been in the way, Gina, in her offended state, would have been looking up at the heavens. "Mama, if only you knew that Papa hasn't brought a woman home in all this time. He only plays poker on Thursdays. Let's thank him."

"Don't be dramatic. Lower your voice."

Gina ignored him. Standing in the doorway, Isabel strained her ears. She knew it wasn't the first or even the second time Gina had brought a friend from school up to her room, or a friend from university, or some foreigner she'd met at a museum. And if it could happen at a museum, who's to say who she met at the bar or at a party? Isabel found this out via the traces left on the sheets. And the hand towel Gina would give them to dry themselves off. After, she'd throw it into her dirty laundry basket.

"Don't you see, Mother dearest, you married a saint, and you're missing out. It's a shame . . ."

"You're being unfair."

Gina ended her comic act and looked away from the ceiling. She decided to glare into her father's eyes.

"That's it. The counsel has spoken. What a great lawyer, who forbids me from seeing my friends."

"Enough, Gina." With a single boom, Manuel managed to silence her. A couple of seconds later, he restarted the conversation calmly. "Listen up, girl, because I'm talking to you seriously."

Her father lit a cigarette and breathed in deeply.

"Bring me the ashtray."

Gina stood up from her chair and reached out behind, toward the drying rack next to the sink. The ashtray, turned upside down, was still damp. Manuel Castro, his breath still hot from his latte, picked up the thread of the conversation.

"I'm just telling you to be careful, know your worth, and realize that in this house there are rules I want you to abide by. This isn't the first time I'm telling you this."

"No, it's not the first time. That's true. But maybe it's the last time."

Precisely because of the seriousness of what she was about to say, Gina knew it wasn't worth working herself up.

"Look, Dad, don't take it the wrong way . . . I recognize you've been the best father you could be. I'm sure it's not easy to become a widower when you have a nine-year-old daughter who you've never bathed or ever dressed nor ever been home when she goes to sleep because you work late."

"What's that have to do with anything now?"

"I'm not calling you out. I'm seriously not . . ."

"Well, it seems like it."

"I'm really not." Gina put her hand on her father's arm, and he didn't dare pull it away. "Quite the opposite. Let me finish. I wanted to say how hard it must have been for me to suddenly become the center of your universe for the next decade. Always watching out for me, you've taken care of me, you've spoiled me, you've worried about me, you've done my homework, you helped me with my integrals and derivatives, you've taken me everywhere: the movies, the circus, Tivoli Gardens in Copenhagen, and Tibidabo Amusement Park. You've taught me manners, you've scolded me when I've acted out, you've given me all kinds of gifts. We spent Three Kings Day here, Santa Claus, and hit the Caga Tió at Christmas. I've never wanted for more. You sent me to Canterbury to learn English for two straight summers with my friends from school. You've told me about my mother, how she was. You've shown me pictures of all the travel she loved to do . You found me the best dermatologist when my face was filled with craters. You let me study the degree I wanted, and you've paid for it all. I recognize all of that. Hats off to you, Dad. It's honorable. I thank you, and I will of course thank you my whole life. And man, it's so hard for me to say it, I love you, Dad. You're the most important person in my life. I love you, you know that?"

Manuel braced himself. Isabel, with the vacuum in hand, not on so as not to disturb anyone, was on the verge of tears.

"But I can't take it anymore, Dad. Just as much as I mean all that, I mean this."

"What can't you do anymore?"

"All the control. You're always hovering over me. You're always watching who I hang out with or stop hanging out with, and for example . . . Every day, every single day, without fail, you comment on how I dress. That's just an example."

"It's a dead woman's clothes. Sorry to say it."

"It's secondhand. I buy them at a shop on Carrer Avinyó, and they don't belong to a dead woman. It's secondhand. Clothes previously worn by someone else, I don't care who. I like it, and I can spend my money how I like. I'm buying it. So what? Don't you see how you're . . ."

"What? Say it."

Only silence.

"Unbearable."

"Nosy. Prying and prying every day. And I don't get it, Dad. I can't handle it anymore."

"Handle what?"

"You. All the control. I'm sorry, dammit. You raised me to be an independent woman. You've taught me to see my self-worth, to be brave. You've made absolute sure of that. But you've come up with all these rules, like you're mad that I turned eighteen."

"We aren't talking about that."

"Yes, we are talking about that. I want a dad, a normal dad, not a bodyguard."

"The fact is that there was a naked man underneath your bed."

"And so what? And not that long before that he was on top of my bed. And look, he was even on top of me." She didn't dare go into the details that her dad could only imagine. Nonetheless, out of her mouth came an even worse challenge.

"And if I feel like it, he'll be there again."

"Not in this house, Gina. And don't speak to me like that, please."

"See! Please. Please what? You say everything like that, without losing your composure and with your tie all straight. Without ever raising your . . . But you don't stop. You keep at it, hammering away, you don't shut up. Blah blah blah, and in the end, you can't anymore. I can't anymore. And I feel bad that Mama had to live with you."

"Stop while you're ahead, missy." He put out the cigarette grumpily.

Gina Homs, who for a couple more days still called herself Georgina Castro, gathered up her courage.

"Look, Dad, I've been thinking about it for some time, but last night I turned it over in my head and I realized that it's better if you and I see each other less. We'd be better off. We might love each other a lot, but it doesn't mean we have to be together so often."

"Goodbye."

"That's what I wanted to propose."

"You can get the hell out of here."

"Don't think you're kicking me out of the house . . ."

"I said 'goodbye.'"

"I'm the one who is leaving."

That damn Bonjoc pride, Isabel thought with her ears pricked. She decided to turn on the vacuum, and with that racket, the conversation ended. She never thought that the hallway carpet could have accumulated so much dust.

4

A Third-Floor Apartment Without an Elevator

Two hard-case suitcases. A Samsonite with small wheels, for a weekend trip. Three duffel bags stuffed with shoes. And a cardboard box with kitchen utensils and some olive oil and vinegar cruets, some oven mitts, and various odds and ends Isabel had prepared so that she wouldn't lack anything in her escape to the student apartment. When you're eighteen years old, the inventory of your life is still portable. No doubt, she was leaving behind a ton of things at her dad's house, Gina thought. If she needed them, she'd come back for them. Nothing was stopping her. Even in the most contentious moment, her father had never told her not to step foot in that house. In fact, his last words before that curt and sluggish goodbye were to tell her that she could come over whenever she wanted to. On one condition: that she was in a good mood. He didn't want any bad attitudes in his house.

As soon as Gina had all her belongings on the street, she noticed a confused-looking man approaching her slowly on the sidewalk. He walked with the gait of someone who was uncertain. He seemed to be carried by the wind. He was looking up as if he were searching for something hidden among the buildings at half mast, and was about to crash into the black suitcase with little wheels.

"Oh, sorry—"

The man, with a head of black hair that seemed to fall with its own weight, moved his hands like he wanted to say something but couldn't quite grasp the words. And he seemed frustrated, not knowing how to express himself in the language of the country. At first glance, Gina found him attractive. He looked rough around the edges, with sharp cheekbones, and a small round nose that didn't quite suit him. By the redness in his cheeks, she immediately guessed where he was from. She had seen many younger versions of him in pubs in Kent County. The man struggled to say something but couldn't find the words. No matter how hard he tried, it was useless. Finally, just as he was about to babble like an idiot, the British man with green eyes and an intriguing air asked the girl with boxes for forgiveness with his look.

"Do you speak English?"

"More or less?"

"I'm looking for . . ." He took a crumpled piece of paper out of his jacket, looked at it, and read it with some difficulty. "Polina Joms."

"Paulina Homs, maybe?"

"Miss Polina, yes."

The guy had done a good job to come to the Sants neighborhood. He was just a decade too late. Maybe he had taken a Spanish train. The Englishman returned his gaze to the piece of paper.

"Rambla de Catalunya, 127."

He looked at the number in the doorway to verify that he was right.

"Yes, the address is right. Are you delivering a package?"

"No, no. A package? Not me."

"Then . . ."

"I came looking for her."

At that moment on July 21 on a hot summer, just as the hourly radio announcements were reporting that the Catalan magical realist writer Pere Calders had died at eighty-one, Gina surprised herself. Maybe it was because she liked what she saw, maybe it because he found her at a chaotic moment, maybe it was because she was still mad at the most important man in her life, maybe it was because that morning had suddenly become a mystery, maybe it was because she still liked to gamble in life, maybe it was because she was ovulating and feeling strange—she looked the Englishman in front of her up and down, and she flashed him a smile she hoped seemed frank and said persuasively: "That's me. I'm Paulina Homs."

They shook hands.

"How do you do?"

"How do you do?"

"Mark. Mark Granger."

"Paulina Homs," she repeated to him even more slowly, looking at the piece of paper. "Paulina *Oms*, the 'h' is silent. *Oms*, just like that. And what do you need from my . . . what do you need from me?"

"Honestly, nothing."

"Nothing?"

"I don't really know. It was a sudden impulse. I didn't expect to find you like this, so quickly, and that you'd be so . . ."

"You came all the way from England, and you don't know what you want?"

"Well, I do work in London, and I live in the East End. But I'm Welsh. I can't say I'm English."

"Look, Mark, you found me in the middle of . . . I'm in a rush. What can I help you with?"

"Help?" The Welshman smiled crookedly. "I should be the one asking you that."

Gina, stepping into her mother's skin, had started a game that, scarcely a minute in, she wasn't sure where it would end. She also wasn't sure how she'd put a stop to it once the moment came to be honest with Mark Granger, who was missing a finger on his left hand, even though she hadn't gotten a good enough glimpse to see if it was his ring or index finger. *"If you're at the ball, might as well dance,"* she'd heard Grandma Lourdes say on more than one occasion, and she decided to go all in. What did she have to lose? And what the hell, carrying on a conversation in her mother's voice was a new and unlikely source of fun.

"Honestly, you can't really help me too much, but if you took a plane from London and came all the way to Rambla de Catalunya 127 to find me . . . As you can see, by the way, you caught me off guard, because I'm in the middle of a move."

"For a trip."

"Not exactly." She also didn't feel like telling him the whole story. *I don't let my dad control me, so why should I let an Englishman or Welshman or whatever the hell he is pry into my life?* "What are you laughing about now?"

"The thing is I didn't come by plane. I drove here."

"From London?"

"Yeah . . ."

"That's crazy. Without stopping?"

"I love driving, but I slept in one of those accommodations on the side of the highway, just past Lyon. A Novotel. When sleep takes hold . . ."

"Of course, of course . . ." Idioms change from language to language, but clichés are all the same.

"It hasn't even been thirty hours since I left home. Once upon a time my grandpa did fall asleep at the wheel. It's a good story. Grandpa Granger owned one of the first Fords in Wales after the war. And one day, many years ago before I was even born, he took a nap at the wheel, but unfortunately, tired as he was, his foot stayed on the accelerator without his realizing it. The car lurched directly forward a couple of meters, and just as he was about to crash into the barrier at a level crossing, he suddenly woke up and had enough of his wits about him to duck his head. And by some miracle, the car passed through just an instant, just a second, before a train passed."

"Lucky man, your grandpa."

"A miracle, I'm telling you. We're lucky folks, us Grangers. We always save ourselves by the skin of our teeth. But after that scare,

Grandpa never drove again. He never wanted to hear about that car again."

For Gina, with her boxes spread across the street, desperate to abandon a secure life and jump into a new adventure, and seeing that skies were turning gray, this story about Grandpa Granger meant nothing.

"So, I'm working on getting my license."

"You don't know how to drive?"

"How old do you think I am?"

"Don't know . . ."

"I'll be nineteen soon. What about you?"

He was forty, and he was missing his middle finger. He had a big hand and strong fingers. At least the ones he had left. His nails were too long for Gina's taste. On a man, long nails make him look old.

"And can I know why, Mark, now that I know about your grandfather, you came looking for me if we don't know each other at all?"

"I didn't come here deliberately. Or not exactly. I had fifteen days off. I rented a room in Salu—Salou," he corrected himself, "but since I was passing through Barcelona and since I haven't been able to reach you by telephone, I thought it might be fun to take a detour, find you, and meet you."

"Where did you call me?"

"Where did I . . . Did I screw it up?" Mark's four-fingered hand grasped from pocket to pocket, but he didn't find anything. "Here it is."

In the inside jacket pocket, he found the paper he had checked earlier for the address. He gave it to Paulina. It was actually her business card. It contained her name, the Catalunya 127 address, a phone number, and something written, that on her first glance, Gina had not been able to read.

"This is an old phone number. No wonder you couldn't . . . Where'd you get this from?"

"From a book about two or three years ago. I found it inside of a book. At first I didn't pay it any attention. I saw that *'Appelle-moi'* was written there, and I kept it for a long time, maybe more than a year.

One day I thought, 'Call, Mark, you have nothing to lose.' And I called. One day. Then another. But no one ever answered. It seemed like there wasn't even a ring tone. I made sure that the Barcelona area code was right, but nothing."

"Let's see. Oh man, it's been years since we changed our number, I have to say."

The more Gina looked at it, the less she understood. What was that business card, belonging to her mother, who had been dead for ten years, doing in the hands of that Welsh man with four fingers who had come to find her on the other end of Europe without really knowing anything about her? Because if he did, he wouldn't have mistaken Gina for Paulina. And she didn't understand that *"Appelle-moi."* That handwriting, written in blue ink, might have looked like Paulina Homs', but now that she thought about it, she had seen so few things written by her own mother that she couldn't verify whether it was or wasn't hers. The game had gotten complicated. She didn't know what to say or do.

"Look, Mark, I'm sorry if you've come up with a whole story, but that's not my handwriting. Someone, who even knows . . . Someone must have needed paper, maybe found my business card on the ground in London and used it to write that down . . ."

"Do you speak French?"

"No."

"Me neither. I went to a work friend, some guy from Calais, who does the north route. I asked him what was written here, and he said: 'Call me.'"

"Yes, yes. *'Appelle-moi.'* I saw that. But I surely couldn't have written that." She had just told the first truth in a while. "I don't get what my card was doing in the book."

"Have you ever been to London?" The question sounded like one from a beginner's English language textbook. *Have you ever been to London?*

"Yeah, yeah . . ." In that moment, she thought as both Paulina and Gina, if she had ever gone to London. "Yes, twice . . . I was sent to Canterbury for two summers to study English, and on the weekends, we'd go on trips to London. But . . ." Paulina returned the card to Mark's mutilated hand. "Where exactly did you say you found it?"

"In a book. You know farther up at Charing Cross? There's a huge bookstore, maybe you've been."

There was a silence.

"I went there. Between shifts sometimes I have some time to wander. I bought a book, and a couple of days later, while I was flipping through, all of a sudden it fell out . . ."

Mark Granger looked for clues that could explain his finding. As lonely as he was, he wanted that *"Appelle-moi"* to be a sign. He needed it to contain an element of mystery or sweetness or poetry that he had imagined for months. However, that Paulina, brazenly young, answered him in prose.

"Look, all that sounds strange to me. Did you say that you have a car nearby?"

"Yeah, about two corners from here."

"How does this sound, Mark? I propose that you help me carry all this stuff. Take me to my new apartment and we'll get a beer."

It took him ten minutes to come back to pick her up. His sense of direction was fine-tuned. Mark was Welsh, but his car was English, a brand and a drab color that only the British bought. They don't export them, because no one else likes them. *It's like their gravies,* Gina thought. But the trunk was plenty big, and aside from the minimal baggage that Mark had brought for his fifteen-day stay in a two-star hotel in Salou, Gina, now Paulina, was able to fit all her stuff. Just as she was about to sit in the passenger's seat, she bumped into the steering wheel.

"You'll have to let me borrow your car to practice, although driving on the right side is hard enough . . ."

"There's a trick to it. For my colleagues who are just starting out, us professionals say that changing sides is like fucking. The more you think about what you're doing, the worse you are."

"And without a finger is it more difficult?"

"Fucking?"

"Changing gears . . ."

"You noticed?" Mark held up his five fingers. The four he had.

"Does it hurt?"

"No. It starts to throb when it gets cold. But it doesn't stop me from doing my job. I'm a . . ." He said it without emphasis. Without humility or pride. "I'm a bus driver."

"A bus driver?"

"For the red ones in London, the double-deckers. I'm sure the first time you went to London you climbed to the upper deck and took a picture."

"Of course. And I'm sure it was yours."

"Why not? I've been driving for a while."

He took his four-fingered hand off the wheel, and held it in front of Paulina's face. "Do you want to know the story?"

"You fell asleep right as a train was about to pass?"

"No, no." He laughed. "It's not hereditary. If we ever see each other again one day, I'll tell you."

Paulina didn't respond. And neither did Gina. She had seen more romantic ways of trying to ask for a date. An amputated finger, what a strategy for getting a date. She decided not to respond and focused on giving directions, "the first turn on the right, straight down the avenue until you reach the plaza, and we'll be right there. It's a narrow street. I'm not sure you'll find parking right in front. This is called Sants."

"Is the Barça stadium nearby?"

"You're also a soccer fan? It's not far."

"*Pfft.* Mark Hughes is Welsh. A beast of a man."

"We're here. Stop, it's here. Let's unload, and if someone comes around, they can wait."

"But . . ."

In the blink of an eye, Mark went from acting as a chauffeur to the porter. He took the two heaviest suitcases from Paulina's hands, and he lugged them up to the third-floor apartment without an elevator.

"What do you have in here that's so heavy?"

"It's just a dead woman's clothes."

The staircase, with white, chipped paint, smelled like cat and humidity. The steps, uneven, made for uncertain footing. Or they caused you to slip or they were too tall or too narrow, but not a single one was identical. Time and use had turned them into traitors, the kind who fail you when you least expect it. No one was at the apartment. They had left the key for her under the mat. Once inside, there wasn't a surprise party or welcome balloons. Just cigarette butts. A blend of black and white cigarette filters that had filled all the ashtrays in the kitchen/living room/dining room for the last couple of weeks. The apartment was a hovel where she'd have to coexist and share—because that's what she had decided on a whim—with a guy and two girls from Reus who studied art history in Barcelona. Judging by the stench they left behind, they hardly aired out the apartment, and they smoked like chimneys.

"Mark, I promised you a beer, and you earned it."

Paulina left the six boxes at the entrance. Without turning off the light, she slammed the door shut and left the key back in the Reus students' hiding place. She let Mark walk ahead, she hit the stairwell switch with her butt, and distrusting each step, she descended down with the intention of interrogating the Welsh driver who, without even knowing it, was searching for her mother.

5

Women Usually Shave

Why? Why did you come? Why did you pick up a business card that fell out of a book and think it was a sign? Why did you keep it? Why did you think you'd find her in person if you'd been unable to track her, track me, down by phone? Why didn't you come until now? What made you think you'd find me? Did you think I'd be so young and fun? What was the bookstore it was in, do you remember? Why do you read? What kinds of books do you like? What's a bus driver doing reading and reading?

By his second beer, Mark had answered that he didn't know to almost all the questions. That he didn't know, or didn't remember, or that it was altogether a coincidence and that he actually thought that sometimes fate sent you messages that you had to catch on the fly. He responded that he had nothing to lose, that sometimes you had to spice things up to break up the monotony, and that he didn't imagine she'd be so young and so pretty. He imagined her to be more like a university professor with reading glasses hanging over her breasts, an older lady, so thin, so bony, more . . . But the thing he wouldn't let her get away with was the offensive question about why a London bus driver might read. Are we idiots? Or do you think only the preppies at Oxford read?

"I didn't mean it like that."

Gina apologized like someone who throws a stone and hides their hand and then pretends to be offended and misunderstood. And at the height of brazenness, makes others feel bad.

"Opening a book, I think, is like discovering new worlds, living other lives, giving meaning to our very own. Traveling forward and backward. Carving out stories. Laughing and crying. Newspapers are always the same. The days look too much the same. Nothing ever happens. And when something important happens, they don't even tell you. To me, reading books is maybe the only way to daydream a little bit. Every one has its own system and concerns. But, it's the best solution, at least to me, to escape boredom and escape the revolving door."

Aside from being handsome and downing beer like it was water, this character was shaping up to be interesting.

"Sorry, what revolving door are you talking about?"

"The one of daily life. Getting up. Going to work. Putting on your uniform. Watching the clock. Doing the same thing all day. Stopping and starting. Routine knocks you senseless. I find repetition makes you dumber. Tower Hill, Monument, Cannon Street, Fleet Street, Aldwych, Stand, Trafalgar Square. And then here we go all over again. Route 15. I can do it with my eyes closed. Do you know what it's like to do the same route eight times every day?"

"Formula 1 drivers go in circles, and they don't complain."

"They don't deal with traffic jams or stoplights. They don't have to brake and start. They don't have to pull out without checking that there's no one walking down the stairs. They don't have to answer questions from tourists who never know where they're going. Do you know how many bus stops there are in London?"

Paulina took a gulp of Estrella. She took it as an opportunity to haphazardly calculate some approximate statistic.

"A thousand?"

"Fifteen thousand. In the city of London alone. And there's more with the Routemasters, because the door is always open in the back, and they don't bother the drivers. But they're starting to change the vehicles.

Everything has to be more secure, more comfortable, newer, more environmentally friendly. They're getting rid of the payment machines on the street. They want us to oversee payment from people, so that no one sneaks on."

"Man, you need a vacation."

"How's Salu?"

"You mean Salou?" How can you be honest with someone who's already reserved a room in Salou . . . ? "Do you like the beach?"

Mark Granger showed his top teeth when he laughed. They were white, straight, each in its place. He looked more like the chauffeur of some elegant sir at Westminster than the bus driver of a city route.

"Asking a Welshman if he likes the sun is like asking a Chelsea fan if they like soccer. Everyone likes what they don't have. Why don't you come along with me?"

Neither Gina nor Paulina knew what to say.

"Me? It's just that I just . . ." she stumbled. The question had caught her by surprise in its directness, without a preamble, from one subject to the next. But she was conscious that deep down she was dying to.

"Two, three days. Just go with me and come back. Whatever you want."

"Why not?" After she said yes, she let out a sigh. "But are you sure that there's a room for me?"

"We'll figure it out."

They both understood. And they felt a surge of excitement and thought about how dazzling the world is sometimes that in the blink of an eye with a snap decision, with four words your lungs can fill up and you feel the bristles of the painter's sweeping brushstroke on the immense canvas of life. Sure of yourself, you dip the brush in the red pot, and, letting the drops drip upon the brown paper, you begin to outline with a sharp gesture, with the genius's certainty. Feelings accelerate, everything is quick, nothing is planned. It's all, in the very end, sexual desire. The call.

En route to Salou, in the middle lane of the highway, as he drove absentmindedly like Georg Philipp Telemann's *Water Music* was playing, Mark thought, *Oh my god.* In just a couple of hours he could be fucking Paulina Homs, the mysterious woman from the business card who had turned out to be a young woman in hippie clothes with curly hair and honey eyes. Gina, with her eyes on escape, thought about how she'd navigate it if, upon arriving at the hotel, she was asked for her ID to register her for the room. How would she hide it from Mark if she had to write down Georgina Castro? Suddenly she felt the four-fingered hand on her knee, strong, warm, and with no intention of moving.

"Is Paulina a common name here?" Mark took advantage of the question to hide his daring gesture.

"Weren't you supposed to tell me what happened?" It was the first time in their two days together that Gina had touched his hand.

"We should load up on gas." He noticed that the gas light had come on. "My finger? It's not that interesting, really . . ."

"You promised," Gina said emphatically without a trace of affection.

"Okay then. Do you like fireworks?"

"Ugh. . . They scared me when I was little."

"What about now?"

"It goes either way. My parents made me watch them with them from the balcony. I didn't want to, and . . . But don't change the subject."

Mark smiled. Gina had come to know that this was her road trip buddy's best expression. When he let loose, he seemed more honest and less British.

"I lit some fireworks at a children's festival near Cardiff. I had to light a row of them. Everything was well organized, laid out perfectly like a professional exhibit. It was all going well: The wick, I just had to count to two, and move back before the firework soared. But on one of the them, god dammit, I didn't have time to do anything. Just as I lit it, my finger was torn off and sent soaring with the firework."

"How awful." Gina bravely dared to ask, "Do you have kids?"

"No."

"You said you were at a children's festival . . ." She tried justifying her reasoning. The question hadn't come out of nowhere.

"I have three nephews. Three brats through and through."

"And a partner?" Now that she had asked. "Do you have one?"

"Does it matter?" He lightly shifted to look at Paulina from the corner of his eye. "I'm on vacation, and I'm far from home. Do we owe anyone an explanation?"

"Not me."

"Me neither."

Half a kilometer south, once they passed under the blue exit sign for Vilafranca, Gina tried to apologize for the question.

"You're not wearing a ring . . ."

"And what if I told you it went soaring with the firework?"

They laughed wholeheartedly, nervously. As the professional driver, Mark Granger knew how to best navigate the situation.

"I'm suggesting you don't pry into my life. You'll end up falling in love with me."

"Oh right. You've made that very clear."

And they laughed again, more honestly.

By the time they stopped to fill the diesel tank, the Welshman could tell that all the signs of attraction were lit up. As soon as he turned the key to the ignition off, he leaned toward Paulina, and with his eyes closed, he sweetly bit her lip before kissing her. She immediately put her tongue in his mouth, moving it without stopping from one side to the other, with a childish feeling of unease, as if with that wet and persistent tip she would have to perforate the tunnel below the Mancha canal.

Once the tank was filled, they continued until they reached Hotel de França de Salou. Mark happily hummed to the music he played on the cassettes in the car. Gina had not recognized even one of the songs. He didn't play any of the Beatles. He didn't even care. She thought about how she had never done it with a man twenty-two years older than her. He was more than double her age. She also thought about the moment she would have to tell him that she wasn't Paulina but rather

her daughter. As of now, tomorrow was another day . . . What was it about secrets that was so addictive and exciting?

No one ever unloads your luggage from the car when you stay at a two-star hotel. There's only ever a German shepherd who can't hold in his farts and responds to the name Sultan, who sniffs you from afar. It was his custom with all the guests. After, overcome by the laziness of age, he didn't pay them any more attention on the remaining days the guests spent in his modest hotel. At this sleepy midday hour, the lobby smelled like sand from the beach and grilled calamari. The receptionist, who had just as little charm as that lobby, desk, and room key, welcomed them without even looking up at them.

"Let me." When Mark was able to use English, he was on top of things. "Granger. Reservation for two weeks. I paid for a room for one, but in the end there will be two of us. Is that a problem?"

"Can I get your identification, please?"

Gina grew worried. "For the two of us."

"Only for the gentleman. The reservation is under his name."

Mark took his passport from the back pocket of his pants, and he left it, open to the page with his picture, on top of the desk. Having ridden in the car from London to Salou, the documents now folded into a U-shape. He had a beard in his license photo.

"There's only one issue," said the receptionist impersonally, without a hint of irony. "Room 24 contains two separate beds."

Mark and Paulina looked at each other complicitly. No big deal.

"No problem."

"And one other thing . . ." The receptionist disappeared into an office and returned with a pair of towels. "We only had you marked down for one person. We change out the towels every three days. Here's one for the bath, the toilet, and the bidet. You have a balcony with a clothesline and pins. You can hang them up there. Room 24 is on the second floor. The staircase is to the right, all the way at the end. There isn't an elevator. Breakfast is on the ground floor from 7:30 a.m. to 9:30 a.m. We lock the doors at 11:00 p.m. If you will be returning later than that, please let us know beforehand. We hope that you enjoy your stay." And here ends my eulogy, she practically added in her mournful tone.

They didn't even take time to open the room window or even look at it. It was dark outside, and with the curtain open, only a streetlamp vaguely illuminated their stay. Not even in the repetition of the play, in slow motion, was it clear who threw themselves at the other for the first kiss. Mark held Paulina's face in his two hands; Gina, on her tiptoes, had her arms wrapped around him and held on to his shoulders. From time to time, they came up for air, only to go back immediately with more desperation.

"Usually, for a first date, women shave, and men masturbate."

"Excuse me?" She wasn't sure she had heard him correctly.

"It's a saying in the East End. They don't say that here?"

"No . . ." Gina did not back down from crude comments. "Well, I must warn you that I haven't completed my end of the deal. What about you?"

"I didn't know that the day would end like this, Paulina."

"Of course . . . That's what they always say. Don't count your chickens before they hatch."

"Shh, don't underestimate me."

Mark silenced her with another kiss. He loved Paulina's moist and tender lips. She undid his shirt, damp from all the driving. The sweat from Lyon to Salou had stained and stiffened his clothing. It looked like the Welshman had bigger breasts than she did. While Gina washed up, Mark moved the nightstands, took the Bible out of the drawer, threw it under the wardrobe, and joined the beds. Paulina, without showing off, came out with an ease wearing only one garment: her panties.

By the time they woke up, breakfast was over. The sun had shone on their weary bodies for quite some time. If they hurried to shower, they might be able to catch the very end of lunch. They had hardly eaten in two days. They walked a bit, went down to the beach for a while in the evening to dip their toes into the water, and above all, they laid out their towels several times on the balcony that faced the cement parking lot of the Hotel de França de Salou. During those languid days, Gina discovered that a body in its forties has a musculature, skin, and even smell that was different from any other that she had experienced until then. Mark discovered that the young Paulina, so silent in her orgasm, liked giving more than receiving. It worked in his favor. He—she didn't know if this was particular to Welshmen—also liked receiving more than giving.

On the third day, while Mark snored to the high heavens, Gina decided she had had enough. She didn't want this lovers' escape to turn into a honeymoon for newlyweds. She thought about the revolving door, she feared ties to a stranger, she suspected that routine could fall apart in fifteen days . . . and if she were honest with herself, she was tired of going by Paulina. She didn't like her mother's name at all. She woke Mark up, and told him that after breakfast she'd go back home. He didn't try to stop her. They took a shower together, made love one last time, and after eating breakfast, they said goodbye in the lobby of the hotel that, in the end, upheld its two stars with dignity.

"Mark, I have to tell you something . . . and promise me you won't get mad."

The Welshman raised his eyebrows. The lobby once more smelled like calamari. But when were they fried up? First thing in the morning?

"I'm leaving now. I'll take the train and go back to Barcelona. On the way to the train, I'll think about these two days, what we laughed about, and what we did. It's been great, but it's just a fling that we have to leave here. It's better to end it like this. Don't come looking for me. We don't want to know everything about each other. What we know now is enough. Keep the business card if you want, but don't romanticize me or my name. Things happen, and that's it."

"We don't have to explain ourselves to anyone is what we had agreed on . . ."

"Forget about me and be happy, you hear?"

"I promise." The bus driver lifted his four-fingered hand as if to swear by the American constitution.

Gina hugged him and gave him one last noisy kiss. Sultan, lazily, opened one eye. He closed it again, and continued resting his snout on the floor, comforted by the cool tile.

"Are you going back to your parents' house?"

He asked it in a practical tone, as if he obviously did not care that Paulina was leaving.

"No, I'm going to the apartment where you brought my boxes. I'm living in Sants with three friends from college. I hope it goes well. Did I tell you that I'm studying art history?"

"Are you that mad at your parents?"

"No, at least not at my dad. It was an excuse to . . . I don't have a mother. Didn't I tell you?"

"Oh man, I'm sorry. What was her name?"

Suddenly Gina noticed that her heart was beating a hundred beats a minute. She hid the sting of the moment and flashed Mark Granger the best smile he had ever seen. Immediately after, before leaving for the station, she decided to stir things up.

"Just like me. Paulina."

6

With a Bottle of Beer in Hand

"Hi, I'm Sara. I left after second grade at BUP. I'm single, and at the moment, I'm happy to stay this way. I own a stationery store that my parents opened right near the El Putxet market. I don't know, what else can I say? I sing in a neighborhood choir three times a week, and we have a fun time?"

"Alfred Sicilia. I'm realizing as I see all of you that all these years have passed, and you have done so many things, but I remain the same. I still have a dog, although it's not the same one of course. I'm still an RCD Espanyol fan, what's wrong with that? I still live in Riera de Sant Miquel, and I still vacation in Blanes."

"And your secret, Sicilia?"

"Secret?" He mulled it over for a second. "I'm not sure if I should admit it, but my older son plays in the Barça kids' league."

School reunions. At first, they're more annoying than anything. Afterward too. But once you're actually there, your drowsiness tends to evaporate.

"Not much going on for me." Mia, the chattiest girl in class, needed no introduction. "I got married in Lloret de Mar to Toni, who is a lifelong friend. We have two kids—they're nine and six—who go to school here because, even though it's not very popular to say it, I have fond memories of this school. I mean, every day I get stuck in rush-hour traffic. Back in the day, things like the Dalt beltway, traffic jams, finding parking, or having to double-park in the mornings or evenings didn't exist."

"Or the tow truck guys making a killing off us," someone yelled out from under the proudest of the pines. The other two had given up.

"Between traffic jams, I work at an agency. Like I said, nothing special."

No one discussed their small, insignificant successes. Aside from the forty-euros-per-person charge (there would be a meal and an open bar), the payment instructions, and suggested dress code, the invitation email contained a postscript that, at first, sounded like a real riot. After updating each other on how life had turned out, everyone would have to introduce themselves and confess a secret. Now that the moment had come, hardly anyone did it, and hardly anyone found it funny.

"I got married at twenty-nine. That morning, before putting on my suit coat and the whole getup, I decided to weigh myself. Better said, in order to be accurate since it's a night for confessions, I jacked off for the last time as a single man and then I got on the scale, in that order." Everyone laughed and applauded. "I wanted to be able sometime in the future to say, 'When I got married I weighed . . .' So anyway I weighed 230 pounds. Five years later I got divorced at 260 pounds. Happy to be single again and eat fast food, frozen pizzas, and microwavable pasta, I ended up at 295 pounds. And then, once I was warned that I had all the risk factors—smoking, high cholesterol, obesity, and erectile dysfunction—I did the one thing none of you should ever do under any circumstances: get a gastric bypass. Sure, I've lost weight without any effort, but look at me, I have extra skin everywhere, and this is no way to live."

Oscar sat down at the table, and all his old classmates applauded again.

"Let's do guy, girl. It'll be fun."

"One after the other."

"Whose turn is it?"

"It doesn't matter. We'll all get a chance to talk," said Gina, who, at thirty-eight, looked a lot like the pictures she had seen of her mother in her thirties.

It had been a while since they had seen each other. They were celebrating twenty years since their graduation, and Maria and Axel, who had kept in touch and were the type born to organize events, had put the whole thing together. They had talked to the school, organized the catering for the dinner, found tables, chairs, and tablecloths from who knows where, and set everything up in the three pines courtyard like it was a wedding with around ninety guests. With their sleeves already rolled up, they put in an order for a lovely evening, serene and mild, so that the girls in their spaghetti-straps wouldn't catch a June cold, which is always the most traitorous.

Egged on by his tablemates, Driki stood up with a bottle of beer in his hand.

"You can say that I've stayed ahead of my time. I started a travel agency just as people started to buy plane tickets and reserve hotel rooms online. Feel free to respond: *Bravo, campione*."

"Bravo, campione!"

"Then I came across a bargain: A photography shop was being sold on the Eixample. It was a good location, a good turnover. The owners were retiring, and I bought it. Six months later, digital cameras appeared on the scene, and no one returned to develop photos, not even their mistress's dirty pics. Respond . . ."

"Bravo, campione!" everyone yelled wholeheartedly.

"I thought I'd use this dinner as an opportunity in case anyone wants to team up with me, because I have a business idea and I'm sure it could be a good investment."

Everyone burst out with laughter about Driki's misadventures. He was the same as always, without an iota of self-pity, and always the first to laugh at his bad luck. When he sat down, all his friends at the table hugged him, squeezing his shoulder and throwing napkins at him.

"Gina, now it's your . . ."

"No, first Maite. Let Maite talk first, because if she keeps drinking like that, soon she won't be able to say anything."

"Thank you so much, dearly missed imbeciles," Maite shot at whoever had paid her the compliment, and then, she looked up at the tables beyond the courtyard. "First of all, let me say that, in these twenty years, the men here have generally been on the decline but the women, we've only gotten better. *Olé* to us! We've taken care of ourselves and look better than you all, who, honestly, after twenty years, there's not a single one of you that's cute or worth a damn. As for me . . . I can't complain about work. Dental assistant: Put in the hours, open doors, fill the little cup so you rinse your mouth, and a few cleanings a week. But if we have to reveal a secret . . ." No one expected for someone to throw a bucket of cold water in their faces at a celebratory dinner. "Hmm, in these last few years . . . I've lost two babies. I've had two abortions, one provoked, the other not. Sometimes I think about what would have happened if I hadn't gotten rid of the first . . . Perhaps the second was a punishment of sorts: You didn't want the first, well, we're taking away the second. The second child was a girl, and was eight months along. But now, doctors don't think we can have children. That said, now that I see I've brought down the mood, I have two questions. One: Does anyone believe in the existence of such a macabre God who does these kinds of things, who gives and takes, who rewards us and punishes us? And second, and most importantly: Has anyone here adopted a child from Armenia and can explain to me how the whole process functions once you get there?"

The people at her table were the first to get up and applaud Maite. The eighty-something other classmates chanted her name, waving their linen napkins like scarves. She plopped down in her chair and could not stop the tears that, in a stream, fell on the damned pine needles that got into shoes of all the classmates.

"Now it's my turn." Slowly, Biel, using his hands like an amateur orchestra conductor, made everyone sit and quiet down, knowing that he would have to disrupt the dramatic, even tragic, mood that was in danger of overtaking the nostalgic dinner.

"I've lived in London for the last seven years. I work as a lawyer at a firm where there are fifty of us suits, not a single woman. And yes, I came back just for this dinner."

They applauded him. Even though he had managed to turn things around, he still needed to keep the crowd going.

"I've come because I was excited to see you all. All the boys and girls. But especially one person. A classmate of yours, who twenty years ago was a girl, and who I see is now a beautiful woman, and read my lips, a girl who had the honor of taking my virginity in her bed at her house."

"Wow!" Soler was the first to react.

"Who is it?" Edu cried out.

"It must be . . ." And here Mec spouted off a list of girls he saw at the party, trying to guess the riddle.

"It's Gina. It has to be Gina . . ." Driki, who knew a thing or two, riled up the crowd.

"I won't name her if she doesn't want me to." Biel, ever the modest one, wanted them to beg.

"Let's see, with all the hints." Gina stood up amid the uproar. Once they all calmed down, after a minute of commotion, laughter, and standing ovations, she continued to speak. "Let's admit that back then Biel was the ugliest in the class. I wanted to do him a solid because if I hadn't, given how dumb he is, he still wouldn't have lost it to this day. Let's just say it was . . ."

"A favor!"

"Shut up, Driki."

"Charity work," Gina shot back, who had to go on the offensive, not embarrassed in the least.

"Charity, charity, charity." All the classmates started to clap to the beat.

Biel, who had not improved with the years, had remained standing. He looked at Gina smiling, challenging her with calculated risks. No one wanted to back down from this duel that brought so much entertainment to their classmates from a school named after a saint.

"If you're gonna tell it that way, like you did me a favor, let's just tell the whole story."

"Tell the whole story, tell the whole story." The enthusiastic audience continued to clap to the beat of the syllables.

"I ended up butt naked under the bed, because her dad came home by surprise." The old friends writhed on the floor with laughter. Gina was also giggling.

"No, no, I'm sorry," she stressed politely. "Let's make one thing clear. You ended up being dragged out from under the bed by my dad, who threw you out of the house with your underwear in your hand."

"Underwear in your hand, underwear in your hand."

They were thirty-eight years old, but a few of them acted like they were stuck at fourteen years old. They continued clapping and screaming like children.

No one could surpass that confession. And if in that old classmate reunion there was someone with even bigger revelations, they knew to keep the mystery to themselves, loyal to the unmistakable maxim that once something is known by two people, it stops being a secret.

Biel, who donned a new black Lacoste polo for the occasion, looked for an opportunity to get Gina to himself. It wasn't easy. She had become the queen of the party with the confession, and everyone wanted to ask her how she was (trucking along like everyone else), what she did (art history professor at the University of Barcelona), if she had kids (no), if she had gotten married (not that either), if she had a partner (not tonight, she limited her response to), how she managed to still look so good (what genetics can't do, a Visa can . . .).

Once they left her alone, breathing in the night air, contemplating the city, Biel came up from behind her. Before turning around, Gina ventured to speak.

"Let me kiss your cheek." She had guessed who it was. "What a scene you caused, little Biel with the big balls."

Gina noticed that Biel smelled like sweat. Biel thought that Gina had picked the sweetest perfume out of everyone at the party. The man, who was going to be turning forty without a single hair on his head, began the conversation with a special formula to test her.

"I'll never forget the first time I noticed you."

"The last time you said that, we ended up fucking. Don't get too excited today, because you're not gonna be as lucky this time."

"I wasn't hitting on you, but . . ."

"And you won't fit underneath my bed anymore." Gina fixed her eyes on his belly. She was going to touch it, but she didn't dare. She thought about how mad she'd be if someone had the guts to touch hers, however flat her belly might be.

"I'm also not in the mood to play tag with your dad. This much is true, he wouldn't be able to drag me now."

They burst out laughing. Gina hugged him again and gave him a kiss on the cheek. A noisy kiss. Biel smoked his cigarette and repeatedly and delicately exhaled the smoke. Gina was thankful that, without asking him, he turned his face to avoid bothering her with the smoke.

"Is he still alive?"

"What do you mean?"

"Your father . . ."

"Oh, yes, yes, of course! Man, he has a new family. At my age, I've ended up with two cute little brothers. They're eight and six years old. They have cosmically bad luck. They don't have a father. They have a grandpa who lets them do whatever they want, who spoils them all day. With those two dictators at home, there's no one who will step foot in that house. Altogether, if you look at it from my perspective, it's pathetic. But if he's happy . . ."

"Does he look happy to you?"

Gina didn't know how to respond. Biel wasn't too interested in his own question either.

"You said you live in London?"

"On the outskirts. About twenty-five minutes on the tube, but I work on Fleet Street in the City. Do you know the newspaper street? It's by St. Paul's Cathedral, where Lady Di and Dumbo Ears got married."

"It's been a while since I've visited. I'm more of a Paris person. Actually, I go quite often to Paris. I have a story, man . . . I'm putting together a ten-thousand-piece puzzle about my mother."

Gina noticed the surprise on his face.

"A ten-thousand-piece puzzle?" asked Biel.

"It's a figure of speech."

"Was your mom a fan of puzzles?"

"No, no, I mean, well, I don't know. I'm trying to piece together my mother's life. Specific episodes. Vital moments. I realized that I knew hardly anything, that I had such few, foggy memories, and that most of all, I had a lack of knowledge about my mother that was keeping me from moving forward. And that, holy moly, I needed to know her. It was an obsession. It is. As if I need to know how she was, how she lived, how she thought, to be able to accept myself. Give me a drag."

"You smoke?"

"I do now." Noticing the surprise in Biel's eyes, Gina had to explain. "What's wrong? I want to. The night deserves it, and I have to tell this story that is the most . . . intriguing, impressive, and inspiring story you've ever heard. I still can't tell if it's a thriller or a fairy tale. I can't believe the things I've been discovering about my mother. Do you have time?"

"Well, ma'am, when you sell it to me like that . . ."

"But I have to warn you that I don't know how it ends and that you might have to help me. That's why I'm saying that I'm in the middle of a sea of puzzle pieces that I'm trying to reconstruct. There are pieces everywhere."

"And in Paris, from what you're saying . . . Should we sit down?"

They returned to the tables destroyed by the dinner. Mountains of wrinkled napkins, a dying candle, and everywhere dirty coffee cups and half-drunk glasses of wine with lipstick stains. The classmates had climbed up to the red courtyard, drawn by the open bar, the DJ, and the three loudspeakers that played loudly even for the dead in the cemetery that was in front of the school. There was hardly anyone left in the courtyard with three pines. They sat in two lawn chairs. Biel brought an ashtray close, and Gina ("What a relief!") kicked off her heels. The tickle of the pine needles among the grass felt refreshing to her.

"My mother had a cousin in Paris . . . well, close to Paris, in Croissy-sur-Seine. The Seine is, just so you know, like the Thames in London."

"You're a dumbass . . ."

"They were inseparable as girls. The two, Paulina and Júlia, were only children, and that's why, as you can imagine, they were more sisters than cousins. Neither of their families were overflowing with money, so, in order to save, they went on vacation together. They rented a cottage in Sant Pol, and the two girls spent the whole day glued to each other. Together they went to the beach or jumped rope in the town, or did homework on the porch, which, from what they tell me, there was shade there and it was the breeziest place in the Can Botey home. They were so in unison they would synchronize their breathing. In fact, they slept in the same room, and they alternated summers sleeping on the highly coveted mattress next to the window. Once they got older, my mom wasn't one for school, but her cousin was sharp. Júlia won a scholarship and went to study at the Sorbonne, where she met Alain, tall as a giant. They fell in love and stayed in Paris."

"At whatever-it-is-sur-Seine."

"In Croissy, exactly. Obviously, my mother went to the wedding. She didn't just attend. Júlia wanted her to be the maid of honor. Recently I saw Alain and Júlia's wedding album, and my mother is in all the pictures, absolutely radiant, with and without the newlyweds, holding the bouquet . . . My mother was beautiful. Like me, but even more so."

They laughed again with the frankness of a friendship between schoolmates who haven't seen each other in twenty years, but still understand each other with only a glance.

"Alain and Julie, which is what they called her over there, had two daughters. My cousins. Actually, Fabienne and Laurence are my second cousins, but because there are so few of us in this family, we don't pay attention to the degree of parental separation. Six months ago, just after the holidays, Fabienne called me crying early one morning to tell me that her mother died of a heart attack in the garden of her house while grafting some geraniums. I dropped everything, I canceled classes at the university, and I went to Paris to be with my French cousins. A whole drama. Well, just as it is everywhere for all families, when someone dies before their time. And it's even worse when it's so sudden. What I mean is that there's nothing that makes it sadder or more tragic or different from the obstacles everyone experiences and has to bear, if you get what I'm saying. I get there, and Alain is a mess, obviously. Collapsed on the sofa to the point that you can't even get him to react. Just imagine a philosopher who is suddenly left without answers. Fabi and Laurence are also shattered. But on we go, we did a nonreligious burial, with a woman who spoke beautifully and some musicians who we got the sheet music for 'The Emigrant' for a string trio so that they could play it as best they could. I spent two days at their house keeping them company. On my last morning, Fabi, who had asked for the day off to accompany me to the airport, went through her mother's wardrobe to make piles of clothes for donation, grouping shoes to throw out, and sorting boxes and hats and . . . All very French, just so you know, somewhere between pretentious and old-fashioned. Nothing I would wear ever. And there in my Tia Júlia's wardrobe, inside a square beige box that my cousin said she had never seen, she took out a handful of papers and began to page through them. She looked through, read them, went back, and organized them on top of the bed. Suddenly, she said, 'Gina, I don't get it. This doesn't belong to my mom. It belongs to yours.' She spoke to me in French and really emphasized the possessives, but despite that,

I didn't really understand. So I said, 'Sorry?' And, among the papers, she took out three letters, without a return address, addressed to Julie Homs, number 2 on some street in Croissy-sur-Seine, with a heading, under the postmark, that said within parentheses, 'To Madame Paulina Homs's attention.' That is my mother. Two of the letters were open, one just waiting to be opened. As if no one had ever read it. Of course I opened them, of course they moved me, so much that on the return flight I read them however many times more, and that since then, and it's been a couple months, I've just tried to reconstruct what it all means and who my mom really was. Biel, I don't know if I should tell you that I would like you to come to my house one day so you could give these letters a look and see if you find another clue."

"I would love to." He cut himself off. If he could be with Gina, he'd be happy. "Do you still live in a student apartment?"

"No, now I live in a professor apartment, if that's any better." Gina got up, with an impulse that was reminiscent of her classmates. "Should we go dance?"

"You go dance. I'm gonna get a gin and tonic."

7

Out of All the Books, One

"I'll go with you."

"To Paris?"

"To the airport."

For a second, Paulina had gotten scared. She would have loved for her husband to accompany her to her cousin's wedding, but in that brief moment of misunderstanding, which didn't last long, her whole world had fallen apart. It was very strange for a stubborn man like him to suddenly change his mind. And she had spent a couple of weeks, perhaps even a couple of months since they had received the formal invitation, telling Julie that she was deeply sorry, but Manuel would not be able to attend. There was a lot of work these days. He had to prepare for the annual Düsseldorf fair, and in four days the year's revenue for the sale of windshield wipers was at stake. People drive their car, and turn on the windshield wipers when it rains, never even considering how someone manufactured the two wipers and how inside there's a rod that sustains the rhythmic dance of the brushes. And the more cars that are sold, the more windshield wipers are manufactured, and automatically, Manuel's machines have to start generating stainless steel rods in three eight-hour shifts. Sure, the workers will change, but the machines don't stop. She had told Júlia all these tales over the phone to excuse her husband, and now, twenty-four hours before the wedding, she couldn't just call her and say, "Sorry, love, but Manuel is also coming. He was able to pull it off. And the guys at SEAT and Renault, who have assembly-line workers twiddling their thumbs because they're waiting on the delivery of the rods, can go fuck themselves." She couldn't change the nuptials plans on such short notice, because she knew that her cousin—a devoted and long-suffering girlfriend—had racked her brains arranging the tables, performing all sorts of balancing acts, isolating unknowns, and taking into account so many variables that she would have needed a mathematical formula to make everything fit together: This is for one side of the family, these people can't stand these other people, these people are business competitors to these other people, this is a bitch that no one can tolerate but the monsieur hasn't had the balls to cross her off the invitation list. And to further complicate operational matters, given that the groom was French and that she was not native to Paris, there was a basic linguistic constraint she had to take into account when putting together the tables of ten. Paulina knew that if she had showed up to church with her husband, Júlia would have been delighted to see him, and in a blink of an eye, would have figured out how to find him a spot at a table. But, since he had opened the envelope with the invitation and learned that Júlia and Alain would be married on June 12, 1981, and that the wedding feast would take place at the Bois de Vincennes, Manuel had no intention of running off to Paris for a couple of days like his wife suggested. Paulina, in the negligee that was capable of achieving the impossible, affectionately sat on one of the arms of the armchair where he always napped.

"Four days for a wedding?"

"It's my cousin. I can't just go, say hi, and then come back. Especially to Paris."

"Three days of window shopping, if you're asking me . . ."

"I know how to go shopping by myself. I'm used to that, but come on, for the wedding."

"Do whatever you want, but don't get me involved."

"Júlia is like a sister to me."

"Then go by yourself." He put Alain and Julie's invitation back into the envelope. "But don't pout."

She hoped Manuel would accompany her. She wanted Júlia's French friends and new family to meet him and say, "Whoa, what an interesting guy your husband is. And so tall! Such a handsome nose! And what a personality." But he had shut down completely, and Paulina didn't want to get upset with him. She knew that her husband found weddings exasperating. He'd complain about having to put on stiff shoes. He'd get angry, because after polishing them, they'd get all dusty before the damned photo with the couple. He worried about arriving without anyone noticing the sweat on his shirt, about parking near the church, about standing up through the eternal cocktail hour, about the doofus waiters who served wine and let it drip all over the tablecloths, about the temperature of the steak that was burnt on the outside but cold inside, about . . . He wasn't like that about his life. Manuel tended to be easy to please. He had his quirks, like everyone, but he kept these hang-ups in check. Paulina generally had nothing to complain about. But they had lived together for years, and she knew that, when it came to weddings, Manuel grumbled about everything before they even left the house until, in the elevator, he took off his stiff shoes. Maybe it was better if she went on her own and left Gina, now that she was five years old and felt a little older, with Manuel at home. Or maybe even with Isabel, who could sleep over those days if it was easier for her. The apartment on the Eixample, old with high, decorated ceilings, had a view to the front and back. The dining room faced the intersection between the Rambla de Catalunya and Carrer de Còrsega, next to the biggest lamp store in the city. In the back, with views of the interior patio, were the primary bedroom and Gina's room. Isabel, who had been asked to vacuum every day because the child still played on the floor a lot, was convinced that as long as the apartment was, it must have at least forty rooms. And one of them, one of the only three that didn't get natural light, was hers. They had fixed it up with a bed, a wardrobe with a mirror, and a poster of the olive trees in Jaén, the landscape of her childhood, so that the nanny could sleep over in situations like this.

"Take her to school and eat dinner at home. That's all I'm asking. That way Gina sees you for a little while and you can be there for her. She's never been away from me for five days. Since I'm gonna miss her, at least she . . ."

"It's five days, for Christ's ache! It's not like it's five months . . ."

"It's 'Christ's sake.' It's 'sake,' not 'ache.' I've told you several times . . ."

"What do you know? You're a philologist now?"

"It's not a matter of language, Manu. It's philosophy. How do you want Christ to ache, if he doesn't exist?"

Manuel hung his head, not in the mood to throw any more stones. He knew that if he kept splashing in the deep waters of his marriage, he might surface a conversation with no predictable end in sight. And at home, anyway, they were polite in their actions and words. They passed the "keyhole test" with flying colors. They loved each other. They respected each other, and they made love twice a month. Three times, in the best of cases. And they were satisfied with that. Sometimes he initiated it. Sometimes it was Pau who would climb into bed without pajamas, waiting to surprise him under the blankets. They were also not keeping track. But they both agreed once, when they discussed the matter, that since Georgina's birth, their habits, their appetites, with how tired they were and everything . . .

"How do you think people would see us through the keyhole of the door?" Paulina asked Manuel, not long after, before she started to leave.

"I'm not sure . . ."

"You've never thought about what people you know, your parents' couple friends, are like behind closed doors when you peek through the keyhole? Everyone puts on a front on the street, at the stores, but what are people like when no one sees them? What surprises would we discover if we peeped at them through the keyhole of a door?"

Manuel had never played at imagining what other people's lives were like the way Paulina did. From that moment forward, he played with his whole heart. Paulina became his wife, and the "keyhole game" became a family tradition like Parcheesi or checkers. "If we could watch Romero," Paulina would say, referring to the neighbor from the first apartment on the second floor, "through the keyhole, I'm sure he wouldn't be as nice as he acts. If we watched Aparicio through the keyhole, the longtime boss at the factory, I think we'd discover a dark side of him. I'm not sure if he likes men, women, or what. And what about us? What do you think they'd think about us through the keyhole?" Paulina would always be the one to ask the question.

"Fine. Normal." Manuel always gave the same answer. "A peaceful family." News at the Castro–Homs household never needed big headlines. The morning that Manuel walked out of the bathroom without a mustache, it was a whole event, and it was the topic of conversation at dinner for weeks. Whether it was deciding whether to vacation at Morros de Torredembarra or put the car on a ferry and stay in Menorca at a seafront hotel in Cala Galdana, they mulled things over without rushing. The same thing happened with Gina's room. Now that they were switching out the baby furniture for decor fit for a five-year-old girl, Paulina decided, and Manu, automatically, gave his approval after looking at the plans and reviewing the budget. Nevertheless, if it looked good to Paulina, he couldn't add much else.

Their tempered feelings also managed to keep them on track. Their happiness was justified. Drama was scarce. There were more kisses than tears, but not much of anything. And a little bit of everything. A little playfulness and some humor. And an absence of fear, which was no small thing. Whoever might have watched them through the keyhole would never have seen a door slam or a "fuck you" or a murder attempt, or to put it in the least vicious way possible, uncontrollable feelings of telling everyone to go to hell. There were outbursts, of course, just like in any other home. But no deep collapse that would cause them to consider what they were doing with their lives or force them to ask how happy they were on a scale of one through ten. Above six? (What is the national average of happiness?) Or were they right on the average? Since they didn't really want to know the answer, they no longer asked themselves these questions.

Perhaps there were no longer any fireworks, but there also weren't any fires to put out. And for Manuel Castro and Paulina Homs, this was good enough. Each of them had their own space. Every Wednesday Pau went out with friends to see some exhibition, and after, they'd go out for a leisurely lunch to a nice restaurant to break up the week. That day, Isabel, who also had to immerse herself in the family routine, knew she had to grab a taxi and pick up little Gina with a snack ready and a water bottle. Manuel's Thursday poker games were sacred—everyone knew this. It didn't matter what was happening—as of years ago, since before they had gotten married, the game with friends was untouchable. Every four weeks, the meetup was held at the house. Paulina made all the preparations—Argentine sandwiches with sliced bread and the open bottle of wine—and then she was off to her room to read. That way they could smoke cigars and drink and bet twenty euros maximum per game until one thirty in the morning, the hour that Manuel chose because nights are for sleeping.

"What will you be taking to Paris, madam?" Isabel asked her.

Isabel wished that she weren't so chubby and that the lady wasn't so tall, because she would have loved to open wide Paulina's wardrobe, try on Paulina's dresses, and go to Paris, another city she knew she'd never visit.

"I still don't know, Isabel. I've been thinking about it for the last few days."

Make and unmake, construct and take apart, grow and trim. A building, a plant, a relationship, even a suitcase. There's a big difference between packing your bag before a trip begins and the moment you return. For the journey there, you have to choose between all of your belongings. Between the things you have dragged throughout your whole life, the ones you have accumulated, the ones that have proven useful and the ones that haven't, and the ones you forgot you had and appear, huzzah, at the least expected moment. Out of all your clothes, this dress. Out of your sunglasses and watches, these will go. And which of your skin creams will you take? Out of all your books, this one. Choosing precisely one, this one, is unfair to the other authors and stories that will have to continue to wait for their turn on the shelf, for someone to pull on the spine and awaken them from their slumber. She chose *The South Seas* for her trip to Paris. The Gauguin painting on the cover drew her attention, and she remembered that it had won the Planeta Award the year before. Her husband had gifted it to her for San Jordi, the day of books and roses, sure that she would like the books of Manuel Vázquez Montalbán. However, Paulina hadn't read any of the Carvalho novels, Vázquez Montalbán's famous detective series, and she figured it was the right time to lay it flat between her makeup bag and a cardigan, just in case.

On the journey back, it's as if nothing happened. Packing your bag is like a sneeze. Taking inventory is fast, because at noon, they throw you out on the street. You double-check that you didn't leave anything in the bathroom or the closets in the room or drawers above the mini bar that, every time you open it, smells intensely of wood, like it's been ages since anyone opened it. You collect your pajamas from between the sheets, you throw them in the suitcase without order or concern, and you head home. The memories aren't packed away or on the hotel bill. They can't take them away from you at the airport.

Paulina counted her underwear sets. Four pairs of matching bras and panties. Five, just in case. So she started from the bottom up. She chose her clothes and left them lying atop the bed. Isabel wanted to help put it all in the bag, but the lady preferred to do this on her own, not wanting to feel controlled. She closed the door to her room and continued the ritual. She chose some Daniel Carbocci cowboy boots and some espadrilles from Castañer. For the wedding, she had bought herself some black mid-heeled pumps from Ferragamo. She continued up the body. She packed some new Calvin Klein jeans, like the ones she had seen on Brooke Shields in *The Blue Lagoon*. Of course, she was a teenager in that movie, and Paulina was dangerously approaching her thirties. To wear with jeans, she chose a white T-shirt, a silk blouse with a bow, and a mustard knit sweater from Ferrer y Sentís, as well as a wide leather belt to place on top of all of that. She was a little more picky with the dresses. At Groc, designer Antonio Miró's avant-garde boutique, she had bought an extravagant geometric dress. The original and modern shapes of the pattern matched the earthy tones and naturalness of the piece. On the three or four occasions she had ever worn it, everyone had told her how beautiful, how elegant, and how svelte she looked. And it was true. She saw it herself when she looked in the mirror. She also chose some brooches, and big flamboyant earrings and bracelets that could not go unnoticed. And finally, the most important thing. From her wardrobe, she took the dress jacket for the wedding off its hanger. She slipped it out of its bag for a moment to look at it one last time before placing it in the suitcase. She was proud of it, and it would not show up her cousin. Suzie Lindberg at the Yves Saint Laurent on the nicest part of the Diagonal had made her the tailored blazer to her size with shoulder pads, straight and almost galactic, in a blue she thought could be all the rage at Júlia's wedding. Either it'd be well liked or criticized in a whisper. The skirt, falling just under the knee, highlighted her swimmer's hips and legs that were begging to be looked at.

"I'll get it!"

The phone was ringing, and she yelled so Isabel could hear her. She picked up from the machine on her nightstand. Her husband, on the other end of the line, seemed overwhelmed when it came to giving an explanation.

"It really isn't a problem, Manuel. I'll take care of it. I'll take a taxi to get to the airport, and that's it. I have plenty of time, and once I get to Prat airport, I'll put it all on a trolley to check in, because I don't think that everything I'm taking will fit in a single suitcase. But don't you worry if you have work. I get it. Really, you do your thing . . . Yes, dear, I know you said you'd come with me, but it's okay, Manuel. It's just a change of plans. I'll call you once I get to Paris, once I get to their house. Don't worry. I'll call to talk to Gina. Sending you a kiss. Yes. Me too. See you on Tuesday . . ."

And then the toiletry bag, and the Montalbán book, and her cardigan, just in case. Once she had everything laid out on the bed—*Oh no, I forgot my nightshirt*—she decided she'd take a big hat. There's not a day that goes by during the spring in Paris where there isn't a downpour. Of course Júlia (a soaked bride was a badly loved bride, as they say) would pray that it didn't rain on Friday. At least in the evening, at La Fermette, on the Île des Minimes, in the Bois de Vincennes, where the hundred or so guests would arrive on a decorated barge for Alain and Julie's wedding. Just in case, at the departures terminal, Paulina would buy herself an umbrella. Her last one had died while in use.

8

I've Seated You Together at the Table

The guest bedroom faced the back patio. With her two suitcases open on the mattress, Paulina drew back the thin fabric of the curtains. She didn't want the neighbors across the street, the Dugarrys, to see her while she was getting dressed for the wedding. Their house was made of exposed brick and was identical to her cousin's. There was a ground floor, a first floor, a tiny attic, a garden in the front, with a portico that fit one car, and a less fixed-up patio in the back where Julie kept the grill, the pile of firewood that hibernated until winter, and two treacherous chairs that, if you didn't sit directly in the middle, can prank you when you try to sit down. In the last week, Julie had laid out on one, without falling, every time the sun peeked its head over Croissy-sur-Seine. She wanted her skin to be bronze for the wedding ceremony, the party, and most importantly, the pictures. These were the kinds of pictures that follow you your whole life, and even beyond that. Your children look at them, your grandchildren inherit them, and one day, your great-grandchildren stop in front of the dresser in the hallway and say, "I think someone said that the people in the picture were my maternal great-grandparents on their wedding day." June 12, 1981, is written on the back of the frame. "Look how tan Yaya Júlia was . . ." But there's nothing left of Yaya Júlia. Only the photo remains, the picture of the bronzed, radiant bride in her sublime hour.

Paulina also shut the door. Between the hairdresser, the iron pressers, the tailors, and the makeup artists, there was too much noise coming from Julie's room. And too many nerves. And she didn't want to catch it. She had already gone through all that chaos some years before. Manuel Castro and Paulina Homs, young and in love, had exchanged vows at the Basilica of the Immaculate Conception in Barcelona, and since that May evening, they hadn't swayed from them. They held the celebration dinner at the Fonda Espanya, and they slept in a suite at the Oriente Hotel on the Rambla, thanks to a gift from the groom's poker buddies. Two days later, in a new car for the wedding, Paulina and Manuel traveled to Venice, down the foggy highway, the one that crosses Italy from west to east. Neither of them had been to the city before, and despite everyone's warnings about the smell that emanated from the canals, they didn't think it was too big of a deal.

Paulina came out of the shower with a towel wrapped around her hair. First while she was naked, then while wearing her bra and underwear, she looked at herself in the mirror the way all women do when they are in their late twenties: in search of defects where there are none.

She stood there for a good while, drying her hair with the professional blow dryer that the bride's hairstylist had lent her. She had arrived at the house with three metallic suitcases filled with tools of different kinds. After, with the skill of having rehearsed it multiple times, she improvised a bun that gathered all her hair, showed off the bare nape of her neck, and gave her more of a stylish edge. It perhaps made her look older, but she didn't mind. In order to avoid any wrinkles, Paulina had ironed the dress designed for the occasion the moment she had taken it out of the suitcase the evening she arrived at Júlia's house. She liked looking at how it hung on the handles of the mirror-wardrobe in the guest bedroom.

Before putting it on, she opened her travel makeup case. She did her eye makeup discreetly, for the night, highlighting her turquoise irises. For her lips, she chose an aubergine-red lipstick, because it was a special occasion and no one knew her in Paris. After, with a tissue, she blotted her lips so as not to leave stains on the glasses and cups.

"You look beautiful," the bride said as a chauffeur opened the door to the Citroën fit for a presidential ride.

"Today, there's only one beautiful woman. Don't get it wrong."

"Do I look fine? I'm not too . . . ?" Júlia needed a little more than reassurance from her cousin, since they were always so honest with each other.

"You're the most beautiful bride in all of Paris. Don't worry. I feel awkward being here . . ."

Júlia had insisted that Paulina go with her in the car to the church. "What nonsense. It wouldn't make sense to go separately if we're going to the same place. No need to talk about it anymore." The last thing Paulina wanted was to get on anyone's bad side during such a nerve-racking time. If Júlia had already decided, if this was how she had seen things going, surely there was no need to go over and over it in her head. There was no more discussion then. On the journey from Croissy to Paris, sitting in the back seat of the car fit for François Mitterand, the two cousins held hands. They could barely speak.

"On days like today," said the bride before sighing, "I miss the people who aren't with us anymore."

"Don't think about it."

"I know, but it isn't easy."

"You can't let yourself. Let's not let your mascara run from that eye look they did on you."

"Too much makeup?" she asked, insecure.

"No, no, no. You look like a movie star."

"You think so?"

"Of course, Júlia. You look spectacular."

"Really?"

"Of course. But I forbid you from crying. Enjoy today. It's your day."

"Okay."

"It'll all work out." She looked at her and squeezed her hand harder. "Come on, don't worry."

"Now I have a headache . . ."

And they remained silent, frozen, until they were two blocks away from the Fontenay-sous-Bois church, where the organist already had his hands on the keys and kept looking at the door compulsively. As they had planned, Paulina stepped out of the car and walked the last stretch. Right on the dot, she let the bride make her own entrance in the Citroën with the radio antenna, door handles, and window wipers they had decorated with bows. Before disappearing into the crowd of wedding guests, she noticed the passersby watching her. Maybe it was the electric blue outfit, or the wide triangular shape of the top of her dress that narrowed at her waist. It was, without a doubt, the prettiest dress she had ever owned. The black lapels and cuffs that matched her shoes, and a single giant button, also drew the attention of the neighborhood people. Some women watched her jealously, but others, she thought, seemed to do it with admiration. Men shot her lecherous glances. With every step, her confidence grew. With her hand, she protected her small round Chanel bag that paired with a long chain that was easy to snatch. For some time she wanted to have a dress like this and wear it out. And she had found the right occasion, the city, and the day. Perfect. Things didn't always work out so nicely. That said, it was true she would have to walk a lot, and she just knew that her new shoes—the mid-heeled pumps—would start to hurt her, and she'd forgotten to put bandages in her bag.

The ceremony went by quickly, considering the way these things usually go. The priest, an acquaintance of Alain's who was highly sought after, got straight to the point. They did not do the Eucharist, everything went smoothly, and they finished like they had to rush out of the church so as not to make the loyal 7:00 p.m. massgoers angry. Seated in the second row, Paulina entertained herself by looking at the statues of the saints, the arches in the nave, and the members of the choir, who, between their Gounod and Schubert renditions, earned themselves a nice tip. Julie looked happy. She smiled, and from time to time looked sweetly at Alain, her husband, which she could finally say in all its glory. But despite Paulina's worries, the bride did not tear up at any point.

As they left, some clouds hid the sun and a dry, evening breeze began to blow, which for a few moments frightened the women with the most revealing necklines.

The Chalet de la Porte Jaune was an old hunting *relais* in the middle of Bois de Vincennes, not too far from the church, on the outskirts of Paris. Over time, the mansion and the wild gardens had grown closer to the city, and the entrepreneurial heirs of heirs decided to rent the space for banquets and conventions. After touring several places that were either too run-down, or too big or too old or too far or too expensive or too dirty or too minimalist, Julie and Alain had finally opted for La Fermette. The welcome cocktail hour would take place in the garden; the wedding reception was in a salon that just barely fit the hundred guests. Based on the decor, it could look like a dollhouse or the mansion of a Massachusetts state senator. Julie chose option A for the most important day of the first three decades of her life.

The guests, dressed to the nines, lined up to take the barge that could, in two minutes, transport them to the restaurant of La Fermette through Îles des Minimes after scaring a few ducks and swans.

Once aboard, Paulina stood next to a huge wooden face, no one having warned her that it was a figurehead. Julie had decorated the entire vessel with flower arrangements so her guests wouldn't think that she had forced them onto an amusement park boat. The green and white of the decor dominated everywhere. She observed the guests who, like her, had restrained themselves in the church and were now heading toward the reception, ready to celebrate to the fullest. Among the ladies, black gowns down to the feet or knee-length red were the most predominant, and from where she stood, she could see no shortage of blue shades, much like her own. There were many padded shoulders, more straps than strapless dresses, more peeks of cleavage than full-blown décolletage. Aside from one woman who had a peacock on her head—more alive than dead—she counted, roughly, more headbands than berets and wide-brimmed hats, more updos than loose locks, more fine jewelry than flashy costume jewelry. Among the men, there wasn't much color or variance. Black reigned from head to toe, whether in a tuxedo or a suit, always over a white shirt. Imagination had only been given free rein when it came to a bowtie. There was one man, though, wearing a light-colored blazer, bold also in its cut. Pipe in hand, he gazed out onto the landscape as if he were the captain of the ship as he whistled the notes of the sirtaki to himself in slow motion. Paulina hadn't seen him in the church. She would have noticed him.

As soon as the guests set foot on the ground, the cocktail hour began. A line of waiters welcomed them with a drink and a potato soufflé stamped with the date and Alain and Julie's names. The bride and groom were not the last to arrive. They had taken a shortcut from Fontenay to La Fermette, and once it appeared that everyone had arrived, they exited from the restaurant, greeting everyone from left to right, distributing kisses and smiles. After the photographs, in front of a kitschy little fountain, Júlia hurried to rescue her cousin, who she saw standing stiff as a board, not interacting with anyone.

"Come. I have to introduce you to someone." She grabbed her cousin by the hand and pulled her along like two girls playing hide-and-seek in the schoolyard.

"Him?"

"I told you you'd have fun today."

"Please, Julie, I don't like surprises."

"I told you, didn't I? Come on, he's very nice."

"Júlia, please . . ." It was too late.

"Jean-Pierre, I'm so happy you could come!"

The bride threw herself around his neck and hugged him with more warmth than mere courtesy required. Paulina had perfectly guessed where they were heading: toward the man in the unusual jacket. She had even underestimated it. Up close, she saw it was a linen piece, white, unstructured, without pockets, fitted at the waist. The stitching on the lapels was visible and in red thread, like the seams of a baseball. One needed elegance, a flat stomach, and a lot of personality to wear such a distinctive jacket without looking ridiculous. His tie didn't go unnoticed either. It was a garnet-colored piqué wide necktie with a horizontal cut that ended three fingers above the belt. Paulina had already noticed, during the aperitif, that Júlia's friend smoked a pipe and removed the stem from between his teeth when he spoke, holing the warm base of the bowl in his hand.

"Jean-Pierre, this is my cousin from Barcelona, Paulina. I think I might have mentioned her to you at some . . ."

"Oh, Poline, so nice to meet you." He bent down slightly to give her three kisses.

"Nice to meet you. Pau—Paulina Homs," she said, emphasizing the correct pronunciation of her name. Back in school, anyone who called her Poline as a joke was annihilated without trial or mercy.

"Sorry . . . Pauline," he repeated in the French version, stressing the *a* and the *u*, eager to apologize despite not having the slightest inkling of her childhood trauma. Without asking for permission, he had already made her name French. "Jean-Pierre Zanardi. It's a pleasure."

"Jean-Pierre . . . I'm not sure we non-French speakers can pronounce the *r* correctly. Jean-Pierre, Jean-Piegue . . ."

"You said it perfectly well," her cousin added. She was already kissing other friends who had pulled her by the arm. Before the whirlpool of people carried her off, she had time to say one last thing: "I've seated you together at the table. You were the only two who came unattached . . ."

Paulina looked at Jean-Pierre and instantly and shyly lowered her gaze.

"So you're alone, then?"

"No, no, not at all . . . My husband stayed in Barcelona, he had a lot of work and . . . and someone had to stay with our daughter."

"Oh, you have a daughter? You're so young."

What a pest, Paulina thought. *My cousin saddled me with the divorcé who's shooting his shot before dinner even starts.* Or maybe he was only trying to be nice to a stranger who, Julie was right to say, had been left without a plus-one.

"Yes. A little girl. She's five years old. Gina." She added details almost like a protective shield. "What about you?"

"Me? No. I don't have any children. I'm *célibataire* . . . How do you say it in your language?"

"Single."

"Yes, single. That's the word. And I think I'll stay that way."

"Oh, you can never say that for sure . . ." She looked around. "It's a nice place, *n'est-ce pas*?"

"Yeah, I've never been here either. When I read on the invitation that it was in the Bois de Vincennes, I thought, oh dear . . . But no, not at all. And you can see Julie's touch in everything: all the details, everything is thought out, everything is nicely arranged . . ."

"Are you on Julie's side or Alain's?"

"No, no, on Julie's. We've been friends—phew—for many, many years." He put the pipe back in his mouth and picked up two glasses of champagne from a waiter passing by with a full tray. He offered one to Paulina.

"To the newlyweds!"

"To the newlyweds!"

They clinked glasses.

"Hey, Pauline, here in France, when you toast, *il faut* look people in the eyes."

Maybe he was only trying to be polite, sociable, but the move was . . . They toasted again.

"To the newlyweds."

"To the newlyweds. Now this one counts." He took a sip, raising the glass by the base.

"It's too bad they can't go away on a honeymoon now."

"Alain doesn't have any vacation time. Not until August. But it's worth waiting for a trip to California."

"California, wow, I had no idea . . . What a trip!"

"Have you been?"

"Yes, yes, I love traveling. Whenever I can, I escape. In fact, I rearranged things so I could be here today. If it weren't for the wedding, I'd have to be in Helsinki right now."

"You travel for work?"

Paulina kept the conversation going just to have someone to talk to. She wasn't interested in the answers of this man—older than she was, well put together, with an appealing look, but who, in any case, clearly wanted to draw attention to himself. Up close, the two layers of stitching made the texture of the tie even more noticeable. She had never seen one like it.

"For work, for pleasure. It's all the same. I'm lucky that I work at what I love. My work is my hobby."

"How nice." *Why should I even care?* she thought.

"I'm in the art world."

"You're an artist?" The quirky jacket was starting to make sense for the character.

"Oh, no, no." When Jean-Pierre laughed, he showed his straight teeth. "I have . . . I have—it sounds very pretentious to put it that way—I have, I have . . . It's an art gallery. I buy and sell paintings. I organize exhibitions, I travel for that, to meet painters, close deals, transport works . . . Are you staying here many days?"

"Me?" *What's it to you, snob?*

"Because I was thinking—I don't know—I was thinking you'd enjoy seeing the gallery. It's over there, on the rue de Seine, by the river. You must have walked past it a thousand times."

"I don't . . ."

"It's a narrow street with art galleries and antique shops, one right next to the other . . . You know the church of Saint-Germain-des-Prés?"

"I'm not sure. I'm familiar with Paris, but usually Julie guides me around. I'm not good at remembering . . ." She set her half-finished glass on a counter among other champagne leftovers. "It looks like they want us to go sit down."

"The aperitif was delicious, don't you think?"

Paulina didn't answer. She was surprised because the man with the pipe had placed his hand on her shoulder to guide her toward the Orchids table. She wrinkled her nose. Julie had wanted each round eight-person table to bear the name of a plant or flower she liked, instead of a number. Someone had told her that at a wedding an orchid symbolized fifty-five years of marriage.

Jean-Pierre, more or less, knew the other three couples assigned to their table, and he introduced Pauline Homs correctly in French, careful to pronounce both her first name and last name correctly. He always added: *la cousine de Barcelone*. It seemed that everyone had heard of her. The women—who seemed sincere, despite being Parisians—complimented her on the elegance of her dress.

"A good choice."

"It looks so good with your blond hair."

"Yves Saint Laurent, *n'est-ce pas*."

Jean-Pierre then tried to join in the compliment. But it was too late. There was no need for him to say that the geometric shape had something cubist or futurist or . . . whatever. Júlia had made sure that Paulina was seated with a view of the head table. From time to time they looked at each other and winked, or sent some secret signal as if to say: Everything is fine, the food is delicious, everything is turning out just as you deserve.

During dinner, Paulina's improvised partner did not stop talking. It seemed that the rest of the table silently mocked him, and he kept talking to her nonstop, saying one thing after the other. Perhaps he didn't know everything, but he did tell her everything he knew.

"Did you like the Schubert song they sang at the church?"

"That was Schubert?"

"The second song, yes. Do you know how many songs Schubert composed?"

"No, no . . ."

"More than six hundred. But get this—he died at thirty-one. By then he had already composed six hundred plus . . . phew . . ." He made a gesture with his well-proportioned hands. Paulina didn't trust men with small hands. "I like Schubert a lot. Each song of *Die schöne Müllerin* is like a drop of honey. And the poor man died without any success at all, without a penny in his pocket, and without ever having premiered any of his operas or orchestral works. Life can be so cruel."

"Yes, and unfair."

"We've been enthralled with his music for two hundred years, but he died in utter poverty, never knowing that, in centuries to come, he would be one of the most performed and lauded composers. Do you know what he died of?"

"Schubert, you mean?"

"Yes."

"Is this a test?"

"No, no . . . Please, Pauline . . ." He didn't want her to feel offended in the slightest.

"Did he commit suicide?"

"No, no. Of syphilis. He died at thirty-one of syphilis."

"I see . . ."

"Schubert was a romantic. To die young, to die of syphilis is a consistent ending for a romantic like him. He had a curious understanding of his own work. When he wanted to sing about love, it turned into sorrow. When he wanted to sing about sorrow, the audience turned it into love. He gave the best diagnosis of his own songs. He was spot on, exact, with what he said. *Die schöne Müllerin* contains twenty songs. It begins with a young man walking along the stream, crossing the fields, and arriving at a mill. And then what happens? He falls in love with a beautiful blond miller girl. *Die schöne Müllerin.* They are delicate and joyful love songs, full of happiness. But, as Schubert said, he wanted to write a song about love, but it turned into sorrow."

"The miller girl wants nothing to do with him?"

"At first the miller girl pays attention to him. They have a relationship, yes—but it's an ambiguous one, and soon she leaves him for a hunter. The hunter is more mature, more of a man, and he wears a green suit that's irresistible. And the young man, feeling abandoned, becomes more and more obsessed, until he ends up imagining a grave from which flowers sprout to symbolize his eternal love for the beautiful miller girl. And then—by this point we're already at song eighteen or nineteen—the young man despairs, throws himself into the stream, and kills himself."

"You see? In the end, there is always someone who commits suicide."

"Don't you find it fascinating, Pauline?"

She was beginning to get a better idea of who this Jean-Pierre Zanardi was—a man perhaps fifteen years older than she was. A man with tact, charm, and worldliness. Dangerous. Very dangerous. A bachelor used to impressing people at first with art and conversation. But later, when you go up to his apartment for what he insists is one last drink, you realize that the place is cold, that he doesn't have even a crumb of bread in his house, and that he will age badly.

Once dinner was over, Alain and Julie stood up and cut the six-tiered cake with a samurai sword. Before tasting it, they opened the dance floor with a Strauss waltz that was different than usual—both the waltz and the Strauss.

"We are surrounded by culture," Jean-Pierre whispered in her ear, to be heard above the applause for the newlyweds, "but they want us to believe that politics shape our lives."

That was certainly not Paulina's life. Politics, for her, consisted of the three consecutive news segments she watched on Telediario when Manuel had it on—nothing more. Her father did buy *La Vanguardia.* He'd done it all his life, mainly to do the crossword after lunch. In his thirty years as a subscriber, he had maybe finished it four times without waiting to see the next day's solution.

"Should we dance?" Jean-Pierre held out his hand to Paulina. They got up from their seats and, hand in hand, walked to the dance floor. They arrived just as the band's bald and stocky Paul McCartney started singing.

"Do you like the Beatles?"

"I like this song, yes. 'Twist and Shout.'"

They danced and shouted. It was mostly Jean-Pierre who shouted unabashedly. Paulina still hadn't let herself go. She danced shyly like she didn't want to be perceived. As everyone applauded the band, Jean-Pierre slipped away.

"I'll be back *tout suite*."

He returned, having taken off the baseball-style jacket, rolled up the sleeves of his white linen shirt, undone the first button, and loosened his tie.

"Ready for some rock and roll?"

"Do you know how to dance to it?" Paulina feared she couldn't measure up. Even if no one knew her, she wanted to spare herself the embarrassment.

"Follow my lead. Trust me."

Alain and Julie were dancing to "Don't Be Cruel." You could tell they had worn out many pairs of shoes. The other guests on the dance floor made space for them so as not to step on the bride's train, which, by that point in the celebration, was turning dark at the ends from being dragged around.

Alain set the pace like a model. But he made overly exaggerated faces. One moment he sucked in his cheeks, the next he bulged his eyes as if he'd seen a UFO. Or suddenly, as though shocked by electricity, he hunched his shoulders and thrust his neck forward with an exaggerated expression. He danced, sang, and shouted between grimaces. Some people must have chalked it up to the alcohol. But that was just Alain. He was a serious philosophy professor at the Sorbonne from Monday to Friday, but he transformed the moment he set foot on a dance floor. Julie, a more occasional dancer, had just married him—and in principle, for life. Both had said yes, in sickness and in health, until death turns life into drama and, after mourning, into a memory.

Paulina watched the newlyweds from the corner of her eye but focused on following Jean-Pierre, who moved his feet skillfully, as if it were nothing to him. He wore polished black lace-up shoes with tips so sharp that if he had kicked a distracted pigeon, he would have split it open. The band followed one song with another without giving the crowd of dancers, who were more and more lively, a moment to breathe. Next it was "Hound Dog," also by Elvis. Jean-Pierre held both her hands, let one go, and spun her with ease, casually like he was twirling a spaghetti noodle. His cheekbones were relaxed; he marked his steps with the raise of an eyebrow or simply by lifting his chin ever so slightly so she knew which way to move. He danced effortlessly in cadence. He hardly needed to bend at all to give his movements a distinguished air.

Paulina followed him with less effort than she had feared. She was having fun. They got along with each other in rhythm and harmony. Suddenly, their eyes met, they smiled at each other, and that dandy—who had seemed so full of himself—no longer struck her as quite so vain. Painted across his face was an inner passion, strong and silent.

"How old did you say you were—forty-something?"

"You shouldn't ask someone their age. But I'll tell you what, I'm going to need a slow song soon." He was panting and sweating more than he would have liked.

"You looked like you were in good shape . . ."

"No need to make fun of me. Look . . ."

The band Julie and Alain had hired for the wedding—a bass, two electric guitars, drums, and a worn-out singer—played a song that let people catch their breath. *There are worse things I could do.*

"This one is from *Grease*." Paulina recognized the slow song from the very first chords. "I love that movie."

"I . . . Can I tell you something?"

"Bien sûr."

"I can't stand John Travolta." He leaned in close to confess something in her ear. "He moves like the groom—too out of step, don't you think?"

Jean-Pierre discreetly mimicked Alain's fidgety movements. They laughed. Paulina had to admit that she found the man who knew everything about Schubert but moved like Elvis rather attractive.

"Don't lose focus, Jean-Piegue. Are you dancing, or are you giving up?"

"You don't know me. Not at all. Me, give up?"

It was the first time Jean-Pierre noticed Paulina, happy and beautiful, and her chest brushing against him. It was the first time in many years that the scent of a woman stirred him. And to think he had sworn to himself never again . . . As the song went on, Paulina might have rested her head on his shoulder, casually, complicitly, to let him know she was enjoying herself too. But she held back—just in case.

When the slow *Grease* song ended, Jean-Pierre surprised her with a sweet and quick kiss on the Île des Minimes. A bold move. Lips pressed against each other. A declaration of intentions.

9

Like the World Around Them Didn't Exist

The taxi driver from Croissy-sur-Seine knew the general overview of Paris's neighborhoods and zones. He wasn't a Parisian taxi driver. He wasn't a specialist of the city. After lunch, when the well-dressed customer, wearing her earth-toned suit, got into the car and asked him to take her to the intersection of rue de Seine and Visconti in the sixth arrondissement, he thought he could manage it. He knew rue de Seine well—it was the one that starts at the river, behind the Institut de France, and leads to boulevard Saint-Germain, close to the church. He even knew that, being such a narrow street, barely only a lane wide, traffic flowed from Saint-Germain toward the river. But rue de Visconti must have been very small, because he had never even heard the name before. Since the client, a foreigner, didn't seem to know where she was going either, he—using the logic honed over more than twenty years behind the wheel, which allowed him to hide his shortcomings as a rural taxi driver—would enter rue de Seine from the top and slowly make his way down until he found where rue Visconti crossed it.

He occasionally glimpsed her in the rearview mirror. She looked like an actress—one of those women who is sure about their own charm. Playing a guessing game, he asked the woman with the large earrings if she worked in film. "No," Paulina answered curtly. "Well, your face looks very familiar," the country taxi driver insisted, just before entering the trap that is the Parisian outskirts, always gray and congested. She stopped responding. She was the type of actress who didn't want to talk, he concluded, suddenly losing the urge to be friendly. Beautiful but rude. Paulina, restless in a way she found unrecognizable, was in no mood for pleasantries, much less to make small talk with a stranger whose French she struggled to understand. The situation unsettled her. She had begun to feel uncomfortable that very morning, with the question Julie had asked her on her first day as a married woman.

The day after the celebration, the sun had taken its time to rise. Everyone had woken up very late. Paulina had eaten a bit of fruit and cheese in the kitchen with the newlyweds, who had just woken up. Afterward she called home. Isabel answered. She told her not to worry, that Gina was fine and had gone out with her father to buy the newspapers and wash the car. Paulina had good timing. She knew her husband's habits and schedules better than anyone. Saturdays in the Castro Homs household were even more predictable than their weekdays.

"Should I tell him, madam, to call you at your cousin's house when they're back?"

"No need, Isabel. Tell Manuel that the wedding went well, that the weather was good, and that everything turned out the way Júlia deserved . . ."

"Don't you want to speak with Gina, madam?"

"Of course, of course . . ." Paulina couldn't stand the maid's insinuations, and even less the tone she used every time she threw a stone and hid her hand. "Give her a big kiss. If it can't be today, I'll talk to her tomorrow. I've got to hang up now, Isabel. It's a long-distance call. Bye-bye."

She hung up on the maid mid-speech.

"Don't hold back on account of us." Alain acted generously with his wife's family's house phone.

"I'm sorry, these calls are expensive."

After hanging up, Paulina kept her fingers on the receiver like it brought her closer to her daughter.

"How's Gina?" Her hair still wet from her first shower as a married woman, Júlia inquired about the baby of the family.

"She's all good, according to the witch." She made the newlyweds laugh. "I get the feeling she doesn't miss me at all, little Gina . . . Feels like no one misses me, really."

She added, "And least of all Isabel, who in the twenty-four hours has definitely made herself the lady of the house. I can just see it."

And suddenly, as if she sensed a hornet's nest nearby, as if she had a built-in emotional danger detector, Júlia asked her a question that, under normal circumstances, would have seemed perfectly ordinary.

"What are you doing this afternoon?"

Bull's-eye.

What could she tell her beloved cousin now? It was crazy not to be able to tell her the truth. After all, it had been Júlia who introduced her to her friend Jean-Pierre. She had been the one who had seated them together at the table. Plus, Paulina had no intentions in going to see him. He had been kind, she had been distant, and it didn't seem right to snub him if he had offered to show her his art gallery and the antiques street . . .

But did she have to tell Júlia who she'd be spending the afternoon with? And who cared? What harm was there in saying? But why couldn't she bring herself to do it? Maybe she felt guilty—preemptively—of what exactly she wasn't quite sure. Perhaps Júlia's innocent, seemingly harmless question had opened her eyes to a reality she preferred not to acknowledge. She had felt comfortable around Jean-Pierre, and she wanted to see him again. These were two truths she couldn't suppress. She just wanted to see him, plain and simple.

But if that was the case, why didn't she dare tell Júlia, the one person she never kept secrets from, that she had arranged to meet Jean-Pierre at his gallery at four o'clock? Why hide it? If she wasn't doing anything wrong, why did she feel like she was?

"Don't stay in Croissy, woman," said Alain, still half asleep. "You'll wither away here."

"Stay bored? No. Maybe I'll go down to Paris," she said, pretending to mull it over on the spot. "Are the shops open on Saturday afternoons?"

"Yes. Well . . . it depends. I answered too quickly. Where do you want to go?"

"To the center. Maybe toward the Rive Gauche, I was thinking, the Latin Quarter, behind . . ."

"That whole area, yes, of course. Take a taxi from the station." Júlia, ever the busybody, had the tendency to manage other people's lives in the blink of an eye. "Look, we'll arrange for one to pick you up, because you can't always find a taxi in Croissy when you want one, especially on Saturdays. Depending on which you get, they can be a bit rickety. We may be half an hour from Paris, but we're still in a village . . ."

"The Tour de France doesn't even pass through here," Alain said, sadly.

"All right, I'll do that."

Paulina felt a weight lift off her shoulders. It was better to say nothing and go about her own business in secret.

Visconti—her first surprise—turned out to be the architect of Napoleon I's tomb. The street's blue sign declared it proudly. He had nothing to do whatsoever with cinema or Italian neorealism.

Her second surprise was far less pleasant. Disturbing, even. The Galerie Anouk was closed.

The lights were off, and it didn't look as if anyone were inside. It was at number 44, rue de Seine. Yes, this was Galerie Anouk. But it was already twenty minutes past four. There could be no mistake, but the shop was dark, and Jean-Pierre was most definitely not there.

She rang the bell. *Rien de rien.*

She waited at the door, but even after two minutes, no one opened.

In her fluster, she hadn't noticed that there was a painting with a torn piece of newspaper glued to it in the shop window. Beneath the Le Corbusier collage were some words glued to the glass door: *"Un quart d'heure avant la fin du monde."*

This had to be the right gallery.

She checked the name again. Galerie Anouk, written in thin, elegant, modernist white block letters. This was the place, no doubt.

Either I misunderstood, or he forgot, or something happened to him. Or worse, he stood me up.

But she would never have thought Jean-Pierre could be the sort of man who would . . .

Paulina looked far down the street, first one way and then the other. It was too hot for anyone to be out walking. Four tourists with a guidebook open in their hands stopped every now and then in front of the shop windows. At nearly half past four on a June Saturday, the street looked dead.

With so few people around, maybe Jean-Pierre had decided not to open the gallery and had been unable to reach her. Maybe . . .

And at that moment of poorly processed uncertainty—when she had decided to give herself five minutes before hailing a cab to go cry for being so dumb in a random corner of the city where no one was expecting her, where not even her own shadow could spot her—Paulina thought she heard Jean-Pierre whistling in the distance.

She spun around, but she couldn't see him anywhere. She looked back inside the gallery. There was nothing there either.

He came into view through the reflection in the glass, a blurred silhouette, appearing among a pile of fruit crates from the shop directly across from Anouk. Jean-Pierre, having traded in his pipe for an apple, came out casually, unhurried. His hair was freshly combed, his white shirtsleeves were rolled up, and he had a lilac tie. She found him even more attractive than she had the day before. The daylight highlighted the tanned skin on his forehead and arms.

"The best painting on this street is that spread of fruit crates. Have you noticed the colors, the composition? If you're able to find a better work of art on this street, I'll buy it from you . . ."

"Everything good?"

Paulina realized that the self-assured Jean-Pierre had no intention of apologizing. In fact, he didn't even seem to realize that she had experienced the vaguest feeling that she'd been stood up. He crossed the street calmly and took out a key from his pocket as he greeted her with two kisses.

"All good, of course. Too good, really. I woke up super late with a headache . . . I didn't think we'd had that much to drink last night. So I said to myself, you know what? I asked Alfred—my sometimes assistant who lives upstairs—to open on his own, and I stayed in bed until lunchtime. Then I took a shower and came on over. Want some?"

"No thanks."

Truthfully the apple peel didn't look too appealing. And this, right at the start, sixteen hours after a clandestine kiss, was not the time to explain how picky she could be or begin confessing her flaws.

Jean-Pierre slid the key into the lock and opened the door.

"Welcome to Anouk 44, my paradise. This is my cave, my refuge"—he switched the lights on, bit by bit, from behind the counter—"and my life. Voilà!"

"It's beautiful."

The old varnished wood floorboards were once railway ties, warped through the years. The reflection of the lights on the long strips of wood brightened them and gave a sense of spaciousness to an interior marked by three iron columns, painted white, that marked the walkway through the gallery. All the walls were also a Grecian white, a Mediterranean white, and judging by the smell, it had only been a couple of days since the paintbrush had gone over them. The artworks, each consciously spaced from the next, popped even more against such a light backdrop.

"Do you like it?"

"It's beautiful, Jean-Pierre. I'm glad I came."

"Very austere, very simple. What you see is what you get. There's nothing more . . ."

"It's very you."

"There's this counter and a chesterfield sofa to contemplate the Vasarely piece. In the back there's a storeroom that functions as a tiny office, a half bathroom, a half kitchen. Really it's just a small stove to make coffee. Would you like one?"

"No, not right now . . ."

"Here. Sit and take a good look."

Jean-Pierre had taken her by both shoulders and practically pushed her onto the single-seat worn-leather chesterfield that faced a green-and-white Victor Vasarely hexagon. It couldn't have been much bigger than a television screen.

"Don't take your eyes off the painting. Keep your eyes fixed."

"Are you trying to hypnotize me?"

"Keep your eyes fixed, don't rush," Jean-Pierre whispered, "in silence . . ."

Paulina lowered her eyelids, trying to focus. She saw green-and-white hexagons everywhere.

"Can I say something?"

"You're getting dizzy?"

"A little . . . how did you know?"

"You'll like this one better . . . Pull your feet in. Be careful."

Before Paulina could even get up from the armchair, Jean-Pierre dragged her by the backrest, past the columns, and left her a few feet from another painting.

"Let's see how you like this one . . ."

"Is it an Andy Warhol?"

"*Marilyn's Lips.* I knew you'd like it . . ."

"What makes you say that?"

"I could tell."

"Well, well, well. You know when I'm dizzy, you can predict what I like . . . You really do know me."

"More than you know me."

"Listen to him, so full of himself."

Instinctively, Paulina touched his hand, running her fingers over the hairs on his veiny hands. After she had done it, she realized she didn't know whether she had permission to do so . . . She felt like they had gone back a few steps, to where things had been left off the night before, and now she didn't know where they were at.

Jean-Pierre had greeted her with two cool, brotherly kisses—on the cheek!—but now, sitting before those multicolored lips, he didn't mind her caressing his hand. He didn't make a face. There was no sign of disapproval. On the contrary.

What game is this womanizer playing today?

Is this all spontaneous—the apple and the chesterfield—or is it part of some grand scene he's directing?

Paulina needed clues, but she had none.

Jean-Pierre had more than enough energy to spare. What kind of apple had he eaten?

"Why do you think people like looking at a painting?"

"I thought I came to Paris for a wedding, not to be quizzed."

"Let's see if you agree with me."

The gallerist wasn't really interested in Paulina's answer. He needed to deliver his own theory—crafted, pondered, anything but accidental. It was, indeed, a rhetorical question.

"I've thought about it a lot. I've talked it over with experts and other gallery owners . . . We live in an age of tremendous noise. Don't you think?"

"Yes, yes." No one in their right mind would interrupt his monologue.

"The radio, the TV, the news. Messages coming from everywhere. A bombardment. Opinions, opinions, information. It's a constant bombardment. Every day, at all hours. At the end of the day, we no longer know whether the things we think are truly own thoughts or just echoes of everything we've heard. We repeat what we hear. We are the echo, and we don't even realize we've become animals of repetition."

Jean-Pierre unbuttoned his collar and loosened his lilac tie like it was holding him back.

"My dear Pauline, I think that art can help us in a crucial way. It can let a person go back inside of themselves. Art draws you away from external noise and helps you find yourself again. When you look at a painting, when you spend some time with it, you discover what you have inside. Little by little you discover what's inside, what you think, and how you feel. You discover who you are, and you likely realize that there's nothing more interesting than that."

"Wow . . . And is that why art moves us?"

"It's why there are people who don't like looking at paintings. Because they sense they wouldn't like what they'd find. The glass on the frame isn't there to protect the painting. It's to protect us from ourselves. It's our shield, our very own shield."

If the peacock had wanted to impress, he had succeeded by fully fanning out his tail. Self-satisfied, he lit his pipe.

"I make sure that there's a variety of works here. There are no two pieces by the same artist. I don't do any themed exhibitions between May and September. I've scheduled things that way for years. I've realized it's better to do a collective show for the summer visitors, a tutti-frutti of colorful pieces from the gallery's archives. I only have contemporary art, dating from World War I onward. These are works I've collected from past exhibitions, and now hardly a week goes by without someone coming in and falling in love with a Lichtenstein comic, or Christo's models before he wrapped the Pont Neuf, or Vilacasas's Planimetrias. I love these bird's-eye views of the city. Or the one in the shop window. Did you see it? A first-rate Le Corbusier. Did you notice the collage? I put the things I like best in the window. It's like an advertisement of myself to the street. A bit of who I am."

"You're a collage?"

"Who isn't?"

"No, I hadn't seen it."

Paulina got up out of the armchair, checked that the clasp of her dress was still properly fastened, and smoothed down the earth-toned skirt from Groc so it would fall right below her knee.

"While I was waiting for you—because honestly you took a long time and I was just about to leave—I had time to notice, at least, the magnificent fruit crates from the shop across the street. The fruit was so beautifully arranged. The best painting on the street. I'd never seen anything like it . . ."

"Don't make fun of me . . . But isn't it lovely to have a produce store right across the way? And so useful. I buy kiwis and apples to take home . . ."

"Do you live around here?"

"Not exactly. I live in Le Marais, but you can walk there. Do you know it?"

"Yes, but . . ."

"Not very well."

"I think Julie took me there once."

"It's very lively there—you'll like it. It's close to where they're planning to open the Picasso Museum."

"Excuse me, but the real Picasso Museum, the good one, will always be in Barcelona."

"You can't expect me to argue with you about this without laughing . . ."

"Agree to disagree?"

"Should we debate it over dinner?"

"Now?"

"We eat early here. I can show you the neighborhood, take a walk, and then have dinner."

"What about the gallery?"

"Do you really think anyone's going to come in? And besides—" He switched off the lights. "The owner gave me permission."

They walked along the rue de Seine so absorbed in each other, they hardly looked at the street. Jean-Pierre, acting as a tour guide eager to impress, pointed out interesting things about the neighborhood while she listened in silence. Where the sidewalk narrowed, their hands brushed, unintentionally, she thought. Skin against skin. And she shivered. They turned onto rue de Buci, packed with tourists seated on shaded terraces, and soon reached boulevard Saint-Germain.

"Saint-Germain-des-Prés is one of the oldest churches in Paris, and Saint-Sulpice is the second largest in the city after Notre-Dame. It looks even bigger from the outside, depending on your view. Saint-Sulpice is right here. You can see it peeking out from here."

Paulina looked at him, a challenge in her eyes.

"Four hundred steps."

"What?"

"From here to there."

"From Saint-Germain to Saint-Sulpice?"

"From door to door. What are you betting?"

"Tonight's dinner."

"Done." She held out her hand. "You'll be paying, Jean-Pierre."

"Your steps or mine?" He clasped her hand to seal the bet.

"They're the same. From door to door, four hundred normal steps."

"Plus or minus ten."

"What's that, honey?"

"A little margin of error, woman. Four hundred might mean three hundred ninety or . . . I'd really feel bad if you're forced to treat me to dinner."

"Thanks, but I don't need a margin of error." She was firm, resolute. "From here to there, four hundred steps. Door to door."

And as soon as the light turned green, Paulina began to walk and count softly under her breath. Jean-Pierre, beside her, was also counting in his head and making sure his strides matched those of a Pauline who, beyond her captivating beauty, clearly had hidden talents.

Once at Mabillon, they walked the whole street from end to end, skirting the Saint-Germain market, which gave off a rather unpleasant smell of fishy water and wilted flowers at closing time. The passersby who crossed their path—unaware of the lovers' challenge—were surprised to see this elegant woman, with her distracted gaze, counting her steps in a quasi-military fashion.

She was at 350 by the time they reached the side of the nave. They still had to walk toward the square and reach the front facade. Door to door, she had insisted on it when she set the rules.

Jean-Pierre's eyes widened. He never could have imagined Pauline would come close, not even by a long shot. Twenty meters from the finish line, she started carefully pacing her steps. Careful not to give the "judge" any grounds to challenge her, she reached her four hundredth step exactly on the final stride.

"Et voilà!"

Paulina couldn't contain her enthusiasm.

"Sublime. Brava!"

"You're paying for dinner."

"It couldn't be any other way." He still couldn't believe it. "But how on earth did you do it?"

"It wasn't a trick. And if it were, a magician never reveals their tricks."

"I had expectations of you, but honestly, this display has blown me out of the water."

"Didn't my cousin tell you I'm somewhat of a witch?"

Saint-Sulpice was an imposing church, full of pretension, somewhat out of place. If lightning hadn't decapitated its dome, it could have been a replica of St. Paul's Cathedral in London. The neoclassical facade, the massive columns, the pale stone, the symmetry.

That was something Paulina noticed: The symmetry was disrupted at the top, by the two bell towers that looked unevenly truncated.

The front facade opened out onto a large traffic-free square lined with a dozen serene acacia trees and a majestic fountain held up by four stone cardinals, a sort of cemetery pantheon, which blocked the view.

Paulina did not get close enough to see that the sculpture was signed by Visconti, the architect her taxi driver had been obsessed with only hours before.

"It's so tranquil."

"That's Paris. You walk two blocks away, and suddenly you find yourself in a peaceful corner seemingly untouched by the world."

"Maybe that's part of Paris's charm."

"Maybe, deep down, that's the charm of life."

Paulina wanted Jean-Pierre to explain what he had meant. They stopped admiring the side of the church like two tourists and faced each other. They stepped closer and reached for each other's hands at pocket level.

"I was saying that sometimes, maybe, in life, you have to step away from the streets you always walk, to see that there are other paths worth exploring."

"Right."

Their eyes glistened with joy and surprise.

"Even if you don't know where they'll take you."

Jean-Pierre's face slowly drew closer to hers.

"Sometimes . . ."

She did nothing to stop it.

"It's just life."

She closed her eyes and let the inevitable happen. A kiss. Passionate and mature. Willing, long, and sweet with all its honeyed flavors. They embraced each other, holding each other tight, and taking turns holding on to one another's faces ravenously.

They opened their eyes and smiled at each other, delighted by the unexpected, and immediately kissed again, playing with their lips and tongues like it was a first kiss among teens, like the world around them didn't exist. On their second kiss, Paulina detected the aroma of the tobacco pipe among the flavors. Sweet, pleasant, even addictive. She had never kissed a smoker before, she briefly thought. But there she stood on tiptoe, hanging from Jean-Pierre's neck.

They stayed in the square at Saint-Sulpice for a while. They did not look at the church again.

Having communicated everything with kisses, so as not to say anything they might later regret, they walked back arm in arm along rue Bonaparte. They didn't count their steps, but they could have counted their heartbeats.

Tactful and full of savoir faire, Jean-Pierre decided everything. He seemed to be the kind of man who never doubted himself.

"We'll have dinner here. It's a historic café."

"Les Deux Magots," Paulina read on the green awning at the corner of the boulevard and the Saint-Germain square. "I wonder if there's anywhere in this neighborhood that doesn't have a history . . . Who came here, Van Gogh?"

"Not that I know of. The surrealists, I think. And they say Sartre wrote something here."

"Outside or inside?"

"Here will be nice."

A waiter with a drooping mustache seated them in two wicker chairs that faced the square, next to a small round table. It was a French tradition. Instead of facing each other, people sat side by side, looking out at the street like they had already seen quite enough of each other and for the love of God needed to look out onto the spectacle the view offered.

The street always provides entertainment, but sometimes you want to have a conversation with someone, but with the tables so close and cramped, only trivial remarks can be exchanged.

Jean-Pierre rebutted all of Paulina's observations, point by point, with economical arguments. Parisian terraces are arranged this way because of tradition, because customers expect it, because it's part of the Parisian landscape, but most of all to maximize space. The fees establishments have to pay to occupy a few square meters of patio are extremely high. They pay many taxes and are highly regulated by the municipal leech, so they have to optimize every inch.

Paulina was already spaced out.

Jean-Pierre said everything with the same conviction he seemed to live with. He did admit humbly, to his credit, that he was repeating hearsay, because numbers weren't his strong suit. He had never really bothered to think about why this particular Parisian postcard shot looked the way it did.

It was an entirely different matter when he discussed art, painting, and culture. There he truly combined sensibility, confidence, and erudition. They hadn't even spent a day together, and Paulina could already attest to it.

"This is an egg place. Omelets, scrambled eggs, fried eggs . . ."

"I'll take an onion soup and a beer." She looked up from the menu. "What's wrong? It's what I'm craving. Why are you looking at me like that? Doesn't onion soup have egg in it?"

"Onion soup in June?"

"It's on the menu." Paulina pointed it out, flashing her red fingernail. "I can't be the only one ordering it."

Jean-Pierre ordered a ham omelet and another beer. They watched people as they ate. Every now and then Paulina came up with a story about the lives of the people walking by on their Saturday-evening stroll, unpredictable and uneven. It was a fun and cheap game she played when she was younger with Tatiana, the neighbor on her floor who was her companion in age and shared secrets. The two friends would sit at a bar in the Sarrià neighborhood of Barcelona, where they had no problem staying two or three hours. A Coca-Cola for each was enough to keep them guessing if the woman passing by with the supermarket bags was happy, if the couple walking silently had any children or not, if he worked at a bank, if she had a lover or two.

Jean-Pierre was astonished by Pauline's novelistic imagination. In no time she'd turn a woman emerging from the hair salon with teased hair into a Madame Bovary. And, just by looking at a young man walking a droopy-eared basset hound, she'd dream up a filmlike story in which the young man was an artist who, in order to pay for his life in

Paris and for his brushes and oil paints, earned a handful of francs each afternoon by taking the pets of the invalid grandmothers of the Rive Gauche out for a walk.

Aside from the people watching, he pointed out to her that, from the patio of Les Deux Magots, the facade of Saint-Germain-des-Prés on the other side of the square looked like a village church. It was irregular, austere, and very Alsatian. Once Paulina had finished playing at imagining other people's lives, she dared to inquire into Jean-Pierre's.

"Anouk. What does it mean?" she asked in a calculated innocence.

"Nothing. It's a name. Like Jean-Pierre."

"Is it a man's name?"

"No, not exactly." Jean-Pierre didn't want to complicate an unforgettable evening unexpectedly. "I think it's a woman's name. It's not very common."

"Can I ask, although I hope I'm not prying, why you named your gallery Anouk?"

Jean-Pierre lowered his head and set his pipe on the table. For the first time, Paulina noticed that the man she'd met at Júlia's wedding, the one who had just given her the best kiss of her life, was quietly wavering. Conveniently a waiter placed the bill that Jean-Pierre had requested wordlessly on the table. It had been enough just to raise his eyebrows and rub his two fingers together.

"Did you know that Marcello Mastroianni lived on the rue de Seine?"

"Is it just me, or are you openly changing the subject?" Paulina figured that she'd also packed wit in her suitcase. It was always as useful as a toothbrush.

"I just thought you might find it interesting. Do you know Mastroianni? The actor, I mean."

"Yes, of course. Now tell me," she replied teasingly, pretending to be intrigued. "What's this crazy story?"

"It's nothing, really. I just thought you'd like knowing that he lived right next door to the gallery, that an Italian like him had an apartment in Paris. He bought it on the rue de Seine, and one day he came into the gallery to calmly look at the paintings. I talked to him. He was a normal guy, very polite, and he was interested in a Pollock that . . ."

"I think you sort of resemble Mastroianni. Sorry, it's not just because you just mentioned him. I swear I thought about it yesterday. I don't know. There's something about you. The laugh, the nose, the look in your eyes, the way you hold your pipe. I'm not sure. Maybe it's the side part and the fact that your hair goes like this . . ."

Paulina pretended to comb through her hair, but only ever so lightly, suggesting that she was tracing an artfully messy coif back from a receding hairline. Smiling slyly, Jean-Pierre tried to look like the actor. He seductively put on the voice of an interesting man, an actor perhaps.

"You're not the first one to say that."

They laughed happily.

"And has anyone ever told you that you're a big show-off?"

She put her head on Marcello's shoulder to soften her words, in case they had seemed too harsh. Paulina sensed he was a bit of a charmer, but an irresistible one at that. How many women had fallen under the spell of such an attractive, elegant, and *charmant* man? How many times had he counted the steps between Saint-Germain and Saint-Sulpice, arm in arm with a tourist or gallery groupie?

Before Paulina could go back to her question about the gallery's name, Jean-Pierre tried to switch gears.

"You know who else lived on the rue de Seine?"

"Who?"

"D'Artagnan."

"Oh, sure." She looked up at him again. "Of course, and now you'll tell me he walked into the gallery one stormy Thursday?"

"No, we hadn't opened yet."

"All right. And did Peter Pan ever stop by? Who do you take me for?"

"I'm telling the truth."

Jean-Pierre took her hand as he realized Pauline was becoming frustrated. She admittedly was starting to feel a little ridiculous with all his bragging.

"D'Artagnan was a person."

"Look, hon, I may not have read *The Three Musketeers*, but everyone knows it's a book. D'Artagnan is a character written by Alexandre Dumas. Is that how it's pronounced? Dumas, Dumàs? How do you all say it?"

A waiter left their change on the table.

"You're absolutely right. Dumas wrote the novel, but D'Artagnan was a flesh-and-bone person. I'm telling you the truth. And so was Cardinal Richelieu. D'Artagnan was actually a Gascon musketeer whose name was something like Charles de . . . something Castelmore. Aside from becoming famous for his swordsmanship, he used to frequent the literary saloons of the Le Marais district, my neighborhood, actually. That's how I know the whole history of the Gray Musketeers."

Paulina was silent, but her honey-colored eyes revealed that she still didn't quite trust him.

"I just thought you'd like knowing that D'Artagnan lived right here four hundred years ago. That's all."

"Honestly? I don't know if I should believe it. Or rather, Jean-Pierre"—she added affectionately—"I don't know if I should believe you."

"*Se non è vero, è ben trovato,* as the Italians say, right?"

"What do you mean, 'the Italians'? I'm from Barcelona."

"Oh, right . . ."

They laughed again. Maybe it was the nerves, or maybe it was because he knew how to rile her up, or maybe it was because he sometimes was a total asshole, but Paulina realized she had laughed more that day than she had in several weeks. Instead of it scaring her, she liked admitting it.

"Shall we go?" He was already standing.

"Let's go. But you owe me something." They both knew what she was referring to. "Or would you rather I ask my cousin?"

"You mean Julie?"

"I was talking about Anouk."

Jean-Pierre wrapped his arm around her, holding on to her shoulder as they walked back toward the river to stroll down the rue des Beaux-Arts. The weather had cooled.

"Anouk. I'll tell you, Pauline. I'll want to tell you myself. But not today, not tonight, okay?"

They walked for a while without disturbing the silence. Like them, the day needed to slow its pulse. Jean-Pierre didn't ask how many steps it was to the river. Paulina wouldn't have known anyway. On the plane, she had read in her Paris guidebook, one of the Michelin Green Guides, that from door to door there were exactly four hundred steps between Saint-Germain and Saint-Sulpice. Everyone has their secrets.

The stall keepers next to the river were already gathering up their spread of old magazines, dusty books—three for the price of two—and vinyl records of *chansonniers* for tourists. With their never-ending grumblings about the day's earnings, the stall keepers, their fingers calloused by their work every evening, packed everything into boxes and tucked them all away into the big green wooden chest that functioned as an open-air shop. They fit everything in a feat of engineering. Afterward, they locked the chest with a flimsy padlock, and then it was good night until tomorrow.

Every so often, Jean-Pierre greeted a street vendor he knew from his midmorning coffee at La Palette. He had a habit of closing the gallery for ten minutes and sneaking away for a small coffee at the century-old bar—wooden on the inside, filled with ivy on the outside—nearby on the rue de Seine. Pipe still in his mouth, he absentmindedly began humming the tune Paulina had heard him hum before.

"Do you always whistle the same song? I noticed you do it yesterday at the wedding."

"It's a sirtaki, it's true. I like it. It sounds Greek, doesn't it?"

"It is Greek."

"Not exactly. It's from the soundtrack of the movie *Zorba the Greek*. Mikis Theodorakis composed it specifically for the movie, and the choreography he created was so impactful that it stuck. Now it feels like a traditional Greek tavern dance. What's wrong? Why are you looking at me like that?"

"You're a movie expert too?"

"I don't know anything, Pau, but the little I do know, I share. It's a salesman's trick. Anything to gain favor."

It was the first time anyone had called her Pau since she had been in school. She liked it. Paulina was too long. She had always complained about it to her parents.

"I love dancing it. I love to mark the rhythm and feel it speed up. Slowly, slowly, slowly." He pretended he was nodding off. "And then quickly, quickly, quickly until you can't keep up anymore. Sometimes, I dance the sirtaki when I'm alone at the gallery."

"You don't even believe what you're saying, Jean-Pierre."

"I swear. I dance it, and it cheers me up."

"So you whistle and dance there in the shop. I'm guessing you move the chesterfield couch out of the way so you don't trip." Sarcasm. It was her lifesaver again, helping her maintain her distance.

"You don't think so? Look." Jean-Pierre clenched the pipe between his teeth, took Pau's hand, and placed it on his shoulder. "Follow me."

"But . . ."

"Do everything I do . . ." He decided to put the pipe, an obstacle for dancing, into the pocket of his blazer.

"Jean-Pierre, no."

"Come on."

She had no choice. Lined up with their arms linked across their shoulders, Jean-Pierre sang loudly and outlined the steps. One foot forward, now the other, one step to this side, another to that side, one leg up, one bend, a second bend, a jump on the other leg until the twelfth beat, then a turn and spin, each time a little faster. Jean-Pierre worked himself up; the faster they danced, the louder he hummed the wordless tune. Paulina feared she'd twist her ankle on the cobblestone wharf in her mid-heeled pumps. She managed to slip off her shoes without interrupting the dance and finish the performance as she panted and laughed.

They were applauded. A couple dining on a nearby moored barge clapped and congratulated them from the deck. Neither Jean-Pierre nor Paulina had noticed that the elderly couple, halfway through a slice of melon, had paused their meal.

"I'm sweating . . ."

"It's the onion soup, lady . . ."

"Sure, the soup. Have you no shame, Jean-Pierre? You don't know what embarrassment is, do you?"

Paulina grabbed her shoes and found Jean-Pierre's muscular arm supporting her as she put them on. Once they had recovered and their pulse was back to normal, they embraced and found the only way they could stop laughing. With a kiss. And another. Slowly.

"You're not wearing the perfume from yesterday . . ."

Jean-Pierre had only meant to come off as observant and attentive to detail. But Paulina felt slightly disappointed. She couldn't let that disappointment show.

"You can't overuse Chanel No. 5. You don't like today's perfume?"

"I love it." The gallerist was quick to clarify. He didn't want it to look like . . . "Perfume is only an adjective. What I like is you."

Tucking her hair behind her ear, Paulina pretended to ignore the comment.

"It took my mother years to save up for a small bottle, and she prized it and guarded it like a jewel to the point that she wore it only one night a year. On her wedding anniversary, when she dressed up for dinner with my father at a nice restaurant, she would open the perfume and spritz a few drops like this on her neck. I loved watching my mother dress up in front of the mirror with the bathroom door open. She curled her eyelashes, put on her eye shadow, touched up her lips, and always—always, always—the final step of the ritual, once her dress was on, was spritzing on the perfume. She used just a little, carefully, like restraint itself made it more effective. You know those childhood things that stay with you, you're not sure why? I loved the way my mother smelled on the nights she put on the Chanel and went out to dinner with my father. He would also come home first to change, shave, and put on a tie. It was their night, and the whole house took on a special scent. I thought it was worth it for my closest cousin's wedding. It's a special occasion for me too, a good day to honor my mother."

"I think that's wonderful. Do you know why that happens?"

"What?"

"Why we remember very specific things from our childhood, but forget so many others."

"Because the things that impact us leave a mark?"

"Because memory chooses for us, for better or for worse. A moment, a conversation, or a scent. Like right now, maybe."

"Like now. Do you think that?"

"You said it yourself. The things that impact leave their mark. Memory engraves, like wood carving, the things you want to keep forever. I'm sure it's happened to you, but at other times, you memorize a phone number for five minutes because you have nowhere to write it down. A short-term memory, according to what's needed at the time, and then it's gone into the garbage."

"Memory can be trained."

"Oh yes. I have a friend who makes a living doing that it. Antoine performs in a basement on the rue de Rivoli, not far from home. It's the kind of bar where they do close-up magic, mentalism sessions, and *je ne sais pas quoi*. He, a bald man with a white beard, a bit of a belly, no charm at all, gets up on a small platform that acts as a stage. The audience yells words at him, one after another, without any rhyme or reason, all the way up to a hundred in a row. And he memorizes them and then repeats them."

"And does he get them right?"

"Almost never."

They burst out laughing. Once they recovered from the joke, they continued following the river in the distracted step of those without a destination.

"You have to meet him—Antoine Fernández—what a character."

"I'm here until Tuesday." *And it's already Saturday,* Paulina thought.

Between the bridges, five tramps, with more sense of the clock than the calendar, started to prepare the cardboard boxes that marked their territory. As was custom, they arranged their bundles—their homeland—to serve as mattresses. They minded their own business. They said nothing to the few passersby still enjoying the last light of dusk. They didn't even look at them. Paulina didn't turn her gaze away either, but she clutched onto Jean-Pierre's arm. Without saying a word, they both decided it was time to climb up the steps to the Pont des Arts.

At around half past nine in the second half of June, the building containing the Institut de France and the Mazarin basilica, visible from the bridge, changes color. The clean white stone shifts into an increasingly lighter and more tenuous burnt hue, until in the last gleam of light, it resembles a pink house. Looking north from the bridge, the sky is a spectacle that melts away moment by moment, second by second, racing against the clock. Almost against its own will. It is a great curtain, glowing red, that gradually darkens the silhouettes of the Grand Palais and the Petit Palais. The Eiffel Tower is always the last to vanish.

On the other side of the bridge, the water becomes denser until at twilight it's hard to guess whether it is flowing up- or downstream. You look for clues through the boats, the way their hoists creak, or through a disoriented duck, to know whether the river is rising or falling. Growing ever more still, the night swallows the Seine right where it branches off, at the angle chosen by so many painters with easels and watercolors who, before the day fully dissolves, also pack up their palettes and satchels.

Jean-Pierre, pipe between his teeth, knew how to choose the perfect moment and landscape.

"Will you come up to my place?"

Paulina opened his blazer slightly and slipped inside, resting her head on Jean-Pierre's chest. She didn't want to answer. She stepped back and looked him in the eyes. He turned his head slightly so the pipe smoke wouldn't bother her. Her answer was not the one she wanted to give or the one he wanted to hear.

"I'm grabbing a taxi, Jean-Pierre. It's time to go back to Croissy."

"Not a glass of wine at my place . . . ?"

"Let's not push things. It's been a magnificent night."

"I've got a chilled Anjou white . . ."

"Let's leave it at that."

". . . for a special occasion."

"Let's leave it at that. Do you understand?"

"Will I see you tomorrow?"

She took a deep breath.

"Is your friend performing? Antoine . . ."

"They close on Sundays. It's a shame. But I have to show you my favorite place. You can't say no. It's important that you see it. If I ever get lost, someone should know where to find me." He knew how to play the Mastroianni role when he needed to. "Will I see you tomorrow?"

Paulina took the pipe out of his mouth and gave him a quick kiss.

"Which side of the bridge is better for hailing a taxi?"

10

In the Shadow of Notre-Dame

Like many streets in many cities, on Sunday afternoon the rue de Seine was dead. Not a soul in sight, not a single passerby. The shutters were closed, and the shops lay in darkness, as if in an effort to let the paintings sleep. Only a bird or two, unaware of unions and work calendars, made music with their wings.

The taxi driver who ferried her from Croissy to Galerie Anouk had left behind the winding of the river and entered the street through Square Honoré-Champion, turning the corner that led to Paulina's destination without realizing she was going the wrong way. Paulina decided it was better to get out there than have the driver go all the way around. She asked her to stop the meter in front of the statue of Voltaire, and in her white shirt and new jeans, she walked past twenty or so shop windows before finding Jean-Pierre again, who greeted her with a kiss and twelve peonies. Paulina forgot all about her cousin's interrogation once she was with the gallery owner. Julie had cornered her at the doorstep and had accusingly asked what she'd done with Jean-Pierre the night before, where they had eaten, what he had shown her, where he had taken her, what they had talked about, what he thought of the wedding, whether she knew what he thought about her husband, whether she had called home, what she planned to do that Sunday, why she was wearing the new Calvin Klein jeans that made her legs look long and her figure slender, whether she would be seeing Jean-Pierre again on Sunday, where they would meet, at what time, whether she planned to go up to his apartment, whether she'd be back early for dinner with Alain at Croissy, whether . . .

More happy than overwhelmed, Paulina played dumb. She smiled and answered laconically, with a simple yes or no in a monotone. She resisted falling into Julie's trap. In this game of questions, any variation might betray her. She only answered that yes, she had spoken with Gina, that everything was fine in Barcelona, that her daughter was the best in the world, that she had enjoyed her time with Jean-Pierre, that he was an interesting man, and that, first of all, they weren't seeing each other on Sunday. But yes, thank you, now that she offered, she could call a taxi to take her down to Paris so she could stroll around Montmartre or Le Marais or maybe, depending on her mood, she might go into a theater to watch *Chariots of Fire*, which she'd heard good things about during the wedding aperitif.

The one thing she was sure of was that they shouldn't wait up for her for dinner. She wanted the newlyweds to be on their own at home. She had played third wheel long enough, and would rather they spend a Sunday afternoon just the two of them so they could realize how rare Sunday evenings are for a married couple. Due to Paulina's determination and because she wore her happiness plainly on her cheeks, Julie guessed her cousin was planning something.

Jean-Pierre had been copying art dealers' phone numbers into a new address book, one by one and in alphabetical order, while he waited for Paulina. He finished his task.

"Ready to walk?"

"You won't be able to keep up with me in my espadrilles."

"You look really . . ."

"You like it?"

"Yes."

"Really what? Can you finish the sentence?"

"Spectacular."

"You don't sound very convincing . . ."

"I've seen you at the wedding, and in yesterday's dress. But the jeans and simple shirt look really good on you."

"Thank you."

"The best cook in the world isn't the one who makes the most complicated dish, but the one who can fry up the best egg."

"Don't complicate things. Just go with it. That knit shirt looks good on you too."

"Let's go."

"What do we do with the flowers?"

Jean-Pierre went into the back room, took out a vase with a handful of water, placed the Santa Clara peonies inside, and set it in the shop window at the foot of Le Corbusier.

"This is the best place for it. You're right."

"'Fifteen minutes before the end of the world.'"

"Can I say something? I don't like that quote you have in the doorway. Who said it?"

Jean-Pierre didn't respond. He locked the gallery and set off down the rue de Seine with the intention of showing Paulina where she should look for him if he ever went missing. Once they reached the Institut de France, they turned toward the Quai des Grands Augustins, above the river in the direction of the Île de la Cité.

"I know where you're taking me. It's not hard to guess."

"Where?"

"To Notre-Dame."

"Do you really take me for someone so cheap . . . ?"

"No, come on."

"How disappointing. You think that if I ever went missing, you should look for me in a church?"

"In a cathedral. And not just any."

"You're getting colder, colder. Careful." He grabbed her hand. "We're crossing here."

In the shadow of Notre-Dame, on the other side of the river, on a corner of a street where two cherry trees in bloom made it appear like a small square, at number 37 rue de la Bûcherie, there appeared, like an oasis, Shakespeare and Company. A bookshop. The capital letters of the shop sign, black against a yellow background, made an impression on any passerby who happened upon that secret corner of Paris by chance on their leisurely stroll. Only the *S* in Shakespeare, painted a blood red, and the two portraits on the facade of the man who authored so many comedic and tragic lives, added any color to a bookshop that introduced itself in English: "Antiquarian Books."

"It's beautiful, Jean-Pierre. This place is so serene."

"Has your cousin never brought you here?"

"Never. I've never even heard of it."

"Well, the bookshop is just like you. It's even better on the inside."

Paulina was too distracted to notice Jean-Pierre's compliment. She was astonished, observing the green wooden enclosure of the shop on each side of the two entrances. The color matched the little Wallace fountain that stood in front of one of the windows and broke any sense of symmetry. Symmetry, palindromic numbers, and proportional gardens had unsettled Paulina ever since she was young.

"If you're thirsty . . ." He pressed the fountain. "You can drink the water."

"Is it good luck to drink it?"

"Not that I know of."

"Does it mean I'll come back to Paris?"

"Not necessarily. But it does quench your thirst, which is enough."

"I do hope I come back." She approached the fountain. "Just in case . . ."

Paulina leaned forward on tiptoe, trying not to wet her feet. She let a good stream of water run before drinking.

"They say there are a hundred fountains identical to this in Paris, but I've never counted."

If Paulina had brought a camera with her, she would have taken tons of photos of the fountain, the facade, the shutters, the letters, the peacefulness, the two winter magnolias in their pink spring bloom, the boxes of books stacked outside on the street like fruit. If Paulina had been able to, she would have photographed those days, those streets, those walks, and that special man.

"Enter. Enter alone, Pau. I don't want to tell you anything. You go in, and then we'll talk."

"You're not coming with me?"

"Enter, and maybe you'll see why, if I ever go missing, you should look for me here."

"But . . ."

"Go upstairs, look out the window, enter every room, don't hold back. Look around, rummage through the books, breathe. Stay as long as you need. I want you to discover it on your own. Take your time. I'll wait for you here." He raised his hand, his pipe was smoking. "George doesn't like me puffing like a chimney inside."

Paulina decided to go in cautiously, like she was setting foot inside a haunted house. Her eyes were wide open, her senses heightened. Ready to feel, ready to perceive—what special days these had been—she crossed the doorway like one opens a book. She let herself be carried away by the magical world of imagination.

The bookshop was narrow, labyrinthine, and crowded. The ground floor, at least, was full of winding nooks and uneven inclines at every step. No two steps were the same. In some stretches she stepped on carpet so worn it had lost its elegant burgundy. In others, her timid footsteps landed on wood or on the original stonework, which was slippery, as if to cruelly remind her that time erodes everything. There were books everywhere she looked, from floor to ceiling, in boxes, on shelves that were warped and crooked. There was the occasional straight one, an exception of nature, held upright by the stillness. Her gaze was inevitably drawn to the ocean of books, many yellowed, most topped by the dust of time and having been untouched by a rag. Poetry, novels, histories of history, titles written in English, in French . . .

She had to let a group of Americans, excitement shining in their eyes, descend so she could climb up to the second floor. She cautiously scaled the only staircase. It was very steep, with narrow, uncomfortable steps. She bent her head to avoid bumping into anything. The paradise of old books widened and brightened upstairs. Natural light, spilling in from the street or skylight, gave the space a gravity and depth the cluttered ground floor lacked. The landscape, though, was the same: spines and more spines covering every wall from top to bottom, without a single gap.

In the room at the back there was an open piano and a wooden chair, giving the impression that someone was about to sit down and play a Chopin nocturne. In the middle of the hallway, she discovered a single tiny office with a low ceiling, where only half a person fit, and not even very comfortably. Both ceiling and walls were covered with scraps of paper—glued, pinned, or hanging—where visitors had immortalized some thought. A portable typewriter with a plastic case from the seventies rested on the tiny desk. Paulina assumed it was merely decorative. She was tempted to step in, sit down, and type a message to Jean-Pierre, but she didn't want to be told off for breaking the rules.

She continued to explore the back of the second floor, guided by curiosity and the beam of light entering through the only window, flung wide open. The final room was the final chapter of the bookshop. It was a room made to function like a library. It was the only place in Shakespeare and Company where book lovers could sit for a while and leaf through the paragraphs of a novel that had caught their eye. No two chairs were alike in the library. There were armchairs, stools, wooden chairs with wobbly legs, and a rickety love seat. And, of course, if you leaned out ever so slightly from the windowsill, you could spot the two towers of Notre-Dame from a unique perspective. She took her time. Jean-Pierre's instructions had been clear, and she followed them. She picked up a book of Baudelaire's poems just as easily as she might have picked any other volume within reach and sat down in the wicker rocking chair in the library to contemplate nothingness. She didn't open the book. She gazed into the silence. The other Sunday wanderers who entered the tiny library respected the focus of those who had journeyed onto the paths of fiction. It was more like a room for prayer. Only the buzzing of a hesitant hornet that flew in and out of the window, every now and then, caused a couple of the avid readers to look up in mild annoyance. Others, absorbed in a good story, were not distracted by anything.

"Do you know what they called libraries in Egypt?" Jean-Pierre had asked her. "The treasure that cures the soul."

When she had had enough, Paulina retraced her steps. She hunched her shoulders to descend the staircase and, dodging other customers who were browsing the shelves, stepped outside, exhilarated, to rejoin Jean-Pierre.

"So, Monsieur Zanardi, if you ever go missing, we'll know to look for you here."

"If I ever go missing in Paris, that is."

"It has a special charm. I get it."

"If you think I'm in Paris, look for me here, or in any of the magnificent bookshops around the world. I've visited many, but I have more that I've yet to discover. I've heard about two secondhand shops in Scotland, in Inverness and Glasgow. One day I'll have to make my way up there to see them. A bookshop is . . ." He paused to think before finishing in a way that wasn't arrogant. "A home of freedom, a refuge of words, a real museum of thought."

"What are you searching for in there? Words?"

"Butterflies. Always. Books about butterflies, catalogs, volumes that might show me a species I've never seen."

"I'd like us to go in together."

"Now?"

"You don't feel like it?"

"After you, milady . . ."

It says a lot when a country's zero-mile marker is inside a bookstore, especially one that houses all types of wisdom, the entire weight of literature, and the passing of history. Jean-Pierre held his pipe in his hand. It was still warm even though some time had passed since he had smoked.

"The owner is an American friend of mine. He recently had a daughter at sixty-seven years old. George Whitman from New Jersey. The man has had a life worthy of the movies. He arrived in Paris, having never been to France, after World War II. He stayed, opened a second-hand bookshop in Saint-Michel, and, not too long after, bought this place. I think this is an old convent."

"Is that him?" She used her elbow to point at an extremely skinny man who was kneeling on the floor and rummaging through a pile of books near the stairs.

"Yes. There he is."

"His face says it all."

"He's an eccentric. A lunatic, a romantic . . ."

"A bohemian?"

"Call him whatever you want. Some days he wears a tie. Sometimes, depending on his mood, he wears the most outlandish blazers. You should see him on the nights he organizes poetry readings here in the shop. He's crazy about books. If only there were more people like him."

Paulina laughed under her breath and spoke quietly so George, who couldn't find what he was looking for, wouldn't hear her.

"Have you noticed the tips of his collar? They could poke your eye out if you get too close."

They laughed at the out-of-style and razor-sharp collar points. George Whitman was a peculiar man in his physique as well. His white hair hung like soggy endives from his head. He had a hook nose and a wiry little goatee that had certainly seen better days. He was himself, a one-of-a-kind man, gaunt, with a whole lot of leg and very little body, and the beginnings of hunchback from a life of bookselling. Or maybe he was asthmatic, as the two conditions often look alike.

"Want to know the best part? Look at how young all the workers are."

"And it looks like they're all foreigners."

"The man has it made. He lets young writers from all over the world, or anyone really who wants to become a writer, sleep upstairs, inside the bookshop itself, next to the piano or in the library. Didn't you see all the mattresses on the ground?"

"I wasn't paying much attention."

"The bookshop has become an unusual writers' residence. They come to Paris without a place to stay, and George lets them sleep here with three conditions. First, the young person must read a book a day. Second, they have to work two hours in the shop daily. And third, they have to write at the very least one page of autobiographical material each day. What do you think?"

"That's brilliant, Jean-Pierre."

"He gets cheap labor, and people line up to sleep and work here for free. All the while he collects thousands and thousands of autobiographies from young writers who, who knows, might one day become famous."

They went back up to the second floor. Jean-Pierre walked ahead.

"Did you see the little desk?" He crouched inside and sat down.

"I loved it. The typewriter ready to . . ."

"They say Lawrence Durrell wrote a fragment of the Alexandria Quartet in here. Have you read the books?"

"Have you ever written anything yourself?"

"Me?" Jean-Pierre felt trapped. "Nothing worthwhile. A few lines in my youth."

"Poems?"

"No, no. A *roman*, a long sort of story." He was embarrassed. "I don't even know if I even kept it."

"I want to see it."

"It's not worthwhile, Pauline, really."

"And what about him?"

"Who?"

"The owner. Has he ever written anything?"

"George? He once told me—you'll like this—that he's only ever written love letters."

"Oh . . ."

"And you know what? I believe him."

"He looks like the type maybe."

Jean-Pierre stretched out to escape Durrell's office.

"Let's head down, and I'll introduce you to him."

"George?"

"If you want?"

"And who will you tell him I am?"

She wanted to meet him but was scared.

"What do you want me to say? The truth? A cousin from Barcelona? A friend, a client of the gallery, a model for ready-to-wear clothing? The perfect recipient of love letters? Take your pick."

She laughed nervously.

"Drop it. I'm embarrassed."

"Look." He seduced her with a new idea. "I'll drop it if you promise me one thing: that you'll never forget this place."

"Not this place or this moment."

Paulina moved toward him, slowly. When she was close to him, she kissed him deeply and wildly. A reader with a face reminiscent of a puppet, who had been leafing through Georges Simenon's *Maigret and the Yellow Dog*, looked up from the page, glanced at them from the corner of his eye, and returned to Maigret's investigation. He was more interested in learning how dogs smell death before anyone else than in the impetuous kiss between two strangers.

Paulina noticed that, with Jean-Pierre by her side, the days went by quickly. Just as they had on Saturday, they had met again on Sunday, at first with a polite caution, a respectful tact, almost an aristocratic refinement. With a certain coldness, she might also say, on Jean-Pierre's part, if it hadn't been for the bouquet of flowers. But as they spent more time together, she felt the hours and emotions piling on top of one another. The calm faded, the intensity grew, and vibrations and conversations spun like a centrifuge inside her. Jean-Pierre showed her new worlds and taught her things she didn't know. He captivated her with his words, his gestures, with a kind of old-fashioned courtesy that enveloped her, lifted her, transported her until she was floating. He was more Marcello than Jean-Pierre. Or as much of one as of the other. Or the exact sum of the two seductive men. Paulina, who did not doubt her own charms but was no longer in the habit of making others fall in love, at times feared she might not be up for the task and had to hide.

"We could go to the movies this afternoon."

"Is that what you want?"

"I've never been to a theater in Paris."

"Well, here you have seats and a screen. They turn off the lights, and a man with a flashlight . . ."

"You were there when there was a conversation about *Chariots of Fire* at the wedding, right? I don't think so. It just came out. Some people have already seen it and loved it. They said it was really good and that no doubt it'll win all the Oscars: for best picture, screenplay, cinematography, costume design. They said the music should win an award. Or do you have a better plan?"

"I have only one plan: Spend time with you."

Jean-Pierre had done it again with his silver tongue.

He picked up a copy of *Libération* from a kiosk, opened it up to check the movie times, and put it back before the vendor, who was counting the days to his retirement, could so much as bat an eyelid.

"If we hurry, we can make it to the Gaumont theaters on boulevard des Capucines. It's right by the opera."

Paulina hadn't expected there to be a line. Had she been with her husband, they would have already turned around or picked another movie rather than endure that snaking line that went down to the corner. Manuel could not stand being cut in front of, and was always suspicious someone was trying to do it. In fact, they probably hadn't gone to the theater at all since Gina had been born. At most, they watched a movie on the living room sofa on a Saturday night. One of them always fell asleep.

There weren't many seats left when they entered the dark movie theater, and they had to sit farther to the front than they would have liked.

By the time they found their seats, the British athletes were already running barefoot along the beach, dressed in an impeccable white. The Scotsman Eric Liddell, a devout Protestant who trusted more in his prayer than his own legs, refused to run on a Sunday at the 1924 Olympic Games, held there in Paris, against the English Harold Abrahams, a Jewish man who held all the records. It was a cinematic duel that might have seemed like it was about sports from the poster, but was actually about religion and culture.

"The music really is good," Jean-Pierre whispered.

Paulina didn't respond. She had been taught not to speak at the movies, and this was sacred to her. She was concentrating hard on the film, with its time shifts, which were even trickier in a language that wasn't her own.

Jean-Pierre reached for her hand after the two runners raced Trinity College's Great Court Run before the clock struck noon. He caressed her fingers for a little while. Then he rested his hand on Paulina's, which rested on her jeans. She noticed that he even traced the outline of her wedding ring like it was nothing.

Had he noticed her wearing it? Was he passing his fingers over it as a way of saying he didn't care? Then, as if afraid someone might see them, they unfolded their arms and dropped their clasped hands between the seats, locking their fingers like an anchor. They held hands tightly. Neither of them wanted to let go before the movie ended. They were happy together, touching, sensing each other. Skin against skin.

"Did you like it?"

Jean-Pierre assumed the no-talking rule had been lifted once the credits rolled. Eyes still on the screen, Paulina took a while to answer. She turned and looked him in the eyes.

"A lot. And I really liked watching it with you."

It wasn't until then, when the theater lights came on, that they let go of each other's hands.

They had dinner at Brasserie Lipp, also on boulevard Saint-Germain, on the opposite side of the church and Les Deux Magots, the onion soup café from the night before. Lipp was perhaps the brasserie par excellence, the place that never went out of style. Its kitchen stayed open until two in the morning, ideal hours for politicians, artists, and other scoundrels fond of conspiring. Jean-Pierre and Paulina entered without a reservation shortly before eight, according to the train-station clock hanging on two chains in the dining room. The restaurant had been founded in the nineteenth century by an Alsatian who had come to Paris to make his fortune and succeeded. Léonard Lipp quickly became renowned for his sauerkraut and beer, and the restaurant carried on this specialty more than a hundred years later. It might have looked like any ordinary restaurant from the outside, but once you passed through the revolving door, it was a paradise of sounds and smells, amplified by the large mirrors covering every wall. Jean-Pierre, whose pipe rested in a pocket of his blazer, made Pau enter ahead of him—out of gallantry, but primarily as not to block her first view of the place.

The floor was a checkerboard of large gleaming squares. The rectangular tables, barely a hand's breadth and a half wide, were so close together the waiters had to pull one out entirely to let a customer reach the brown moleskin bench next to the wall. There was no more than two fingers' width of space between each table, the exact amount needed to set a clean linen tablecloth after each meal.

"Should we share a chateaubriand with béarnaise sauce?"

"I won't eat much, but that's perfect. I'm not too hungry." Nerves always manifested in Paulina's stomach.

The annoyingly sweet waiter took their order in a scribble that the kitchen could probably only decipher due to long practice. Even in the nice June weather, all the waiters wore suit coats, vests, and black bow ties in the darkest black shade. They wore a perfectly ironed white apron over their pants that hung down from their waists to their ankles.

Paulina was surprised at how sharp, straight, and impeccably folded the crease line was. She would have to mention it to Isabel, who never ironed so meticulously at home.

"Look." Paulina pointed at the little sign on the table in front of them. "You'll have to restrain yourself here."

The scent of perfumed tobacco bothers most of our clients.

PIPE SMOKERS,

PLEASE NO SMOKING IN THIS ESTABLISHMENT.

"I don't smoke perfumed tobacco." He finished reading the sign. "Haven't you noticed I don't smell like a Dutch sailor?"

"You're right. Your pipe doesn't smell like pipe smoke."

She responded that way even though what she really wanted to say was *You always smell wonderful.*

"I smoke fine-cut tobacco. It's not pipe tobacco, but I like it better. It doesn't make my tongue sting. In any case"—Jean-Pierre signaled toward the sign with his eyebrow—"don't worry, I won't smoke. I don't usually smoke while I eat."

"One day, mark my words, smoking won't be permitted in restaurants."

"You think so? It's part of the business."

"People will be able to taste their food better. And I think our clothes won't reek of . . ."

"Impossible. Who's going to outlaw it? No one would dare."

"You should know when my father was young, he once said one day people would sell bottled water, and everyone thought he was crazy."

"What a visionary."

"I'm telling you now on Sunday, June 14, 1981, that one day they'll outlaw smoking. We might not live to see the day."

Voilà!

The meat, cut up and red, was brought on a silver platter. It came with french fries, four spears of asparagus, and a hot béarnaise sauce, with its aromatic scent of butter, shallot, and the seventeen spices of happiness.

They unfolded the giant napkins and placed them on their laps. Jean-Pierre liked enormous napkins; Paulina liked well-set tables. She amused herself with the play of mirrors; he explained to her that all those mosaics of painted tiles decorating the restaurant, dominated by greens and yellows, were by Fargue, a master ceramicist of Paris who had . . . Paulina interrupted him. The images the mosaics depicted weren't very Alsatian: bamboo, palm trees, and parrots hiding between modernist lamps that illuminated the tables. Their white lights that did not conceal the *saignant* chateaubriand, cooked perfectly.

Focused on the steak, the sides, and the company, they didn't notice that a decadent cupid painted on the ceiling, hidden behind one of the seven wrought-iron lamps, was pointing an arrow at them.

"Why do you love butterflies so much?"

"Don't you?"

"I do, very much. But I don't collect . . ."

"Because they fly high, because they fly far. Because the more you look at them, the more fascinating they become. Because they are miracles of nature. Because they come and go. Because when they flutter around you, even for just a moment, those seconds are magical. Because . . ."

He could have listed a thousand more reasons, both poetic and prosaic. He would have liked to explain why he traveled the world hunting for butterfly books he still didn't have in his collection, but the attentive waiter slid out the adjacent table, table number seven, so two elderly ladies could slide in. The ladies were so old and so decked out in jewels that their earrings served as counterweights to their canes to keep them from tipping over.

"Why did they take down the photo of Picasso?" asked one of the ladies as soon as she sat on the bench.

"No, Madame Rentz, it's in its usual place," the waiter replied to the ninety-year-old woman. "There, you see it? It's hanging at the foot of the stairs."

The two ladies squinted to focus on the faraway item. If they couldn't even make out the frame, they sure couldn't see the photo. The waiter took it down from the wall and brought it to their table. Jean-Pierre and Paulina could not help but look at the black-and-white image that the waiter, holding it from behind, rested on the ladies' tablecloth.

"So now you see it!" said the overly made-up nonagenarian.

"See what?" replied her friend, from the same vintage.

"That Picasso is smoking."

"No, no," answered her friend, who had overdrawn her eyeliner. "On the contrary, dear, I told you he was lighting a cigarette, but you said he wasn't."

"There you go again . . ."

"What now?"

"Saying that you said what I actually said . . ."

Jean-Pierre looked at Pauline complicitly.

In order to restore peace between the ladies, the waiter used the one tool that has prevented so many wars. Diplomacy.

"Just so you know, mesdames, the photo was taken at this very table. Number seven was Picasso's favorite."

"Oh, really?" the two old ladies replied, before turning to read the menu and never thinking of *Guernica*'s painter again.

The amused Paulina pointed out another detail she had noticed by chance in that image of Picasso smoking at Brasserie Lipp with his plastered bangs.

"Do you see how long his fingernails are? He almost looks like a woman . . ."

"Who?"

"The man in the photo." She didn't want to name him in case the old ladies overheard.

"I suppose they're for opening paint jars."

"Don't make fun of me."

"I'm telling the truth. I don't know if that was the case for him, but I know several painters who grow out their nails just to open jars."

"They don't own a screwdriver? Or a knife to pry open the lid?"

"I don't know, Pauline."

"Anyway, it's enough just to have one long nail. No need for all of them to be sharp."

"I see the subject really interests you," he teased.

"It just grossed me out, what can I say . . ."

"Well then. Let Picasso's market value drop. Madame Homs does not approve of the painter's fingernails."

"You're such a . . ." She preferred not to finish the sentence, because she didn't mean whatever it was.

Don't poke the bear.

The waiter finally managed to hang the picture on his fifth attempt back on its nail near the foot of the stairs.

"Do you know what's upstairs, Pauline?"

"The bathrooms?"

They laughed again.

"If you need those, they're downstairs. Upstairs is hell." He shrugged lightly as if to shake off the evil. "That's what they call it here."

"Like purgatory, you don't ascend into hell. You descend."

"They call it the 'staircase to hell' because upstairs is where they put three types of customers: American tourists, Japanese tour groups, and the undesirables."

"We were lucky to get a table down here then."

"Table eight. The corner table. What more can you want? The best vantage point for observing the whole restaurant. A little tip does miracles."

"Is this where you bring your lady friends to impress them?"

"No. It's the table the communists always requested, because they felt like their backs were covered at this angle, and they couldn't be ambushed from any side."

"Now I know it's not your table."

"What's that supposed to mean?" he asked playfully. "Hey, girl, I have standards, and I smoke a pipe . . ."

"Also to impress women?"

"No, to scare away mosquitoes."

The two ladies—one on the bench and the other with her back exposed, vulnerable to any attack—had ordered enough food for four and a bottle of champagne, which they received with applause before splitting it in half. The widows' celebration did not interrupt Jean-Pierre and Paulina's romantic dinner. They amused themselves with eavesdropping on the neighboring table's conversations without having to strain their ears. Paulina understood almost everything, and each time a comment made her laugh, she kicked Jean-Pierre's knee under the table.

The ladies—Madame Rentz and Madame Bourvil—began competing to see who slept less at night. After arguing up and down, the winner was apparently the one who proclaimed she slept barely an hour. Paulina, appalled by Madame Bourvil's exaggeration, nearly contested the result. She wasn't too successful when the check was to be paid either. Despite her insistence, the waiter deferred to Jean-Pierre's expression that clearly said *If you don't take my money, I will never set foot in Lipp again.* Pauline acted offended, because men paying for everything was a thing of the past. But Jean-Pierre's linguistic advantage tipped the scales. They moved the table aside, wished the ladies a courteous good night, warmly and earnestly congratulated Madame Rentz on her birthday, asked the waiter to take a photo of them at the foot of the stairs, and left Lipp. In the front dining room, which was now the exit for the lovers, Paulina noticed one last sign. She found it funny.

WARNING

For public health reasons, we request that customers

DO NOT FEED DOGS

with food from the establishment

or let them jump onto the chairs.

"Since you're a visionary, what do you think they'll outlaw first in restaurants: smoking or dogs?"

"If it were up to me, both. Come on, silly. Don't make fun of me, you hear?"

There was a lot of tenderness in that playful poking.

Once they left the brasserie, they wandered aimlessly toward the Sénat and the Luxembourg Gardens. They walked slowly, hand in hand or arm in arm, like they were afraid that one of them might slip away at any moment. That night, however, neither had the slightest intention of doing so.

"I'm not going to ask you again if you want to come up for a glass of wine at my place."

"Right . . ."

"Right what?"

"It seems like you are . . ."

"No, no . . . On the contrary, I said I wouldn't insist. I wouldn't want to impose on you."

"You sure are a gentleman."

"We Zanardis are like that. Respectful and . . ."

Paulina didn't let him finish. What she had to say was too important.

"Jean-Pierre, can I tell you something?" Her heart raced a million miles a minute before and after speaking. "I would really like to see your house."

Jean-Pierre gave her a sweet, sugary kiss.

By the time Paulina opened her eyes again, he had already hailed a taxi and opened the door for her.

"Number 5, rue du Trésor, in Le Marais, please."

They held hands in the taxi in silence. Was it nervousness or anticipation that kept them from speaking? Or both things, tightly entangled?

Because it was nighttime, Paulina didn't notice he lived on a narrow, dead-end street that was landscaped with flower beds on each side. She did notice, however, the solid wooden door that was varnished, with bronze handles that were easy to grip. It struck her as noble, befitting him perfectly. They took a stately elevator up to the fourth floor. Jean-Pierre, just behind her, gently took her by the waist with both hands. Their closeness sent a shiver through her spine. He was whistling again. Paulina realized that this tic betrayed him. It was something he did unconsciously when he was nervous or not fully in control of a situation. She was glad to discover she wasn't the only one navigating unknown waters. She said nothing. She was sure that if she opened her mouth, her voice would tremble.

"This is my den."

He suddenly switched on as many lights as he could.

"Wow. It looks like a continuation of the gallery. Everything is so . . . white, austere, neatly arranged. What's the name?"

"What?" He was startled. "Whose name?"

"The designer."

"No, no, I did it all myself."

He approached her from close behind.

"I like simple things, refined things. I'm a man with taste."

He kissed her neck.

". . . And a touch."

"If that's what you say . . ." She turned around to bring her lips to his and look him in the eyes to make sure that they both really wanted the type of night that was accelerating toward them. "But it's true. You have taste, and you have a touch. There's no denying that."

After the welcome kiss, Jean-Pierre grabbed her hand, and, quickly, they walked across the living room, they passed through the kitchen, he showed her the little office that looked out into the inner courtyard, and at the end of the hallway, they reached the bedroom. It took up practically half the apartment between the walk-in closet, the bathroom with its sliding door, and the reading sofa. Standing, they began kissing again. Since he had first tasted her, Jean-Pierre had been longing for Paulina's thick lips. Looking into her eyes, he skillfully unbuttoned her white blouse, one button at a time. Paulina did the same with Jean-Pierre's knit shirt, from top to bottom. They let their shirts fall to the floor at the same time with a sort of reverence. After gently biting her ear, he casually unfastened her bra with a precise snap of his fingers. She lifted her shoulders so the straps would slide down on their own, letting the garment fall down the length of her torso. They embraced, body to body. Both needed to feel the warmth of the other's chest against their own. The perfect fit. Soft, warm, welcoming. They stayed like that for a while, saying nothing. Thinking of nothing.

Then, without letting each other go, they slipped off their shoes, and, facing each other, they repeated the ritual. Jean-Pierre unbuttoned her jeans while she unfastened his pants in the very same second. Each stepped out of their own clothing, and they let themselves fall onto the bed before the impetuous dance they had been nurturing for hours.

Perhaps, without knowing it, for an entire lifetime.

After the initial unrestrained and passionate blaze, their gestures gradually tempered. Paulina, naked in Jean-Pierre's arms, was in heaven. She noticed that his lean, well-built body smelled like tobacco, freshly cut grass, clean sheets, a box of Caran d'Ache crayons, and the afternoon snack of toast with chocolate from her childhood in Sant Pol. She embraced his torso and found concentrated there many moments of her own happiness. With Paulina's hair fanned on his chest, Jean-Pierre couldn't stop caressing her velvety and celestial peach-like skin. From her legs to her bottom, from her back to her shoulders. Her breasts, whiter, well proportioned, held themselves up with the pride of her almost thirty years. Delicately, Jean-Pierre tended to her nipples with a respect no one had ever shown her. *With a violinist's fingers,* she thought.

Jean-Pierre knew a thing or two when it came to making love. And Paulina was delighted. All the sensitivity and artistry in every aspect of his life had taught him to appreciate bodies, to respect them, and to understand that, beyond penetration, there is play and life and fire. What a gift. With his expert fingers and inquisitive tongue, Jean-Pierre knew how to approach delicate places. Paulina appreciated that he came to her sex with consideration, without roughness. But also with the necessary gesture of masculine confidence to carry her up to the clouds.

They made love twice. Slowly. They kissed, they sweated, and they said beautiful things to each other.

"I've felt things I never thought I could feel."

"No one has ever said anything so flattering to me."

"I wasn't just talking about sex."

After that, Paulina got up to lower the curtain so that no one in the building across the way might see them. Jean-Pierre admired her young, strong legs.

"You're incredibly sexy."

She really was proud of her legs.

"Didn't you say you have a white wine from . . . somewhere?"

"In the fridge."

He hid the reluctance he felt about getting up.

"Would you like some?"

Jean-Pierre returned from the kitchen with two glasses and the open bottle in an ice bucket. He served them both. They toasted, sitting at the foot of the bed, and then lay down again, proud of their bodies and the moment.

Three glasses later, she told him not to move. He was lying on his back, looking at the minimalist lamp inspired by a Calder mobile hanging above the bed. Paulina pulled back the sheet and kissed him all over his body, noting that some of his hairs were beginning to turn white. After caressing his arms and lingering around his navel, she climbed on top of him. She braced him between her knees on the mattress, and guiding him with two fingers to remind him of the way, she suddenly had him inside her again. She began to ride him, very slowly. In a rhythm. Softly, so softly. Occasionally she arched her back and supported herself with her hands on his thighs. At other times, with the same soft cadence, she bent forward against his chest, to feel him better, more deeply. She realized her hair falling over his face might bother him, so she skillfully tied it back before continuing the languid, tranquil rocking. "Softer, softer, love," she whispered.

Feeling liberated and unfamiliar with this version of herself, she liked setting the rhythm. Being in control. She wasn't used to it. It was something different.

"*Ne bouge pas.* 'Don't move,' I said."

Jean-Pierre, motionless, grew even more aroused under Paulina's command. Her extremely slow movement—softer, softer—the perfect lubrication, the sensitive friction. He felt every point of contact as if it were new each time, slowly, up and down. The pleasure was long, intense, almost too much to bear. "Softer, softer," she repeated in his ear. And the more she insisted, the softer Jean-Pierre felt himself making love to Pauline—fully surrendered, in another world, in a field full of butterflies with the most colorful patterns he had ever seen flutter anywhere. He felt his head and his heart and all of him on the verge of exploding. With each thrust, closer. *"Softer, softer,"* Paulina repeated, her chest growing rosier each time. And he let her do as she pleased. Let himself be carried. And they felt every flavor of it. And they opened their eyes, now and then, to acknowledge that they were together. And they waited for each other. And at the same time, matching each other's breath, they delayed the final moan as long as they possibly could.

Overcome by pleasure, they fell asleep in each other's arms.

The first sunrays entered the room in Monday's rudeness. Paulina, who had slept soundly, without judging herself, without even thinking about who she was or what she was doing there, lifted her head inches from the pillow. Through the window she saw a slice of the blue sky. On the nightstand, the ice had melted into a puddle. The bottle, upside down, had shed its label, which now floated in the water like a dead body.

When she turned to caress Jean-Pierre, he was no longer there. Before she had time to worry, she heard the sound of the shower. The frosted glass sliding door didn't let her see his silhouette. She stretched and let herself savor her laziness while taking in, left and right, the sanctuary of her . . . lover. After spending a night at his place, could she call him that already? At what point in a relationship, Paulina wondered, does another person become your lover? Is a lover measured in kisses or in feelings? Is sex what defines the term? And if it is, what kind of sex? Is it a matter of how many times, or of intensity? In the calm of the morning, Paulina didn't regret anything she had done or said since Julie had introduced her to Jean-Pierre. That morning she felt, for once, transgressive. Not exactly proud of it, but not punishing herself either. She would think about it on the plane home. The plane home! She didn't want to go back. She didn't want it to end. She knew she could keep this story in the required secrecy. But again, the words troubled her. Why did she think of it as a story, an affair, when she was feeling things she had never felt before? Where was it written that her relationship with her Mastroianni had to be just an adventure, or a fling, or one of those euphemisms invented to soothe guilty consciences? Why limit it from the outset? Why not surrender to Jean-Pierre as much as he seemed to be opening himself to her, and later they would have time to decide what label to put on it? Words are sometimes more incriminating than actions. And she began turning all this over in her mind. Perhaps the man in the shower had broken down a few of her barriers. How many, my love? How many, beloved?

From the bed, she could see that, next to the reading sofa that Jean-Pierre kept in the bedroom, in addition to a standing ashtray and a vintage lamp, there was an antique piece of furniture holding a telephone, some books, and a few photographs. She got up to look at them closely.

There were three pictures.

There was an old black-and-white wedding portrait in an extravagant silver frame. Based on the groom's features, she had no doubt it was his parents' wedding outside the church of Saint-Germain-des-Prés, in interwar Paris.

A second faded photograph was clearly of a proud young Jean-Pierre, pipe in mouth, shaking hands with a painter she didn't recognize. Judging by the joy on Jean-Pierre's face, he must have been a renowned artist.

The third photograph on the piece of furniture unsettled Paulina much more. In a chipped ivory frame was a photo of a little girl. It was a close-up taken at the gallery on rue de Seine with a Polaroid camera. Based on her features, she was a few years older than Gina but nowhere near as cute. She had to be six or seven, eight at the very most. She was dark haired, with two Peruvian-style braids, and smiling at the camera in a way that showed off her fairly separated two front teeth.

She didn't look like an Anouk, a name Paulina thought better suited to a woman than to a girl. No matter how hard she searched, she found no resemblance whatsoever to Jean-Pierre. He had told her he had no children at Julie's wedding, and after the two days, and one night, they had spent together, this was not the moment—please no—to catch him in a lie. There would be time enough later, if necessary, to untangle that mess.

She decided to go wish Jean-Pierre good morning. She slipped off her panties, went into the bathroom, and, without him hearing her enter, stepped into the shower with him. She poured the shower gel into her hand and slowly soaped him, as carefully as one cleans a Renaissance David. Under the generous stream of water, the gallerist had stopped whistling.

"Did you tell your cousin you weren't coming home to sleep?"

"Shit!"

11

Bulgarian Love Songs

She came back with breakfast: two rather toasted croissants, a baguette, half a pound of smoked mortadella sliced on the spot, and three peaches she thought were at their peak. Paulina had gone down to buy breakfast, and before entering a bakery, she looked for a phone booth to call her cousin.

Jean-Pierre had insisted *"S'il te plait"* that she call from the apartment, that she not put it off any longer because Julie must be anxious. But Pau needed time to think about what she would say and, above all, to draw up her speech, since she could feel her life falling apart. Anyway, she felt embarrassed having to explain things in front of Jean-Pierre. She didn't want to talk about him in front of him, and she didn't want him to overhear her getting caught in some lie or a half-truth, the coward's way of evading.

"Honey, are you okay? Where the hell have you gone? It's been agony! Do you know what time it is? We've been waiting for you. Alain and I spent the whole night worrying. He even said we should call the gendarmerie. I thought of calling Jean-Pierre's apartment, because you are with him, huh? Just say yes or no if you can't talk. Look, yesterday, I noticed something in you when you left the house. I don't know. The shirt and the jeans, you had fixed yourself up in a certain way . . . I saw something in your eyes that . . . We've been like sisters for too many years. We can't hide anything from each other. I won't ask questions. You tell me whatever you want, or whatever you can, and I won't judge you. But Paulina, please, be careful with Jean-Pierre . . ."

"Why should I be careful?"

Paulina, who had endured Julie's tirade, waiting for the end of an interrogation from someone who had had a sleepless night, suddenly snapped. Before going back up to the dreamlike apartment on rue du Trésor, she wanted to know why she supposedly needed to be cautious with Jean-Pierre. What was she getting into that she herself couldn't see? What did Julie know, if anything at all, that she hadn't told her yet?

Her cousin was suddenly silent. She wanted to make Paulina believe that her "be careful" didn't mean anything exact, that it was just a vague, general warning, a manner of speaking. But she had thrown a stone and, with the strategy of someone who was jealous, was now trying to hide her hand.

"Are you mad, Julie?"

"Me? No . . ."

"Is it because I didn't tell you I wasn't coming back? I'm sorry, it slipped my mind. Or is it because you think I'm with Jean-Pierre?"

"I'll get over it. I've been up all night and I'm not in the mood to . . ."

"Don't wait up for me today. I'm letting you know now. That way you won't worry. You two do your own thing and I'll manage."

"Yeah, it's quite clear you're 'doing your own thing.'"

She was very upset. But Paulina didn't want to make a scene. She hung up, went into the bakery, ordered two well-toasted croissants, just the way she liked them, and thought no more about it. She wanted to get back to Jean-Pierre and have breakfast with him in the kitchen with the windows open. The window overlooked that interior courtyard that gifted them the proud blooms and scents of late spring. On the way home, she thought that by day rue du Trésor was far more charming than at night, when she had arrived in a rush and with an unfamiliar feeling that burned through her—that strange mix of excitement and dread—that had already hinted at what might happen. She thought that cul-de-sacs had something of an impasse, a calmness, an intimate mystery. This was even more true when cars weren't allowed.

From the café Les Philosophes at the corner to the entrance to rue du Trésor to the unremarkable white fountain that blocked the view at the far end, the street was full of small restaurants with shaded terraces and discerning decor shops. White hydrangeas overflowed from the planted beds so densely they imbued the scene with an exotic, glorified air.

Jean-Pierre was waiting for her with a kiss, a freshly squeezed orange juice, strained with care, and an awareness of knowing that it was not a moment for questions. What had been said between the cousins stayed between the cousins. And it was entirely Pau's choice to share with him whatever she wanted about matters between the cousins.

"Why is it called rue du Trésor?" Paulina was the one with a question. "I'm guessing they must have found some treasure . . ."

"A small chest, yes. With gold coins. They knocked down a hotel, and in the rubble, with one blow of a pickax, a chest full of gold coins was found. It belonged to a king. John the Good, I think."

"And here I thought you were the treasure."

They sat down at the nicely set table and had breakfast in silence. Jean-Pierre quietly slipped a cassette tape into the stereo system.

"Let's see if you like it."

"What is it?"

"Something unusual." He didn't want Paulina to see the label. "I'm warning you. It's peculiar."

The first track was a women's chorus that seemed to be singing a cappella in a language Pau couldn't recognize. She let the second song play before she ventured to guess that it might be Indigenous music or from some Eastern European country, or maybe . . .

"They're Bulgarian love songs."

"Wow, I was close."

"Do you like them?"

She thought it over before saying anything.

"They're original."

"I heard them in a church in Plovdiv. On the way out, I bought the cassette that the women were selling at a little stall."

"Do you know what they're saying?"

"Not a clue."

"They do sound like love songs, once you know it. More so than funeral dirges, of course."

"Songs of *amour*. And the more you listen to them, the more you hear it."

Jean-Pierre had just peeled a peach. He sliced it, wiped his fingers on a rag, and set the bowl in front of Pauline. No one had peeled a peach for her in maybe twenty years. Back at home, her father had always been the one in charge of peeling fruit for everyone. Since then, nothing. Until Paris. Until Jean-Pierre's kitchen the morning after a passionate night. She savored the peach, listened to the Bulgarian voices, and looked into Jean-Pierre's eyes, eyes with a back room to them, more green than brown, an interesting wrinkle beginning to show at the outer corner. His eyebrows were thick, brushed from the inside out, without a single hair rebelling and daring to go astray. Her eyes in his eyes. Her emotions overflowed. The peace, the quiet. Bulgarian love songs, his trusting gaze, and there was no need for words anymore. If only that moment could last forever. She would never forget it.

Always, never. Paulina knew that absolute adverbs had to be used like salt—sparingly and at the right time.

They didn't want to speak until the tape ended.

"Will you teach me how to light a pipe?"

"You?"

"What's wrong with that? I want to."

These were days for trying new things. She could never have imagined herself doing this. She found it sensual the way Jean-Pierre, with the skill that came from routine, shredded the filamentous tobacco from a square, pressed packet of cut tobacco, and packed it into the bowl.

First he let the tobacco sit loose inside the chamber. Then, with his pinkie, he pressed it down toward the heel. In just a few days, Paulina had seen him with two different pipes. Pipes are like friendships. Sometimes you have to let them rest, Jean-Pierre explained, surprised that Paulina wanted to start smoking.

One pipe was made of briar root, the other of cherrywood. Both were straight, flat, with a perfect right angle that matched Jean-Pierre's facial lines.

"They're more comfortable. Bent pipes weigh more. You need stronger teeth, and a stronger jaw, to hold on to them. And these flat ones are easier to clean. You see?"

In no time at all, Jean-Pierre opened the briar pipe. He removed the stem and ran a small brush through the smoke chamber. He gave it a sharp, dry puff to clear it before screwing it back onto the body of the pipe.

"Do you dare?"

Paulina took apart the tobacco and followed Jean-Pierre's steps, each of them with a pipe in hand. He let her fill the cherrywood one, the only Dunhill he owned.

"The mouthpiece is a bit chewed up," he apologized.

"It doesn't matter." In fact, she liked seeing that Jean-Pierre trusted her with something so personal.

"Do I have to do it with my pinkie?"

"Not necessarily. Whatever works. Actually, there's a tool for it that I don't have that . . ." This was new for Jean-Pierre too. He had never shared a pipe with a woman. He liked Pauline's innocence and her appetite for adventure.

"And to light it?"

"Blow out and inhale. It's instinctive. There's no trick to it." Using a Zippo lighter, he lit both pipes. "Blow out and inhale without swallowing."

"Oh, it's working . . . How do you hold it between your teeth?"

Everything was a game with Jean-Pierre. Pauline got up, took a couple of steps while swaying her hips, perfectly aware how nicely those jeans fit her, and, pipe in hand, sat down on his lap.

"Have you ever kissed a woman who smokes a pipe?"

The Bulgarian voices, with a kind of alpha-Gregorian undertone, had hypnotically fogged the morning. Or maybe it was the tobacco smoke? It wasn't long before they lay the pipes to rest in the kitchen ashtray. Pauline kissed him all over, while unbuttoning his shirt. She liked that strong, well-built body. She slowly tousled the white hairs beginning to appear on his chest. She lingered at his belt buckle. Once undone, she knelt in front of him.

"Can I?"

A question or a plea. She looked up—a plea—playfully.

"Come on, just an appetizer." Pauline, trying on her most seductive voice.

Jean-Pierre nodded, eyes closed, before being transported to heaven.

From the kitchen to the bed. They returned to the scene of the crime for the sake of comfort. And to conjugate life by saying tender and intimate things, the kinds of things you don't say with your clothes on. Every now and then, they made love. Like a poem they were continuing, they surprised each other with every verse, refining the rhetoric, and stripping the language bare until they reached the essence of love.

By the time they got up again, lunchtime had long passed.

That afternoon, they talked. Overcome by a longing for Gina, Paulina realized she needed to do it. She needed to tell Jean-Pierre something that was very important to her. She hoped he did not get the wrong idea of her. She was not the kind of woman who went around with a wedding ring on her finger, trying to seduce men whose last names she didn't even bother to ask. She wanted it to be clear she didn't go around animating her life with the first guy who came along without bothering to dig into his past or care about his present. She suddenly felt the need to sit on a bench in the shade of la Tuileries and apologize for something she wasn't quite sure of. But she felt she had to say it out loud, to confess to someone who might be the only one capable of understanding her. After a few unforgettable days, he was the center of her secret. They sat side by side on a wooden bench in the middle of the gravel path, their legs crossed. She leaned back against him. His body was the perfect support for the two bodies to fit together, drawn to each as they were like magnets. Paulina liked feeling Jean-Pierre's strong arm behind her neck, over her shoulder, his hand holding on to her arm. For once, it was easier to speak without looking at him, her eyes drifting into nothingness, or toward the passersby—tourists and vendors of plastic souvenir Eiffel Towers—who walked invisibly in front of her. She thanked him for the hours they had shared. She praised him for his sensitivity and his tact, and told him about the whirlwind of new, unexpected, indecipherable emotions that were shaking her. Most of all, on the verge of tears, she asked him not to think that this was usual behavior for her. It was important that Jean-Pierre believe this was not just another anecdote, a weekend fling in Paris, sex for the sake of sex. She didn't just jump into anyone's bed. It was much more than that. She did not go to bed with anyone. He could ask Julie if he didn't believe her. Actually, it was better not to mention anything to her cousin.

But he had to understand that she, Paulina Homs, was not like that. Or if she was, she didn't know it. And she was just discovering it with him, walking beside him, listening to him talk about Braque, dancing a sirtaki by the river, lighting a pipe, and kissing him at the foot of Saint-Sulpice. She wasn't running away from anything by running toward him. In fact, in Barcelona she had a tidy, well-organized life, without speed bumps. She needed Jean-Pierre to understand that she had a daughter who was her whole world and a family she loved, who she thought she might be failing. But in that moment her desires were breaking out so forcefully she could not hold them back. She neither wanted to nor could repress them. She was feeling things she had never felt before, and now that she was here, she could not stop experiencing them. To their fullest extent. Even if it was only for a few days. Perhaps there was a bit of regret, but it was mostly excitement. She felt she had one foot in paradise and the other on the edge of a cliff, and she needed to share that, just like they had shared everything else those days. So she told him. And that was all. Paulina would not have felt at peace if she hadn't cleared her conscience, if Jean-Pierre didn't hear her out at least once about the doubts that occasionally plagued her. To be clear, it wasn't remorse, she insisted. They were only feelings. Passing worries that sometimes, like the echo of a cramp, sent her a signal and then disappeared.

He listened to her empathetically as a good listener. He wordlessly let her pour her heart out. Once her moment of catharsis was over, he gave her a soft kiss on the ear, gave a Mona Lisa smirk, and said only three things, the kinds of things people say when they're not sure how to respond.

One: "We'll figure it out."

Two: "Don't be afraid."

Three: "I'm okay if you're okay."

They were maybe not the words Paulina would have most liked to hear. But the calm and distant steadiness with which Jean-Pierre said them helped settle her nerves. Sometimes calmness is contagious. She noticed then that Jean-Pierre primarily radiated security.

"Let's go." He rose from the wooden bench the moment he noticed a cocker spaniel approaching to sniff their feet.

"Where to?"

"To Rivoli. Didn't you want to meet Antoine? We can't get there halfway through the performance."

One pencil, two chocolate, three rocket, four Bible, five stream, six funnel, seven telephone, eight clock, nine tin (Antoine Fernández knew that there is always at least one joker in the audience), ten stamp, eleven ball, twelve bed, thirteen water, fourteen glasses, fifteen calendar, sixteen pepper, seventeen domino, eighteen cauliflower, nineteen belt, twenty scalpel, twenty-one wheel, twenty-two racket, twenty-three church, twenty-four bore (and there is also always a mischievous person), twenty-five baton, twenty-six triangle, twenty-seven swing, twenty-eight . . .

"Why does he say a number before each word?" Paulina whispered into Jean-Pierre's ear with surprise.

"It's a mnemonic trick. It's much easier for him to remember each object if he associates it with a number."

"But then . . ."

"Shh, it's our turn . . ."

"You say it." Paulina passed the ball to him to give herself more time to think.

"Thirty-seven, butterfly." Jean-Pierre blurted the first thing that came to mind when it was his turn.

"Thirty-eight . . ." She hesitated. "Thirty-eight, pipe."

She was nervous about ruining Antoine's list and anxious about speaking in front of others in another language, getting the word right. Paulina's slightly sweaty hand clutched Jean-Pierre's, and he squeezed hers with understanding. He was pleased that she had chosen a word associated with his world. Only a few days had passed since they'd met, and he realized they were already creating a shared universe.

Forty-four sunflower, forty-five raffle, forty-six cow, forty-seven condom (and, without fail, there's always someone trying to be provocative), forty-eight mattress, forty-nine coin . . .

"Do you see how he sweats?" They spoke softly, careful not to disturb anyone.

"Every day he ends the day soaked. The mental energy. It seems like nothing, but . . ."

"Why did he blindfold himself?"

"So he can concentrate. It helps him not to . . ."

"Lose track of things."

"Exactly."

"And I think so people don't accuse him of peeking." Paulina nodded her chin toward the waitress, who was writing each number and word in neat cursive on a mounted chalkboard.

Sixty-six coffin, sixty-seven pen, sixty-eight ship, sixty-nine sex (a predictable one), seventy harpsichord, seventy-one clog . . .

"Are you and Antoine very close friends?"

"It depends . . . I like coming here and watching him. I've come maybe ten or twelve times. One day"—he lowered his voice even further when two people shot them dirty looks—"we held a performance in the gallery. We hid an object, and Antoine had to find it guided by the telepathy of one of us even though he was blindfolded and didn't know what it was."

"And?"

"Crazy. He found the pencil sharpener inside the . . . Wait, it's over."

Sitting down with his eyes covered and sweat rolling down his head, Antoine Fernández was breathing heavily. He panted like he had just run a marathon and crossed the finish line. Either this was part of the show in that dimly lit basement on rue de Rivoli, or he was having issues with hyperventilation that were getting worse by the minute.

"And now?"

"This is the part where they ask if there's a doctor in the house."

"Shut up."

In bursts, Antoine Fernández recited each object from one to a hundred patiently and confidently, a few stumbles here and there. The crowd was unanimous in its applause. "Bravo" someone shouted from the back of the cabaret. He proceeded to recite the list backward, from a hundred down to one, without a single mistake, but with even more difficulty. All the way from "snail" to "pencil." The audience, numbering around thirty people, gave him a standing ovation. No one cared that the act never seemed to end. Then, acting like it was easier for him, the mentalist in his sweat-soaked shirt asked the audience to call out any number. He would instantly respond with its corresponding object. And vice versa.

"Butterfly!" Paulina shouted.

"Thirty-seven," Antoine answered triumphantly.

"He's a machine."

"If every show went like the one tonight, he wouldn't be here," Jean-Pierre said, chewing the stem of his pipe as he clapped. "He'd be filling the seats of the Odéon every night."

Acting as disoriented as a castaway, by the time the exhausted yet satisfied Antoine Fernández removed his blindfold and recovered his human appearance, he could no longer spot Jean-Pierre and Paulina. The lovers had slipped away quickly for a pizza and beer before returning home. Paulina had left her worries behind in la Tuileries, on the bench of words.

On the last evening, on rue du Trésor, their thoughts came out in streams. It felt like time was slipping away from them, like they didn't have enough time to say everything. Did you know that Dante only saw Beatrice once? They didn't even exchange a word, and he wrote *The Divine Comedy*. Dante was nine and Bice Portinari was only eight. I've never had the patience to read it, don't hold it against me. What about *Madame Bovary*? Yes, *Madame Bovary* I have. I'm sure she would have gotten divorced if she had lived today. Back then you had to suffer, and you suffered. In the past, love wasn't love. People tend to think it's easier if there's not anxiety about love ending, but no. It's the opposite. It's actually harder. What do you know? Paulina had said this to Jean-Pierre, taking a risk, knowing nothing about the forty-five years of his life before Julie's wedding. Love is like life. If it didn't have an expiration date—they agreed on that at least—it would be terribly boring. The grace of it, what moves us, the engine that makes us throb and suffer and strive, is that we don't know when it ends. Love and life. It can last into old age, or it can end tomorrow. It can end suddenly, or it can slowly wither away or arrive gently, like sea-foam. The key is the illusion that love exists. There are people who pass through this world without ever catching its scent. Even if you and I, and the neighbors downstairs, and Julie, and Antoine Fernández, and everyone wrote down our own definitions of love, no two would be alike. We could put all the definitions in an envelope, open that envelope up, and pull out as many forms of love as there were people who have participated. The two lovers wanted to believe, however, that their definition, based on what they had said and shared up to that point, would be very similar. Perhaps with some variance.

Paulina hid the dramatics of believing it was her last night. Jean-Pierre, who didn't want to take stock of his emotions, experienced it like a drop of honey.

"A drop of honey?"

"You don't like it?"

"Honey? More now than when I was little. But I don't eat it much."

"Drops of honey. Did you study Latin in school?"

"Yes."

"Do you know who Lucretius was?"

"No."

"He was a Latin philosopher from before Christ was born. He committed suicide in his early forties. They say he went mad because of some love potions he drank. But that's all a legend, because no one has ever been able to prove it. The only thing we know is that throughout his whole life Lucretius wrote a single book, *De Rerum Natura*. And he wrote it in verse. This was his greatest contribution, my dear Pauline. He knew he had to explain something as complex as Epicurus's doctrine through atomic physics. And he believed that the best way to disperse that knowledge in the period was through poetry. He believed that it would be easier for people to understand his message in verse."

"Don't lie to me." Paulina was getting to know him better, but every now and then she still felt Jean-Pierre enjoyed pulling her leg.

"I'm serious, really serious. *De Rerum Natura*, his book, was written in the form of a long poem, because he thought people would understand it better. But Epicurus, who was more into physics than rhymes, was annoyed at the didactic way Lucretius treated his discoveries. So

Lucretius pulled a metaphor that still endures to this day out of his sleeve, out of the sleeve of his tunic. He said that when children refused to take a medicine because it was too bitter, a drop of honey made it easier to swallow. He argued that the verses were the drops of honey, the honey that is poetry, that helped sweeten his message."

"The pleasure of the senses."

"For me, drops of honey are the moments life gives us. The dance at the wedding, every kiss, every one of your caresses, the visit to Shakespeare and Company, this morning's breakfast, the Bulgarian voices we listened to with our hearts. Buying a painting. Going to a concert. A sunset on the river. Holding a book I've spent months looking for. Dinner with a friend. Seeing your smile, like it is right now. All drops of honey. We're not here to give moments away, Pau. It's always later than you think."

"Oh, Jean-Pierre, I love you so much. Will you say it to me?"

She threw herself onto Jean-Pierre, sitting on top of his legs, and they kissed with a whole lifetime's worth of passion. Paulina felt sweaty. She was uncomfortable. She thought Jean-Pierre might notice.

"I haven't told you about Rosseta, have I?"

"It doesn't ring a bell."

"I'll take a shower and then tell you."

Jean-Pierre played some motets by Giovanni Pierluigi da Palestrina and sat down on the sofa. Paulina reappeared twenty minutes later, clean, refreshed, ready for her last night on Trésor. She had tied a thick white towel around her body and a smaller one around her head so that her soaking hair wouldn't drip.

"You smell great."

She liked that Jean-Pierre had noticed.

"You smell different," he continued.

"Maybe it's the lotion I put on my legs. They felt sore. But maybe it's because today is the day we walked the least."

"It smells like coconut. It's nice."

It wasn't just her scent. Paulina knew how to play with the opening of her towel, revealing her sensual, gleaming, carefully well-maintained legs. She knew which way to sit so she showed off her long thighs, her round knees, her strong calves, her well-proportioned ankles. There was not an ounce of excess skin anywhere. Paulina had a real obsession with her legs. Her mother had always said she should be euthanized when she got to the age where she had turtle legs, wrinkled legs with toes twisted by arthritis and mussel-shell nails. It never came to that. She still had perfect legs when she choked on a chestnut, mere days after turning sixty. Her father, Senyor Homs, an accountant at a textile company on Carrer Casp in Barcelona, had seen Ava Gardner's legs at the movies and went back three Sundays in a row. *Mogambo*.

"For a couple of years my parents and I spent the summers in a house in Espinavessa, not far from the lake . . . Does Banyoles sound familiar to you?"

"No."

"You're missing out. Espinavessa is near Girona and Banyoles. It's a combination of wheat fields and forests. Landscapes made to be painted. I must have been six or seven, no older than that. We lived in a modest home that I thought was ours until, much later, I discovered we only rented it for the summer. There, where everything was quite flat, I learned how to ride a bike, and once I knew how, they sent me to fetch the milk every morning. At night, my dad and I counted bats. Every afternoon, my mother and I ate a snack at the spring below the village, on the path to the washhouses.

"One day my mother said to me, 'We're going on a hike today.' She had packed water and sandwiches into a backpack, slung it over her shoulders, and said, 'I've found a path we've never walked. We'll take it all the way to Orfes.' It was an adventure. Seven kilometers there and seven back, along a little trail that ran through the middle of nowhere. It didn't seem we'd run into any fields or pass through the threshing floor of any house. We hardly saw any farmhouses.

"Suddenly, once we were already quite far from an abandoned home, we heard a dog barking. The barking quickly got closer. And soon we saw a dog galloping straight toward us at full speed. 'Don't worry,' my mother said. I was paralyzed. I grabbed her hand and noticed she was just as frozen as I was. 'Don't be afraid,' she said. All the while the wolf dog, and its gnashing teeth, kept getting nearer and nearer. The idea of what it intended to do scared the living daylights out of me. I remember that feeling, Jean-Pierre, of thinking, *This is it. This is where my mother and I will die, eaten up.* It was the most scared I've ever been. The creature was probably four meters away from us, when my mother suddenly let go of my hand and screamed 'Stop!' She motioned her hand at it. She screamed at that dog and threatened it in a way she had never done to me. The wolf dog suddenly stopped short, frightened either by the gesture or the yell. I don't know. The truth is that the dog took two steps back. We stood there for a few seconds, motionless.

"Tired from its run, it looked at us with sad eyes, its mouth open and tongue lolling out. Our hearts racing, we looked back at it, not knowing whether we should retreat or keep moving. At least now it was no longer barking. It had stopped, and it didn't quite have the look of a serial killer. On the contrary. Now it looked like a dog who had been mistreated, like it had taken a few beatings.

"'Walk slowly and don't look at it,' my mother said, grabbing my hand again. 'Let's see what it does.' But it did nothing. We walked past it, and it didn't come any closer. It just started walking a few steps behind us, matching our pace. She was a girl dog. She was a thin German shepherd, with a short, light coat. She was older, and, according to my mother, was rife with fleas. I couldn't tell. I did notice, though, that she was wearing a pink collar, with some kind of plastic Barbie medallion on it. It looked like she belonged to a little girl who had forgotten that she had put a necklace on the dog as part of a game.

"To our surprise, the dog followed us along the entire path, like she was watching over us from a distance. Or maybe she wanted to keep us company. We didn't know where she had come from, but it looked like she had been abandoned or lost for several days. She no longer looked like a beast that wanted to attack us. Prancing behind us with her ears flopping, it felt like she was asking for our friendship. When we couldn't hear her, we looked for her out of the corner of our eyes to make sure she was still with us. And so we walked, maybe three kilometers, which is a long time, carefully, watching each other.

"My mother and I gradually relaxed when we realized that this dog was a gentle soul who wouldn't hurt us. Just when we thought the situation was all under control, our little path came to an end. We emerged out onto the paved main road that would take us to Orfes. The road was very French. It was narrow, straight, lined with big trees on either side, and at the very end, there was a village with the cemetery at its entrance. You know what I mean when I say it was very French.

"We walked along on one side of the road so that the cars heading our way could see us. Traffic in the Empordà, especially in those years, was very light. But instead of moving aside, the dog walked down the middle of the road. When a car came, they honked for her to get out of the way. She paid them no attention, and then they honked at us, because they thought the dog was ours and that we weren't doing anything to get her off the road. That was the first time we felt like the dog could be ours.

"'Mommy, let's give her a name. We can call her Rosseta—Blondie—because she's a little . . . blond.' My mother loved the name. She and I were beginning to grow fond of that dog, who was more she-wolf than dog but gave us a pleading look.

"As we walked through the streets of Orfes, Rosseta stayed with us like it had always been that way. She would wait for us at the next crossroad if we lost sight of her around some corner. I wanted to pet her, but my mother said no, because she was dirty and had fleas. When it was time to go back to Espinavessa, we thought that Rosseta would want to stay in Orfes, or that maybe she belonged to some family there. But that wasn't the case.

"In what was the most intense experience of my childhood, Rosseta followed my mother and me all the way back home. She had adopted us, and she hoped we would adopt her. She endeared herself to us very quickly. It didn't matter that, on the last stretch of the walk, it began to rain. In fact, there was a torrential downpour throughout the final leg, and the three of us were absolutely soaked. Like it was a sign, Rosseta followed us right up to the front door of the house.

"I begged my mother, please, please, to let her come in with us. She said no. I ran to the window to watch her once we were inside. She was still there, with those little eyes. That was when I asked my mother again, please, please, if we could keep her and take her back with us to Barcelona. My mother said no, there was no way we were bringing her to our apartment. I continued, telling her that it would mean so much to me, I never asked for anything, it was what I wanted most in the world. Based on what she told me later, I think she was starting to give in. I kept insisting, please, Mommy, we couldn't leave her alone. I felt so sorry for her. I thought more about Rosseta than I did about myself.

"Finally, in a moment of weakness, my mother said, 'Ask your father.' But my father said no. And my father's no was much more final. 'Go change, you're soaked,' he added. After the third warning, I went to change. Through the window, I said to her, 'Rosseta, don't move. I'll be right back.' I put on some dry clothes as fast as I could, but when I pushed the curtain aside and looked out the window again, Rosseta wasn't there anymore. It was still raining hard outside, but Rosseta was gone.

"My mother tells me that I cried. I opened the door and ran out calling for her, but Rosseta was gone. And she never came back. They said I was very sad that day. I talked about Rosseta nonstop. At six years old, I said something at the dinner table that my parents never forgot: 'I feel so sorry for Rosseta. I wish today had never happened.' Can you imagine that? And then my mother, who was the kind of woman who knew when to strike the right tone, explained to me that even if it hurt right now, it was better to have experienced and known Rosseta than never to have experienced it at all, because I would remember her for the rest of my life. It was hard for me to see that she was right. It took weeks. Maybe months. But she was right."

Jean-Pierre, who had listened to Pauline like she was recounting a tale, took a while to react. He resorted to his sense of humor, a defense against the transcendence this moment might have for them.

"Did you just compare me to a dog, or am I just making that up?"

"No, what are you talking about?"

"Now I'm not sure if you're Rosseta, or if I am . . ."

"You've never had a dog?"

The happy Jean-Pierre started to slowly sing in her ear in his deepest voice, "When the hours of this day run out, I'll invent new ones for you."

More than singing, he was reciting the song so as not to go off key. Calmly, he opened her towel and delicately moved his hand from her bare feet up to her hips. Up and down. Perfect legs. Ava Gardner's skin. The sensual smell of coconut he noticed when he kissed the inside of her legs. They let the hours pass slowly without thinking about what would happen next, careful not to get too worked up, never going beyond caresses, in silence—relaxed, unhurried, biting their lips and kissing each other all over. Without saying it aloud, like a game of strategy, they focused on the journey and avoided their genitals, carefully, skimming close, passing right alongside until, at the height of their attunement, they synchronized themselves. When Jean-Pierre inhaled, Pauline exhaled. When he exhaled, she inhaled at every point of contact between them like there was nothing beyond. It took little effort for them to find the rhythm until excitement, carried by measured breathing, led them to a mutual, loud, simultaneous orgasm. It was a new, tantric experience for both of them.

Aroused and astonished by their shared discovery of spiritual sex, they understood the point. *La joie de vivre.* A drop of honey.

12

Fifteen Minutes Before the End of the World

"What's bothering you, Júlia?"

"Me?" She answered with the utmost surprise.

"That I've just stopped by to pick up the suitcases?"

"No, no . . ."

"I know I was supposed to stay here every day, but I also thought you two newlyweds would be better off on your own."

"Oh, you were doing it so you wouldn't bother us, huh," she said, returning her sarcasm.

"Yes. The house is big, but what is that Chinese saying about guests?"

"That they're like fish?"

"That by the third day they start to stink, yes. Exactly."

"You're never a guest in my home. And you won't be one in ours either. Alain and I are fine on our own, we're fine with you, we're happy . . ."

"Friday, Saturday, Sunday, Monday, Tuesday. Five days of marriage. I'd be worried if you weren't."

"You're right. We're still on cloud nine. We keep talking about the wedding, what our friends said to us, my dress, and . . ."

"But?"

"But what?"

"I can tell, Júlia . . ."

"It's nothing. You just could have called the first night. We were worried, but that's it. I already told you. It's over. You and I don't have to explain ourselves. Do whatever you want. I just want you to be well."

"Anyway, look, you were the one who introduced me to Jean-Pierre. Don't try to wriggle out of it now. You paired us up, you sat him next to me at the table. So what are you complaining about now?"

"I'm not complaining. I'm just telling you. It's your life."

"Or maybe I'm sensing something?"

"In me?"

"Yes, yes." Paulina, who had been joking, suddenly caught a strange look in her cousin's eyes. A spark of jealousy, perhaps. "Honey, what happened between you and Jean-Pierre?"

"Please. Nothing. What could have . . . ? Don't turn things around on me now."

"Did I catch you?" Paulina teased, although she had a nagging suspicion.

"With Jean-Pierre? Poor guy. No, no . . ."

"Something happened there . . . When? You're blushing."

"Stop tickling me, stop it. You know I can't stand it."

Paulina had chased Júlia around the kitchen table. She cornered her on a chair and pounced on her the way they used to do when they were little, playing on the beach at Sant Pol, throwing themselves on top of each other to pin the other down and tickle each other until they nearly peed themselves laughing.

"Come on, tell me. What's his bedroom like?"

"No, really, I'm telling you I—"

"What painting does he have above his bed?"

"Stop, stop. I've never been to his place, I'm telling you. And leave me alone, please. Not here."

The gardener, who was trimming the hedges as he did every Tuesday from ten to twelve, watched the cousins through the window. He heard them giggling and was dying to come in and join the party uninvited.

"Don't joke like that, Pau. I'm a married woman."

"Right, right."

"As married as you are."

"Now that you mention it," she said, as if suddenly remembering, "what's Gina's father's name?"

Paulina let Júlia go. Júlia stood up, straightened her T-shirt, and poured herself a glass of water from the tap built into the refrigerator door.

"What's that?"

"A wedding present. Alain really wanted it, and we got it. It's American."

"I've never seen one. Can champagne pour out of it?"

They laughed again.

"When are you leaving?"

Paulina looked at the kitchen clock. It reminded her of the one she'd seen at Brasserie Lipp on the night of Picasso. She noticed that as soon as she was away from Jean-Pierre, everything reminded her of him.

"You can call me a taxi now. I'd rather get to the airport with time to spare. I'd rather waste away there than have to worry about rushing. Order it for . . . I don't know. Have them send one as soon as it's available."

"Is Manuel still that afraid of flying?"

"Who?"

"Manuel, your husband."

"Oh, Manuel, right."

"You're shameless. I don't even recognize you."

"'Afraid' is an understatement. He always says the same thing to me: 'If you ever find out I died in a plane crash, it's because an airplane fell on top of me.'"

Why on earth had she had to bring up her husband and all his misery? It really hadn't been necessary. Júlia picked up the phone and, from memory, dialed the number of the Croissy-sur-Seine taxi dispatch.

"Pour aller à l'aéroport, oui." She covered the microphone to speak to Paulina. "To Orly, right?" She took her hand off the microphone. *"Oui, oui."*

Once she hung up, she launched into the interrogation, racing against the clock.

"So? How was it?"

"Really good."

"Really good?"

"Really, really good. What a man, Júlia. He's attentive, he's intelligent, he knows how to talk. He can talk about the city, art, life. He talks about drops of honey, and leaves you . . . Wow. And he's so tactful, you know. And he knows how to always make you feel good."

"You look like you've had a lot of orgasms."

"Don't be gross, honey."

"Fine, don't tell me if you don't want to." She was shamelessly inquisitive. "But come on, what happened?"

"I've already told you. Really good. I picked up earlier that you were asking about sex."

"'Really good' means he's a man who's discovered there's more to things than penetration?"

"That's it, yes. Jean-Pierre, the discoverer. And he's patented it."

"And I introduced him to you."

"I don't understand how a man like that is alone. And it seems he likes it. He's not exactly young anymore."

"Yes."

"Did you know he's obsessed with butterflies?"

"No, no."

"Don't pretend. You knew?"

"No . . ."

"He goés all around the world looking for books. Not just butterflies. He inherited his grandfather's cases and keeps them all there in a room like a museum, with special lighting. But it doesn't bother him at all to get on a plane and go to the ends of the earth to look for a book he thinks exists only in that corner of the world."

"Did he ask you to go with him?"

"Me?"

"Yes, what's wrong?"

"Júlia, please . . ."

"Did he ask you?"

"How could he ask me that?" As she said it, she realized it stung a little.

"Did you say goodbye?"

"What?"

"Did you already say goodbye."

"Yes, yes. Yes, of course."

"And?"

"Well. What do you want me to say? It was sad, happy . . . serene, I don't know. It was a bit like . . . We agreed we'd write to each other."

"You'll write to each other?"

"And this is where I have to ask you a favor. As a cousin, as a sister, as a confidante. We agreed he wouldn't call me, at home, not there. I asked him not to . . ."

"Why not?"

"Why do you think? With Isabel hovering all day, she'd ask too many questions. Too risky."

"You're more worried about the maid than your husband. That's really good."

"We agreed that he should write to me here, if he writes to me."

"But?"

"Does that bother you?"

"No, no . . ." Yes, it did. "It's a little . . ."

The gardener knocked on the kitchen window. His knuckles were hairy and black, like a chimpanzee's.

"Julie, I'm off." The man spoke, one boot in the garden and the other in the kitchen. "Everything is okay. I thought I saw some aphids on the apple tree so I sprayed a bit of that stuff, just in case, but I don't think it'll get any worse. Maybe it was just a larva. If you don't need anything else, I'll see you on Tuesday."

"See you on Tuesday at ten."

"Au revoir." The gardener said goodbye to Paulina, in awe of her beauty and the cowboy boots she wore for her return to Barcelona. With the boots and new jeans, she was really something.

The chimpanzee hadn't even made it out through the back gate at the end of the garden when he came back and shouted: "There's a taxi outside, Julie."

"Yes, yes, thank you. It's ours!"

"Okay!"

Paulina ran to the living room, where she had left her two suitcases, closed and already packed. She set them back down on the floor and hugged Julie.

"Little cousin . . ."

"I love you."

"I love you too. So much. You know that."

"Take care, you hear? Enjoy time with Alain."

"Any last advice?"

"Have kids."

"Another one."

"Keep things in the bathroom private. Always keep the door closed."

"Another one . . ."

"Have fun together, but keep your own space . . ."

"I like that one too. One more, quick."

"Don't always give in to him whenever he feels like it."

"Pau!"

They hugged again and exchanged three long kisses, cheek to cheek, a seal of sisterhood, understanding, and a secret.

"I'll walk you to the door. It's heavy."

"Give my regards to Alain and thank him very much. I'm sorry I couldn't say goodbye to him."

They exchanged two more kisses. Paulina got into the taxi, closed the door, rolled down the window, and blew two more small kisses to Julie.

"Come visit us in Barcelona soon . . ."

The taxi had already pulled away, and Paulina wasn't able to hear her cousin's reply. As soon as she spotted the sign marking the exit from Croissy, she coughed lightly so the driver would look up at her in the rearview mirror. She took advantage of the moment when their eyes met.

"Where did they tell you I was going?"

"To Orly, madame. To the airport."

"Oh—no, no . . . Sorry, there's been a mistake. My flight doesn't leave until this afternoon. We need to go to Paris, to the rue du Trésor. A cul-de-sac in Le Marais. Do you know it?"

"*Bien sûr.* We'll find it."

Jean-Pierre came down to unload the suitcases.

"No need, really. I'll come up. If there's an elevator . . ." But he was eager to spend every last minute with Pauline.

"What have you been up to?"

"Missing you . . ."

"I was gone for less than four hours, round trip. You're a real comedian."

He opened the door to his apartment. On the key ring hung a butterfly.

"I went to the gallery and made lunch for you."

"I don't believe it."

The table was set with a red-and-white checkered Italian tablecloth. They had never sat at it, never laid out a tablecloth. From sofa to kitchen and kitchen to sofa, they had eaten in a few quick bites.

"Did many people come to Anouk?"

"This morning? One tourist who had to use the toilet in an emergency, and lots of gawking."

"Did you let him in?"

"What would you have done?"

"Told him to look for a bar, a hotel, like everyone else . . ."

Jean-Pierre could have pretended not to hear Pauline's question, or that she had no intention behind it, but that wasn't the case. Before sitting down to eat, he figured this was the moment to face his past.

"We still owe each other a conversation."

She was silent. She couldn't really play dumb and say "Oh, really?" when she'd been waiting three whole days for Jean-Pierre.

"Anouk."

"That's right. You told me 'I think it's a woman's name,' when I asked about the gallery."

"I know I owe you an explanation. Of course it's a woman's name. You asked me about the name of the gal—"

"No, not if you don't want to."

"If I didn't want to, I wouldn't tell you. But I want to, Pauline, because I don't want there to be any secrets between us. I'm going to tell you something no one knows. 'No one' means absolutely no one. Only Anouk, of course."

He took the pipe out of his mouth, with the gravity of a poet who has just torn up his last verses upon realizing they aren't particularly good.

"If you'll let me, I'll start from the beginning."

Paulina was startled by the serious air Jean-Pierre had taken on. For once, it seemed hard for the art dealer to begin the conversation.

"You may have noticed that there's a photo of a little girl in my bedroom, on top of the cabinet."

"No." The lie didn't hold up, and she apologized with a shrug. "Yes. Is that Anouk?"

"Anouk is her mother."

"And you're her father."

Paulina had adopted her most neutral tone to show that she was not affected by whatever information she might learn. She was neither hot nor cold. Everyone had a past life, and anyway, the two of them had only met on Friday. It was now Tuesday, and in just a few hours she would be boarding a plane back to routine in hopes that Gina would be waiting for her at the airport with her father. But she was surprised that Jean-Pierre didn't respond, neither yes nor no. She hadn't asked. She had stated it as fact, and Jean-Pierre hadn't denied it. But he hadn't admitted it either.

"Monique. Her name is Monique. She was seven in that picture."

She had hit the nail on the head. Paulina curled up on the sofa, tucking her legs in and placing a cushion behind her back. She prepared to listen to the story. However convoluted it might be, nothing would change about what she had experienced on rue du Trésor or rue de Seine. Jean-Pierre stood up to pour himself a little bit of malt into a cognac glass.

"Would you like some?"

"I'll have a little of yours."

"I always spent the summers with my parents and brother in Capbreton, in Aquitaine, right by the Basque Country." He took a sip, set the glass down on the table piled with magazines—the monthly *L'Oeil*—and sat at the foot of the sofa. "My father, a notary here in Paris, loved the sea and owned a sailing boat in the port of Capbreton. Whenever the Atlantic permitted it, we'd go out and get seasick for a while. My brother, Nico, who's four years younger than me, had it worse than me. He was as wobbly as soup the first three hours on the boat. When he got home in the evening, he was so pale he went straight to bed. He'd lie there and be sick for two days until my father decided the weather was good enough to go out sailing again. That's how our summers went for ten or twelve years.

"We stayed in a somewhat isolated villa with beautiful views of the sea, though as a kid you don't know how to appreciate these things, nor are you really even interested. We did notice, however, that to do anything in town you had to bike ten minutes, back and forth. Our next-door neighbors, the Letroux family, good friends of my parents who we saw every summer, had a big brown Great Dane, a beast that was taller than I was. I liked dogs, but not horses. And especially not one that could cross the entire garden in two steps and looked like it was going to tackle you to lick you. His face was bigger than mine. Nougat was Anouk's dog.

"Anouk Letroux, the only child of an Alsatian father and a Norwegian mother, was my neighbor, and I couldn't stand her for many years. She was a—*comment dirais-je*—diabolical and twisted girl. I was so afraid of her dog that I ended up disliking her. My brother, who liked Nougat better than the boat, got along with Anouk. They were the same age and both restless as all hell.

"Little by little, of course, we all grew up, and there was a summer that Anouk also changed when the Letroux family returned to Capbreton. Breasts. Lips. She had grown up and calmed down a bit."

"You weren't as scared of the dog anymore."

"Exactly. We can put it that way. I don't know what year it was. I was seventeen and she must have been thirteen. She had completely mellowed, and one night, under the pines beside her house, we kissed. It was nothing, just a kiss. The next day we saw each other again, went out, and the relationship, if you want to call it that, lasted that whole summer. We just kissed and nothing more. An innocent, childlike thing our families never knew about.

"During the school year, we wrote to each other three or four times. I was in Paris, and she was in Colmar. The following summer, when we met again, it was as if nothing had ever happened. But from then on, our friendship grew. She hung around with our group, with the older kids. She maintained a certain character, which she always had, but it no longer had to be only her way all the time. You could talk to her, laugh with her, and she was a pretty, normal, proper girl, like my brother or me. Anouk told me everything, asked me questions, and we had a good time together. But there was never anything else. We saw each other in the summers, and that was it.

"A couple years later, one day out of the blue, she calls me. She never called. And she asks if she can come to Paris for New Year's, because she has something to tell me. I say yes, of course. She takes the train from Strasbourg, shows up at the station, and the moment I saw her coming toward me on the platform that December 31 at seven in the evening, I saw the devil in her eyes again.

"She threw herself around my neck, hugged me, and started crying, sobbing. 'You have to help me, Jean-Pierre, you have to help me.' She kept repeating it, and she wouldn't say why she was crying. She slowly calmed down. I took her bag, and I held her. We managed to make our way out of the station. Maybe twenty minutes had passed, and I still didn't know what was going on. We sat on a stone bench in the square, in front of the Gare de l'Est, and I'll tell you as directly as she told me: She was pregnant."

"I had guessed as much. At seventeen?"

"At seventeen. She had a hell of a problem, and she was begging me to help. She didn't want to tell me who the father was. She never told me, and I never asked either. But she did tell me the boy wanted nothing to do with it. He washed his hands of her, just like that, and left Anouk at seventeen years old like that without knowing where to turn. He told her to do whatever she thought was best, because he couldn't have gotten her pregnant.

"You can imagine what kind of New Year's we had. The two of us shut in my bedroom, sitting on the bed, her crying, and me offering solutions to a three-months-pregnant girl without the slightest idea of what I was doing. Not even a little, no . . . Not at all. I was twenty-one, without having grown up with women in my family. I didn't know how any of it worked. I told her I had some money saved, that we'd find a doctor, a place where . . . But she didn't want to hear it. She wanted to have the baby, she said. She wanted it no matter what. She wanted the baby, but she had to be able to say who the father was . . ."

"No . . ." Pauline saw the bind.

"With every chime of every hour, I kept asking myself what I was supposed to do. Anouk begged me to be the father, to be the father in everyone's eyes. Her parents would kill her for getting knocked up, but they would finish her off for being an unmarried mother. They couldn't be grandparents to a bastard. She pleaded with me to help her, said she and I would be fine, but please, please . . ."

"And you let yourself be taken in? Please tell me you didn't . . ."

"On the 20th of May, Monique Letroux was born, a wonderful baby girl. She was hairy, with dark hair . . . like her father's, I suppose. We gave her Anouk's surname, though. I gave up Zanardi—naturally . . ."

"I can't believe it."

"Those months, from the end of the year until Monique's birth, were a nightmare. We went to see her parents in Colmar, to show our faces and say it was an accident and that we didn't know how it could have happened, but that we were prepared to go through with it. You can only imagine how they took it. They were the kind of people who went to Mass and kept religious icons. They wanted to kill her, but really they wanted to claw my eyes out. I was of age, but Anouk . . . it was like I'd taken advantage of her.

"I remember they insisted for weeks that we get married before the child was born. They didn't insist. They demanded it. I pulled Anouk aside and told her I'd stepped into that situation out of friendship, to help her, to pull her out of the biggest mess of her life. But not marriage, not in a million years. And we didn't. My mother, also upset beyond words, got involved too. It was a debacle the size of a cathedral.

"I'm telling you this now because many years have passed, but back then it was one nightmare after the other. The roller coaster had started, and there was no stopping it. And then, in the middle of the upheaval, someone did the math and realized that at the end of September, Anouk and I hadn't been in Capbreton. So she made up a story about how she'd actually been with me on a weekend she had said she'd be staying at a friend's. I'd gone all the way to Mulhouse, because we were so in love. I've never been to Mulhouse in my life. No desire to go either, but anyway. It was lie after lie."

"Why, Jean-Pierre? To save her?"

"What do you want me to say? Yes. Out of pity, I don't know. Out of friendship, because I saw a friend who was really desperate. Because of the recklessness of youth. Because she was the devil, and I could see I should run away from her, but some strange force wouldn't let me. Because I guess I liked her, or loved her, or thought I loved her. Why? Don't make me say it. Because I guess I thought I was doing a good deed. I don't know."

"And where is Monique? With her mother?"

"Hold up. Don't rush. Everything up until now has been the pretty part of the story."

"I can't believe it . . ." Paulina pitied him, but at the same time she felt like she had been stabbed. He had helped Anouk, because he loved her.

"Those were the happy days. The child was born. She was a healthy, calm, and magnificent baby. Anouk came to live in Paris, near here, in a little flat that was not associated with this one. There was no elevator, only two small rooms, a stench rising up from an unknown source. We both worked so that Monique could want for nothing. Our parents told us we'd have to manage on our own. I was Monique's father in everyone's eyes. In fact, I did act like her father. After a year, she was walking. After two she was talking. It was that whole natural evolution that Anouk and I learned together, side by side. From all appearances, Anouk and I were a couple. Things weren't too bad at home, but it was more like a student apartment with a child added on. We slept in the same room, in a narrow bed, and I won't say no. There were some days, yes . . . We held each other, we finished each other off. Young people things, you know. We were so overworked that we didn't have the time or desire to look for anything else outside the house.

"In the mornings I worked as a librarian at the faculty of medicine. In the afternoons I started to work at a gallery in the Latin Quarter. Monique called me 'Dad,' and of course I loved her like a daughter. I don't know if I loved her well enough. I don't know if she sensed some subconscious wariness in the way I treated her. I don't think so, because I did everything for her. I bathed her, changed her, made her dinner, fed her, read her bedtime stories, cut her nails. Everything. What can I tell you that you don't already know?"

"It's twenty-four seven."

"Twenty-four seven." Jean-Pierre squeezed her big toe to show he understood. "One day, when Monique was six, Anouk disappeared. She disappeared just like that, just like I'm telling you now. I came home from work and I could already hear Monique fussing as I was climbing the stairs. I went in and she was alone in the apartment. She told me her mother had left hours earlier. She was hungry. She'd wet herself, and she wouldn't stop crying. That night Anouk didn't come back, not the next day, or the one after. It was a scene.

"Ten days later, she called me from Norway with an incredible amount of audacity. She told me she couldn't take it anymore. She needed to breathe, and she'd gone to Marifjora, her grandmother's village. She didn't say she was sorry. She didn't even ask about the child. It's like her daughter didn't exist, and she hung up."

"What did you do?"

"I spoke with Anouk's mother and asked for the grandmother's phone number in Norway. I called and spoke with the old woman, who didn't understand anything I was saying. Anouk wasn't there. She hadn't been there in years, and she wasn't expected anytime soon. And there I was, with the kid at home, not knowing what to tell her about her mother.

"One week, two weeks, three, four, a month, two months went by, and before the third month, Anouk came back to Paris. She turned up at Monique's school, picked her up, and took her away. I never saw either of them again. Never again. To this day."

"But—"

"To this day, Pauline. Where are they? I don't know. Why did they leave? I have no idea. Why hasn't she given any sign of life, or an explanation, or a letter? None of those. Never, nothing at all. It's like the earth swallowed them. Her parents in Colmar died—first her father, then her mother—without ever knowing what had happened to Anouk and their granddaughter. There was no news of their daughter. She didn't even come to the funeral. There's no evidence that she even knows her parents have been dead and buried for years now.

"In fact, according to my father, their notary, they left everything in their will to Monique. Her parents were hurt and wanted nothing more to do with Anouk. They left everything to the girl, but there's been no way to locate her. And that's the story . . . You asked me whether I was Monique's father. What do you think?"

"My God, you must have really worried."

She realized, though, that if that story hurt Jean-Pierre so much, it was because, deep down, he loved Anouk. Or perhaps, deep down, he missed Monique more than Anouk. Maybe he needed to hear a child running up and down the apartment again, or he missed picking up the drawings the little girl with braids had left scattered all over the floor. And to think that for four days Paulina was scared he might think she was too naive. From the night of the wedding, lips pressed up against each other's, she had been convinced he was some kind of hero. Only now did she realize he was a survivor.

For the first time since they'd been together, she didn't feel inferior to Jean-Pierre, who, with the last sip of malt, tried to choke back the emotion from a life of setbacks.

"What do my friends know? What does your cousin know? The same as everyone else. Anouk left me from one day to the next, went away, and took our daughter with her. What do only you know? That I was not the child's biological father. That I didn't get Anouk pregnant."

"How cruel, Jean-Pierre, this whole story. To trade in your life to help a friend, however close a friend she may have been."

"It's not a pretty story, no."

"You loved, and you were used."

"Long ago I decided not to remember. The right to forget should be a fundamental law."

"Memory isn't a set of folding chairs that you can store behind the door once your guests leave. It's a terribly sad story, but it's yours." Paulina slid her feet off the sofa and set them on the floor to feel closer to him. "And I'm very glad you trust me with it."

"So you still love me, then?"

Like a little kid, Jean-Pierre scrambled up onto the sofa and hugged her hard, putting his cheek against her. They couldn't stop crying for a while. He had spent years as a hermit, carrying his grief the best he could, missing Monique and cursing Anouk. Even if he didn't show it, the wound was not as healed as he had thought. She, feeling pity for him, felt terrible seeing Jean-Pierre come undone. And she couldn't understand how the sparkling man she'd met, confident, *charmant*, and cocky, could hide a tragedy so big, so unjust, the kind that marks an entire lifetime. How did he live with that pain parked somewhere inside? Would she have been able to go on after a similar loss? And if Anouk was such a bitch, why hadn't Jean-Pierre changed the name of the gallery? Maybe he still thought that . . . And if she came back, would he forgive her?

She kept those doubts to herself. Paulina was ready never to mention Anouk, Monique, or any part of that bitter episode ever again if Jean-Pierre didn't bring it up ever again. In any case, she was leaving that afternoon and didn't even know whether she would ever again speak to this man who had made her feel more a woman than she ever had, more valued, more attractive. Starting tomorrow, could she manage without the person who had taught her how to live every moment like it was fifteen minutes before the end of the world?

Once they had wiped away the tears, Jean-Pierre packed his pipe and slid the lock over his past again. He thought it had been good for him to let it out. He had finally found someone to confide his story in, in detail and out loud. But now he only cared about the future and about a person who had knocked down his barriers and worries.

"Don't move. We'll eat in a second. But there's something we still haven't done, and I really want to. I want you to taste something. Don't move, okay?"

"No, no." Paulina obeyed.

Jean-Pierre got up and went into the kitchen. She listened, trying to guess what was happening in there. The refrigerator opened. A wine bottle was stubbornly uncorked. He filled the ice bucket with a clatter that foiled any surprise. He opened the fridge again and lingered there before closing it again. He rummaged around in a drawer like he was searching for a tool among ladles and tongs. A can opener, probably. If she listened closely, she thought she could hear the dry crackle as . . . A handy man like Jean-Pierre wouldn't have so much trouble opening a tin. A little plate—that sound, she recognized.

"Close your eyes—I'm coming over."

"Done." She squeezed her eyelids shut.

First he set the ice bucket and two glasses on the table. Then he passed his hand right in front of her nose, like a greeting, to make sure Pauline wasn't cheating.

"I love you."

"Can I look?"

"No!" And his steps disappeared back into the kitchen.

He grabbed something and came into the living room, trying not to make noise. He came close to Paulina. His breathing gave him away.

"Don't open your eyes now of all times."

"But . . ."

"Trust me."

She heard him cut something on a plate. It must have been a small coffee saucer based on the light clink.

"Wait with your eyes closed. Open your mouth. Just a little. I'm going to put something in with the knife. Be careful. Okay?"

"And if—"

"Just trust me. You'll like it, believe me. Don't worry. When it's in your mouth, keep your eyes closed. Don't bite it. Let it melt in your mouth. Okay?"

"Okay," Paulina said, more nervous than filled with desire.

She scraped the knife with her teeth, hiding her tongue, careful not to cut herself.

"Mmm . . ."

"Don't open your eyes."

"It's foie gras!"

"Savor it. Enjoy all the flavors. Let it melt. Don't chew. Let it dissolve like a soft caramel."

She did as he told her. In the meantime, he also slid a small piece into his own mouth and poured two glasses of Riesling. He didn't say anything. He watched her taste it with pleasure. He had gotten Pauline to take note of all the flavors: a slow, fresh flavor; a faint aftertaste of bitter fruit, tobacco, salt, little drops of fat; a vague hint of chocolate melting, little by little—unctuous, smooth—dissolving between her tongue and palate.

"It's delicious, Jean-Pierre." She opened her eyes. He was waiting with a glass in hand, ready to bring it over to her. He sat down beside her.

"It's goose. Smoother than duck. I like it more."

"When I met you I thought you were one of those bachelors who doesn't even have a teaspoon at home . . ."

"Hidden talents. You can't take advantage of me, but it's one of life's pleasures."

"So this is lunch, my love?"

He cut her another little cube that Paulina let melt on her tongue. Instinctively, she closed her eyes again, and from then on she always closed them when she ate foie gras, to concentrate on the flavors and to remember Jean-Pierre's surprise. The man who knew how to make every instant special.

"You've had home field advantage these days. That's not fair. You've taken me places, shown me things, surprised me with the foie gras, and the wine, and your music, and the drops of honey. You must think I don't have—I don't know—initiative. That I'm boring."

"Then stay. Stay here and show me you have hidden talents too. Stay with me."

Paulina covered her face with her hands. They had broached the conversation both of them knew had been coming. It was the first time he had said *"Stay."* She wanted him to say it. She longed for it with all her might. But she was afraid. Afraid to hear those words—and even more afraid that Jean-Pierre, prudently or because he was happy for their love to have an expiration date, might never say them at all.

"Stay," he repeated, more emphatically, resolute.

"Don't do this to me, Jean-Pierre."

"Stay, stay with me. We'll live here or wherever you want. We'll work together at the gallery if you want, we'll travel the world, or we'll stay here forever. We'll do whatever you want . . ."

"Don't say that . . . You know that I . . ."

"Of course I'm saying it, Pau. This time I'm going to think about myself. Now it's my turn. I've helped enough people, I've been burned enough, I know what it's like to lose what you love and never see it again. I know that opportunities like ours come only once—or they never come at all. Let's risk it all."

"You're a bachelor. You wouldn't be able to get used to . . ."

"Don't use me as your excuse. I know what I want. I know the only thing I want to happen to me over the next forty years. Let's risk it together."

"I've got a whole life already, I . . ." She laid her head on his belly. "Jean-Pierre, my love, don't say it again. Don't say it twice."

"Three times, as many as it takes, if you tell me I have a chance . . ."

Jean-Pierre bent to kiss her forehead. He waited for an answer. But he sensed Paulina didn't want to say anything else. He waited, tousling her bangs back and forth, like a pendulum of a clock slowing its speed.

"I understand it's easier for me. I also understand that you have a life already, but that's exactly what this is about. About life. We're given one, just one, and we have to make the most out of it. You're too young to drag around, your whole life, the sorrow of not doing what you wanted. We love each other too much to scold ourselves forever for not being together, if that's what we want."

"What I *want*? How can you say that?" She lifted her head again and looked at him in a lover's desperation. "Of course I want it. Don't doubt that, please. Whatever happens, never doubt that."

"Then . . ."

"It wouldn't work out, Jean-Pierre. It's been four days. You're used to being alone. I have a daughter . . ."

"Bring her . . ."

"It's not that easy."

"Bring her. I've already thought about that . . ."

"It's not the same. You and I here with a little girl . . ."

"I already know what it's like to live with a little girl. I was a good father . . ."

A thought suddenly stabbed Paulina, sharp as a needle. What if Jean-Pierre was proposing they settle there to recover a daughter, and not for her? She tore the thought out of her mind forever. She couldn't afford to fall into the trap of neurons working overtime. Not for an instant did she want to entertain—even remotely—the idea that Jean-Pierre needed Gina to recover from losing Monique. Her love couldn't be that twisted. Jean-Pierre couldn't be one of those people. For a second, she noticed he was soft, but she couldn't be weak in that moment.

"My daughter aside—I don't want to drag her into this conversation—living together isn't the same as four perfect days. 'Perfect' meaning 'flawless, unsurpassable, unforgettable,' but it's only been four days. I'm telling you this with all my heart. That's how I experienced it. For you"—she didn't want it to sound accusatory—"what have these four days meant?"

"It's not the days. It's you. My love, my salvation. We don't know what will happen later. Life has many periods, and we don't know what's waiting for us even tomorrow. This isn't a painting, not a finished work of art, framed and hung. We can paint it together, with whatever colors you want. I—now that we have each other, now that we've found each other—I don't see why we should set limits."

"Jean-Pierre . . ."

"Whatever happens going forward, we know that you and I have saved each other. We met so that we could save each other. I'm sure of it. I'm in love. I know what it means to be in love for the first time, and that's something we'll always have. I've opened my heart, and I'm so happy. I didn't know it was possible to feel all this. I thought that many years ago, maybe in college, I had been in love, but now I realize that this is what love is. A new feeling, truer than any other. Incomparable, unmistakable. Of course, I've known other women, married women, attractive women, sophisticated women. I don't know what your cousin may have said about me, but no one ever meant anything. What have you, only you, succeeded in doing, my love? I had to wait forty-five years to know what it was like to be in love. Let's celebrate life; let's celebrate it together. That's the greatest miracle."

Paulina, who didn't want to say anything she might regret, struggled not to let herself be swept away by Jean-Pierre's fervor.

"My father used to say that his parents, my grandparents, said 'I love you' so often that, in the end, they accepted it like it was nothing, like a 'good morning' or 'good night.' Emotionless. They grew old and lived together all their lives, but their feelings had worn down . . ."

"We're not ninety years old . . ."

"My father said that 'I love you' is the only phrase that has to be said feeling each and every letter. And I realize—"

"That he's right. Until yesterday I hadn't told you I love you. And I said it deliberately. And you said it to me, in French. And since yesterday, every time we've said 'I love you,' and we haven't counted, we've said it feeling every letter. And we've accepted it like it was the first time or a last wish."

"I know. And I feel the same way. It's like that, Jean-Pierre, and I wish you could go inside my head so you could see that I feel exactly the same way you do."

"But?"

"But."

"What can I do to break through your armor, Pauline? I'll always love you with the height of emotion of these days. We'll earn our happiness together. You have to desire and work for happiness. Everything has a cost, and fighting for love costs much more."

"Jean-Pierre, I wish that I could . . ."

He backed off. He saw a tear in Paulina's eye and knew to be quiet. He let the drop slide down her cheek, put his hand to her face, wiped it away with his thumb, and caressed her other cheek.

"There are decades when nothing happens, and weeks when decades happen. And this is our week."

"That's beautiful, Jean-Pierre." She tried not to cry.

"It's Lenin." He raised his eyebrows, mischievously. "I told you. I'm a man of the left."

They laughed. They laughed together again, freely, to get rid of their nerves. It hadn't all been orgasms, looks, and conversations throughout the four days. They had also laughed a great deal, heartily, free from everything. The two of them alone in the world.

"Should we eat?"

"Let's make love . . ."

They didn't say it though it was on the tip of their tongue. Neither dared. But both of them knew that the unfinished sentence would have continued in a tormented and conclusive "for the last time."

"You'll have to help me with something." She sat down on the edge of the bed. "Can you pull off my boots?"

The silence between bodies enriched the farewell.

She put her boots on by herself. She fastened the clasp of her bra, and before pulling the T-shirt she had bought on Saint-Honoré over her head, she went into the bathroom to brush out her hair with the long-bristled brush she always carried in her bag.

"What time does your plane leave?"

"I wanted to be at Orly by five."

"We'll have to hurry."

It's better that way, Paulina thought. That way the farewell could be shorter. She hadn't wanted to think about it for even a moment, but now that it was approaching, one thing was clear: They shouldn't linger. Hardships are best gotten over as quickly as possible. Jean-Pierre hauled the suitcases over the cobblestones of rue du Trésor to the garage where he kept his car. She didn't want to say goodbye to the apartment, or the elevator, or the cul-de-sac of Le Marais where she had discovered the most intimate version of herself. She had never been so far from home and yet so close to herself.

In the car—a Citroën with a big trunk, ideal for transporting paintings—they spoke very little. Neither of them wanted words to take on the weight of farewells. The grayness of Paris's outskirts didn't inspire anyone to say anything even vaguely romantic. Jean-Pierre hesitated over whether he should make one last attempt. Would it be too brazen to say "Stay here"? He was tempted to give in and say, "Look, Pauline, my beloved, my love, you're wrong to leave, you'll be happy here, and you know it, even if you can't admit it. You know you're going back to a husband who no longer excites you, to a life you live by pure inertia, the way you get used to the hum of the refrigerator."

"Wow, your car smells nice."

He held back. He believed Pauline had already put on her armor for returning home.

"I like the lemon air freshener. It lasts about ten days. After that . . ."

He didn't say it. He didn't dare say that everything fades quickly. At the last moment he couldn't bring himself to parade his cynicism. Paulina wouldn't have understood. And she didn't deserve it. She was leaving because she had a ticket, because even before leaving Barcelona she had known she would return home on Tuesday to her five-year-old daughter and to a husband they had prudently avoided discussing for four days. Once on the highway, when he was in fifth gear, she placed her hand on the gearshift, and Jean-Pierre didn't let go of it until it was time to put the car in neutral for the parking slip.

"All your clothes are in that suitcase?" Jean-Pierre unloaded the car, showing no outward signs of effort. The struggle was internal.

"I gave things to Julie. So it wouldn't weigh so much."

"I won't know how to act when I see your cousin."

"Just be yourself. That's the best thing."

The elevator took them straight to Air France's international departures terminal.

"Should we have a coffee?"

"I'd rather do it inside. These things . . . it's better to be inside and do them inside the airport."

"Then let's go." Orly was a second home for Jean-Pierre. Between art fairs and butterflies, he took about thirty flights a year.

"Keep our story to yourself."

"Of course, Pauline."

"I'll write to you soon . . ."

"You know where to find me if I ever go missing, right?"

Paulina looked down. Jean-Pierre lifted her chin with two fingers so she could look up at him again.

"Have a good trip."

"You too."

A laugh escaped them, unwillingly, just as Paulina's "You too" had slipped out in reflex, a purely cultural formality. They kissed quickly on the lips, a brush of a kiss, and she wanted to be the one who, before letting go of their hands, said the last thing.

"I love you. With every letter . . . do you hear me? *Je t'aime.*"

She saw in Jean-Pierre's eyes the red veins of missed opportunities. They couldn't say anything more.

Shattered, she went through security. Her heart pumped, all at once, anger, disappointment, sadness, a jolt, anxiety, excitement, remorse, and already, in that very moment, the longing for the four days she was leaving behind. The policeman, protected by glass like a zoo monkey, looked at her photo and mechanically looked up to check her face. She wasn't the first woman he had seen crying at the airport. It was the first time in years—this he did notice—that the woman in the ID photo looked more beautiful than the one standing in front of his cage with her sorrow held in. The monkey-policeman stamped the seal—Orly-Paris-France, 16 June 1981—continuing to chew his gum.

"Allez-y."

"Merci," she muttered as she slipped the document back into her bag.

Past the checkpoint, she didn't turn around. She walked on toward the future, toward the past. She couldn't let herself do anything else. She didn't want Jean-Pierre, in the last moment he saw her, to see a tear. She didn't dare look back at him. She ran the risk of turning around and flying—despite taboos and customs agents—straight into his arms. She knew that a single gesture from Jean-Pierre would have been enough to send everything to hell. Just one kiss blown with two fingers as he held his briar-root pipe, and Paulina wouldn't have had the willpower to lose herself down the terminal among Toblerones and perfumes.

Had she turned around, though, she would have found Jean-Pierre alone, standing under the dim terminal light, hands in his pockets, pipe between his teeth, eyes wide open. He had the look of a guilty man listening, without any possible appeal, to his sentence. The verdict—cold and merciless—didn't let him even blink. He was sure he was letting the love of his life slip away, and this time it was happening right under his nose, and he wondered whether he had fought hard enough to stop it. Like in a German requiem, he bore the pain in unconditional solitude.

As soon as the arrivals screen at El Prat Airport announced that the Air France flight landed, Gina climbed onto her father's shoulders. She wanted at all costs to be the first to see her mother when the translucent glass automatic doors opened.

The plane's engine gave its final sigh, stopped on the runway, at 8:21 on a Tuesday, the day when there was a little more love in the world. And a little more sorrow, too, because you never get one without the other.

"Mama! Mama, over here! What did you bring me?"

13

Crossing a Wasteland

Gina received Biel at her penthouse on Carrer de Tuset, without having had time to tidy up the apartment. He showed up with a medium-sized box of iced truffles, a two-week-old beard, and a justification: "The hair I used to have on my head is now on my face." Gina laughed. He was probably still the ugliest guy in their class, but he'd had his eyebrows shaped, and she thought bald men had a charm to them. She sat him down, served him a raspberry tea, and, unable to wait any longer, handed him the three letters she had recovered from Aunt Júlia's box after her death. While Biel read, she took the opportunity to change the sheets and wipe down the kitchen counter with a damp rag. With all her hours at the university, she had found the perfect excuse to neglect the apartment from Monday to Friday. Inevitably, on the weekend, she had to put it all back in order.

Biel wasn't there when she returned to the living room. He had opened the terrace door and gone outside to finish reading the third letter.

"Are you crying?"

"Me? No, no . . ."

"It's the last one, I'm guessing . . ."

"How emotional, the poor man." He wiped his tears with the sleeves of his shirt. "Jean-Pierre, your mother, your cousin. What a triangle. Sending the letters through Aunt Júlia, you can't tell me that wasn't weird as hell . . . This one . . ." Biel checked the envelope of the letter he was holding, to be sure. "Yes, this is the one Jean-Pierre sends directly to Júlia, after your mother's death."

"Aunt Júlia was the only one who knew everything. That much is clear. And she never said a word to anyone."

"Not even to her husband?"

"To Alain? No, I don't think so."

"You don't think so, or you know?"

"I know. Well, let's say I'm sure."

"Did you ask Alain?"

"I asked my cousins to do it. I thought that he wouldn't have dared with me, Paulina's daughter . . . Assuming he knew anything at all, maybe he wouldn't have told me anyway. Alain was never interested in gossip."

"In one of the letters—I think it's the first one—Jean-Pierre tells your mother that he didn't want her to have to lie in order to hide their story. That's intense."

"Yeah, at the end of the first one."

"And?"

"Do you want to know?" Gina sat down on the wooden bench on the terrace. "I went to see my father . . ."

"How is he?"

"My father?" She couldn't hide her disappointment. "I don't recognize him. I hope I don't end up like him, with the years . . ."

"What do you mean, you don't recognize him?" Biel sat down beside her. That way they could talk about nothing, without having to look at each other.

"Nothing, just impressions. The whole thing, I don't know." She noticed Biel wanted more of an explanation. "He's in a bad mood, with those two little kids, my brothers, who he had far too late, honestly.

He never really raised them, he's hardly there for them, they've turned the house upside down, he's let them do whatever they want, and now there's no way to get them back on track. They're two tsunamis. And he's not a father. He's a grandfather. And she, Mire, his wife . . . what can I say? One pulls this way, the other that way. I don't really know whether my father remarried because he didn't want to be alone and was talked into it . . . In love? Maybe at the beginning he thought he was. Not anymore. Now everything is flat. He lives through pure inertia, and it seems it would bore him to even consider anything other than just letting the days pass by. And that's despite the fact that, physically, you can look at him, and he's an impressive man. Even without the mustache, he looks younger than he is."

Gina wasn't embarrassed by her father. What pained her was that he had settled for an insipid life, like a soft-boiled egg. "Pity"—that was the word. She had never said it out loud, and as she struggled to describe the situation to Biel, it hurt her to speak of her father in those terms.

"Didn't Manuel play cards?"

"Thank God for poker. It's still sacred. A couple of nights a week he goes off to play with the same old friends. But one of them, one of the regulars, died from a heart attack watching a tennis match on TV. Now they miss him and had to find a replacement. But he says it's not the same. He says they've gotten old, you know, and sometimes I think I would have liked to see what my father's life would have been like with my mother by his side."

"Do you think he knows anything about what happened in Paris?"

"That's the point, Biel."

One Sunday, like so many others, Gina arrived home, at the place that had once been her home, right at lunchtime. Her father had fully immersed himself in his new family, but he had made only minor changes to the apartment on Rambla de Catalunya, near Còrsega. The living room was the same as the day before Paulina was to come home from Paris. Only a few paintings had changed, along with the upholstery on the sofa and armchairs. And they would soon have to reupholster everything again, with two children climbing all over everything with their shoes on. Except for the appliances, the kitchen was also just as it had been, with the light Formica cabinets she had so often opened and closed as a child. The magnets, with their poles attracting and repelling each other, were one of life's great mysteries for her. Her bedroom, on the other hand, was gone. Even the poster with the black-and-white photograph of people wearing 3D glasses had disappeared. Gina's room had become Edu and Nico's battleground. Her brothers, eight and six years old, slept in bunk beds, and to keep them from fighting over who got the coveted top mattress, they settled it each week with a PlayStation match that usually ended in tears and punches. Gina had prudently not gone back into her parents' bedroom since her father began living with Mireia. She left her jacket and motorcycle helmet on the sofa, and kissed everyone twice. They sat down to eat before she could tickle Edu and Nico, who were already waiting eagerly to roughhouse. All names were shortened since Mire had entered the home. It probably wasn't Mireia's fault. Her name was Georgina, and everyone had always called her Gina. At least Manuel, her father, was still Manuel, all six letters, around all the women.

Mire's rice casserole was a relative success. Edu pushed aside the peppers, Nico the mussels, and Gina swallowed every bite without complaining so as not to appear rude. With every forkful, she felt how the strong onion sofrito would come back to haunt her all afternoon. Before dessert was even served, without anyone even forbidding it, the children were playing soccer in the hallway with a foam ball, so they wouldn't break anything, that is, if there was even anything that still remained intact. After the decaf coffee, Mire discreetly disappeared like she did every Sunday, so father and daughter could have some time alone. Manuel and Gina cleared the table, left the dishes soaking, and went into the living room. Gina sprawled on the sofa without shoes on, and her father turned on the TV once he sat in his armchair.

Absentmindedly, he flipped from channel to channel, looking for a game that might interest him. Gina, always direct and never one to mince words, for once didn't quite know how to approach the subject. Her father still intimidated her. They had never truly understood each other. She decided to get straight to the point.

"When I was in Paris, for Aunt Júlia's funeral, I went through photos with Fabienne and Laurence. We looked at her wedding album. Everyone was so young. Did you not go?"

"Where?"

"To Aunt Júlia and Alain's wedding."

"Oh. No, no."

"Only Mama appears in the photo album."

"That's true. She went alone, yes."

"Why?"

"What?"

"Why didn't you go?" Gina picked up the remote and muted the TV. If he wasn't going to take his eyes off the screen, the least he could do was listen.

"To Júlia's wedding?" He didn't want to give the conversation any importance. "Work, I'm guessing."

"But she was Mama's cousin. She was like a sister to her."

"I don't know, Gina. I must have had work." He tilted his head. "And you know how I feel about planes. Unless it's absolutely essential . . ."

Gina thought it was time to move up a notch.

"She looks very happy in the photos . . ."

"The ones from Júlia's wedding?"

"Yes, of course."

"I don't know if I ever saw them."

"She's wearing a blue dress, she looks . . ."

"Well, your mother was very beautiful, what do you expect."

"Don't you remember the blue dress?"

"No, no . . ."

"She stayed a few days in Paris, I think. Is that true?"

"I don't remember, dear. Your mother loved Paris. It was her favorite city."

"She liked to travel, didn't she?"

"Yes. Very much . . . At first, we didn't go out much, because I didn't like to. Her desire to travel came about in her later years. She wanted to go everywhere. With me or without me, it didn't matter. She just wanted to go. With Júlia, actually, I think they went to Venice."

"Yes, yes. Venice and Milan." She gulped and stared at a second-division match. "Do you know if anything happened to her on that trip to Paris?"

"In Paris?"

In the pause before her father answered, Gina crossed a wasteland. An experienced lawyer, her father knew how to play dumb when it suited him.

"In Paris for Júlia's wedding, you mean? I don't remember anything special."

"I don't know," Gina insisted. "I just wanted to know if, when she came back, you found her more . . . if she was different."

"Different how?"

"I don't know, I wasn't there. Happier, or sadder, or just . . . different."

"I don't know what you're getting at, Gina. It was a long time ago. How many years has it been?"

"The wedding? It was in 1981 right before the summer."

"Just imagine. Barcelona hadn't even hosted the World Cup or the Olympics yet." He kicked the ball out-of-bounds like the mediocre soccer players on the TV screen. "Happier, sadder . . . I don't see why this matters now, Gina."

"It's nothing, really. I just thought about it when I saw the photos, and I realized I need to know more things about Mama."

"Or are you trying to tell me something?"

For a moment, Gina was reminded of that dry tone of her father's that she hated. It was a reproachful manner, the one he took on, her father who, back in the day when she was Edu's age, would have made her eat in the laundry room for pushing aside a pea, or sent her out onto the landing if she had broken a Bavarian vase with a ball, or scolded her for wearing a dead woman's clothes when she was a teenager. They repelled each other, like magnets.

"No, no . . . I just wanted you to tell me things about Mama."

"Anything in particular? Something you think you know, and I don't?"

"That's not it, Dad, dammit."

At that moment, both of them realized that the other knew something. Maybe only a small part of an incomplete story. But the father had no intention of reconstructing the puzzle, and the daughter was not convinced it was entirely worth unraveling the thread. Like one of the sacred Thursday poker games, it was all about bluffing and hiding your aces. Neither of them knew what the other knew about Paulina's four days in Paris, but both had the feeling that the other knew more than they themselves did. Having read and reread Jean-Pierre's three letters, Gina did not want to betray her mother, even though she thought she might have already gone too far. And Manuel, inclined to keep details to himself, was not willing to dive back into a chapter he had long since considered closed. He decided to end the conversation with a closing argument.

"I have only good memories of your mother. Not a single thing otherwise. Not one. Ever. Of course, living together has its problems, you'll see one day, but she always rose to the occasion. Always. I think I did too. What happened in Paris? I don't know. And I don't care. Paulina was happy, she loved you madly, she loved me, and the three of us had a wonderful time together. It didn't last long. It was much shorter than any of us would have liked or needed, but until the day your mother died, the relationship was perfect. You don't remember because you were very little, but we had a ritual you loved that you would ask us to repeat from time to time during the day. You were just starting to talk. You must have been two, three, or four at the latest, I think. You adored it. Your mother or I would pick you up, the three of us would hug each other in a little circle, bounce a bit like we were picking our feet off the ground, and shout: 'We are a family, we are a family, we are a family.' You had a blast. You tried to say it in your own way, but could only do the vowels. We thought you were adorable. You hugged us tight and asked us to do it again and again. Your mother, you, and I were a family. We were. Don't you understand? And whatever happened in Paris—if anything happened, which is something I don't know or want to know—was just four days. Four days don't amount to much. They don't make a mark on an entire life. We can agree on that, can't we?"

A clear reveal. Biel understood that Manuel more or less knew everything. Gina was sure that her mother had given her father an explanation, maybe out of remorse, maybe to lessen the burden, maybe to evaluate future options, maybe because she had been acting strangely, maybe because she had been caught. But how much? She didn't know. And never would. But both decided that time had wiped the slate clean. For her father, it was maybe for the best. If they wanted to know more about that story, it was up to each of them to investigate.

"Biel, there's a lead you can follow since you live in London. That is, if you feel like it, of course."

"Well, since we're here now, why not?" He couldn't hide it. They had gone almost twenty years without seeing each other, he had lost all his hair, but he was still hopelessly into Gina. And she was ready to take advantage of it.

"Years ago, many years ago, not long after my father dragged you out naked from under my bed, I met a Welsh guy. A man, really. A bus driver in London. We spent a weekend in Salou, and I never heard from him again. Never. It was the best for us both, I guess. It was three days of fun and goodbye, end of story. How did I meet him? This part is important for you to know. Mark showed up at my house—you'll like this—with one of my mother's business cards. With her business card in his hand. Paulina Homs, this and that, Rambla de Catalunya, her postal code, her phone number, the whole thing."

"A business card, wow." He took a cigarette from a pack and offered one to Gina. Was it jealousy that was starting to gnaw at him?

"No, thanks. On the card, 'call me' is written in French . . . '*Appelle-moi.*'"

"But why did your friend have the card?" He lit up the cigarette.

"Hold on. That's what we need to find out. He told me he found it inside a book. First order of business: Which book?"

"He didn't tell you?"

"No. And that's an important clue. Second: Where did he buy the book?"

"Could your mother have given him the book?"

"No way. He told me he bought the book, and inside . . ."

"What's your English friend's name?"

"Don't call him English, that'll mess it up. Welsh. His name was—is, I guess—Granger. Mark Granger."

"In London alone, there must be . . ."

"But there can't be more than three who are bus drivers, the red double-deckers, the old-school ones."

Biel let out a breath to communicate he'd be looking for a needle in a haystack and couldn't make any promises.

"Gina, I'm a lawyer, not a detective. I'll do what I can, but . . ."

"Wait, Biel, there's something you need to know, in case you find him." How could she explain this now? "Mark doesn't actually know my name. If you tell him you're coming on behalf of Gina from Barcelona, he won't know who I am. He thinks my name is . . . Paulina."

"Excuse me?"

"Yeah, look, it's complicated, but that's just how it is. He showed up with my mother's business card. I couldn't say no, the lie got bigger and more bitter, and after three days I couldn't bring myself to tell him that . . . You get it, right?"

"Not really. I mean, yes, I get it—I'm not stupid—but sometimes you . . ."

"It's good to role-play once in a while, isn't it?" Gina became affectionate to butter him up.

"And if I look for Mark Granger and I find him, then what?"

"What do you mean, 'then what'?"

"Will you and I fuck again one day?"

"Biel, please . . ."

"What?" He protested dramatically. "It wouldn't be the first time . . ."

"You're pretty desperate, aren't you?" She said maliciously, "I bet you haven't done it again since my father caught us."

"It's been twenty years, woman . . ."

"That's exactly what I'm saying."

They laughed. But she didn't say no. And holding on to that hope, and remembering the silent orgasms of his former classmate, Biel was set to head back to the city with a concrete assignment and an uncertain reward.

14

It's Flowers That They Want

Paris, Day 9 Without You

Dear beloved Pauline,
I received your letter only a few hours ago, and only with a wide smile can I approximate the joy it gave me to hold it in my hands and read it again and again. I read it maybe twenty times!

I had a premonition today. Did I tell you that I never take the mail out of the box until midday? This morning, though, I couldn't wait until lunchtime because of some strange inkling—maybe I caught the telepathy bug from the mentalist we saw on Rivoli. At ten o'clock, when I raised the shutters of the gallery, I slipped my hand into the slot without even looking, convinced I would find good news inside. The surprise went far beyond anything I could have dreamed. A letter from you without a return address. I didn't even need to look at the postmark. My name in your handwriting was enough. I went into my office with a teenager's excitement, opened the envelope, careful not to tear it, and read it with the same level of urgency we experienced throughout those four days of passion in every minute, conversation, glance, and kiss.

And you know what? I didn't expect you to tell me what the best moment of your stay in Paris was. In fact, if I'm going to be honest, I didn't expect us to take stock of every scene and situation. Everything had just the right amount of magic, atmosphere, tone, care, tenderness, and mutual trust. We were good together. Calm. Nothing was taboo or shameful. There were no risks or questions. We respected each other—in words and silence. Do you know how important it is to still understand one another when we say nothing? Do you know how precious it is to stay quiet and love each other? Did you realize that? Did it ever happen to you before? "The man who feels deeply speaks little."

(I could swear someone important said it, but you could hold a gun to my head, and I still wouldn't be able to tell you in this state of effervescence I'm in as I write to you from the gallery counter.)

Pauline, my beloved, since you've left I've been living in an ocean of doubts. There are two of us now, I suppose, based on what you write. But I've become certain of many things, and there's one thing I am sure about: Both you and I managed to break down our barriers. We freed ourselves, one before the other, one with the other. And, we will always have that, dearest, most beloved Pau. I was going to say *for ever and ever.* But I prefer to say: As long as we're here. As long as we want. The drops of honey.

I was telling you—forgive me for jumping from one thing to another, but my ideas move faster than my fingers when I write to you—that I didn't expect you to tell me that listening to Bulgarian love songs in the kitchen at home and looking into each other's eyes, a glass of Riesling in hand and letting the foie slowly melt in our mouths "like a delicious caramel," was *The Moment.* Now I can tell you that I did see a tear slip down your cheek, but I thought you were enjoying the goose foie gras, straight from the knife to your mouth, no bread or toast to mask it. "*Savoring*," that's the word we were probably looking for and didn't know how to say. Savoring. Art, foie gras, love, the moment. "A kiss to build a dream on," like the song. Four days to build an entire lifetime on top of them.

While you walked through my life and my neighborhood, there had never been so much morning light on rue de Seine. Never had the grass at dusk shone like it did on the days we laughed there together. Every afternoon I've remembered the light of when we walked arm in arm, but since you left it has never been the same. Did you know Salvador Dalí hated sunsets? He said he felt sick if he saw one. But I would be healed just remembering the one we experienced together by the river.

Did you see? I also use adversatives. It's not just as you say in your letter. "I remembered the light, *but* it has never been the same again." In every statement, every memory, every thought of the future, we could use a "but." It's true. Maybe you'd like to share in my trick, but I prefer to live without fear, without remorse, proud of what we've lived and aware of what we've done. Why should we limit anything? Why should we always rein ourselves in with another "but"? Why hold ourselves back with a sentence that kills off the previous one, like a card game where the king kills the queen and the ace kills everything? Doesn't nostalgia castrate us enough already? Let's not let the adversatives help it. For example, I should have written that I remembered the glow of dusk when we walked through the Luxembourg Gardens and was moved by a brilliance I'd never seen before, not even in movies. And that would be a truth as great as our love.

I think, beloved Pauline—my happiness and life—that I'm expressing more by letter than I dared say in person. I want to believe that all this, which I held back, you picked up in a gesture, a kiss, or when you let me sing in your ear. *When the hours of this day run out, I'll invent new ones for you.* I write as it comes, without fuss, without censorship, without leaving out anything that dances through my head. I write from the heart, because there is nothing freer, nothing more candid, than expressing what you feel in a rush. In a handwritten love letter, like the one you sent me and I am now returning, nothing restrains feelings, encloses them, or highlights them. Words emerge out of a bright, vigorous impulse. Irrepressible, I think. We can hold back words, but heartbeats can't stop. They haven't stopped for a second since our first dance at the Bois de Vincennes.

How's my day-to-day? You can imagine it. I am surrounded by paintings, remembering how you looked at each of them one by one the first afternoon you entered the gallery. Carefully, not daring to come too close, just as you did with me. Now I arrive, turn on the lights, and I can no longer look at the works with these eyes that are accustomed to auctions and appraisals, but with yours: younger, less contaminated, more authentic. I try to guess which you liked most and which you didn't like so much. I think the original Christo drawings for wrapping the Pont Neuf. Or maybe the Vilacasas planimetria, which captivated you. Did you know that he lived here in Paris in the fifties? I got to know him. His dealer took me to his apartment in Barcelona to see his work. I think the street was called Conseil du Cent?

Today some American tourists, a married couple, came in, and they fell head over heels for the Vasarely, the one from the Homage to the Hexagon series. I'd bet you liked the zebra one better, even though the first time you looked at it you got dizzy. Surely I told you it's a characteristic of Vasarely's optical art. That's what makes it special, different from all the copycats. As I was saying, the Americans sat on the chesterfield couch facing the hexagon and spent a good while commenting on the optical illusion, the perpetual motion, the *je ne sais pas quoi*. They asked me the price, and I told them many more francs than it's worth, because all of a sudden I realized I didn't want to sell it. And the man insisted they loved it, and wanted to take it or, if possible, have it properly packed and shipped to Vermont. He even pulled out his checkbook in a swift motion to show me that if it was a matter of price, he was good for it. In the end I had to tell them it was a sentimental matter for me, and that I wasn't going to sell the painting, period. The Americans were offended. They left a little angry and told me something that, if I understood correctly, has some truth to it: *"You may as well open a museum, if you own an art gallery and don't want to sell anything."* Maybe it really is time to change careers if I'm not able to sell any of the works you looked at and liked, because I won't make a penny anymore. It's like one of those absurd Chekhov stories. Have you read them? I could have given you one when we were at Shakespeare and Company. I missed my chance. I'm glad, dearest Pauline, that you liked the bookshop as much as you say you did. I will probably use the coming months to travel the world and visit bookshops where, from what I've researched, I think I might find a book or a catalog I don't yet have for my collection.

"Why do you collect books about butterflies?" you asked me the evening we dined at Brasserie Lipp. Because they are flowers that fly. Because they are a surprise of color. Because, as angelic and fragile as they are, they hide some mystery. And because, poetry aside, I inherited boxes and boxes of butterflies from my grandfather, which he himself carefully pinned onto cork using the headed pins I handed him one by one. My fascination, like so many things, comes from the past. Perhaps, beloved Pauline, I'm not looking for butterflies. Maybe I'm simply trying to return to the glory days of childhood with my grandfather, my hero, at my side. Doesn't that happen to all of us in the end? Don't we spend our lives searching for traces of past happiness? Isn't that exactly what's happening to you and me, here and now?

Beloved Pauline, you ask me with a certain type of fear whether I intend to answer your letter. Why wouldn't I? You will have silence only when I understand that you want silence. When I have no news from you, I will know that you need me to take a step back and disappear. Do you know how long a butterfly lives before it vanishes? They rarely live past two weeks. Depending on the species, they can last at most a year. I, frankly, hope to live in you far longer than that. Just as you will live in me. Even if we don't speak or see each other, we will have each other. Always. Without "buts." We will have each other. That is the absolute truth I have written in this heartfelt, emotional letter, unlike any other I have ever written.

Yours. Always yours. Proud of you and of us.

Jean-Pierre

PS: As you asked, I'm replying by mail through Julie, the most radiant bride ever to walk down the aisle. Your cousin will decide whether this letter deserves to be forwarded to you and the best way of getting it to you. I wouldn't want to betray you. I would never forgive myself for putting your stability at risk. I wouldn't want you to have to tell lies to hide a story that is so real.

15

A Terrace on the Watergate Walk

Gina knew the assignment she'd given Biel wasn't easy. It wasn't something you could do overnight. But all things considered, a week had already gone by since he'd started, and he still had no results. Even worse, there was no information, either. Every so often—whether she was running on the gym treadmill, curled up on her sofa at home, or teaching a class on light in Piero della Francesca to fifty university slackers who were only interested in their phones—a wave would hit her. She thought she couldn't let another night go by without calling Biel in London to ask if he'd managed to speak to Mark. *No news, good news,* she tried to convince herself. But she knew it wasn't always true. In this case, the anxiety brought on by the lack of news was starting to irritate her.

And then, just then, one Tuesday in October, in the absolute darkness of half past eight, in the professors' parking lot at the faculty of art history, just as she'd started the car after a two-hour seminar with a group of third-years, her phone rang. Biel Santos. Seeing her lawyer friend's name on the screen, she turned off the radio, the headlights, and the engine again.

"Tell me you found him."

"Jesus, Gina, don't you even say hello anymore?"

"Tell me you have . . ."

"Yes, yes, yes." He was pleased but not as pleased as she was. He let her hear it.

"What's going on?"

"Nothing . . ." He needed time to explain.

"Something is going on. I know you."

"Honestly, he doesn't seem like the same person you described. Not even close. If we're talking about Mark Granger, he's sincerely a man on his last legs. He's not even sixty, you were right, but he's already hung up his hat. And from what I've seen, and I assure you we spent a good amount of time together at Gordon's, I don't think he'll pick it back up ever again. He probably has a reason, but I was only able to find that out later. It was actually hard just to locate him, find him, and meet up with him. The leads you gave me were accurate, but they were scarce and out of date. You told me he worked as a bus driver in London. It was a good starting point, but the moment I began the search everything became silent and mysterious. It was easy to figure out who ran the buses. Transport for London contracts Stagecoach Bus, which is the company that keeps the staff on payroll. I asked about a driver, Mark Granger, with no other information, and I got nowhere over the phone. I didn't have much more luck online or over email. After a week of trying, I went in person, and it was even worse. They didn't trust me. 'Why do you want to know? Who are you? Don't you know our workers have a right to privacy? Where do you think we are? Spain?'

"And there I was, being scolded like I was asking who killed Kennedy. They genuinely made me feel bad and everything. In the end I left the office and opted for a more direct route. I waited at a bus stop near the end of the line and tried to speak to a driver who was using his five-minute break to smoke a cigarette. Nobody knew him or could tell me anything about him. Mark Granger, they said, is a very common name.

"Only one woman, a driver on Route 15 who spat like a man, could give me a clue.

"'Mark Granger? He rings a bell.' She thought for five seconds. 'Do you know if he's missing a finger?'

"'Yes, yes. That has to be him.'

"'Then you won't find him here anymore. I think the company made him go on pension early.'

"'Do you know where I can find him?'

"'No idea, mate. Try a pub.'

"She spat on the ground, got back on the 15, and started the route over again.

"Lacking more precise directions, I tried to go through my colleagues. I looked up Stagecoach's lawyer and introduced myself. I came up with a story about there being an inheritance in Barcelona, and declared we had to locate Mark Granger at all costs for his own good. He scrunched his nose. I suppose he sniffed out the lie, but he stood up, left me alone in the little visitors' room where he'd welcomed me, and remained standing when he came back. He simply placed a scrap of paper with a phone number on it.

"'I didn't give you anything.'

"'No, no. You and I didn't meet.'

"'Granger doesn't work here anymore.'

"And he left without shaking my hand or telling me why Mark was no longer a bus driver. I called Mark from that same little room at Stagecoach, but he didn't pick up. I tried again that afternoon. No luck. That night, though, around ten, he answered.

"'Mark Granger? Listen, I—'

"'I'm not up for bollocks. What the hell do you want?'

"'I'd like to talk—'

"'Who are you?'

"'My name is Biel Santos. I'm a lawyer for—'

"'Lawyers are useless.'

"He didn't sound drunk to me. Or especially out of it. Plenty of sober people think that way about our profession. And just as I thought he was going to hang up, I played my trump card, in desperation.

"'Paulina Homs! I'm calling on behalf of Paulina, a girl you met in Salou, some years ago. Well, you met her in Barcelona, but I understand you went to Salou for a few days . . . Mark?'

"He didn't say anything. Surprise, or nostalgia, or the strain of remembering kept him from speaking. I could hear him breathing, but that was all. Finally, he spoke up.

"'I don't want any more problems. What happened?'

"'No, no. Nothing. She's fine.'

"'So what do you want?'

"'To meet and talk about her, on her behalf. She has a question for you. I'm in London, and we could—'

"'Tomorrow. Gordon's on Villiers. Six o'clock.'

"And he hung up.

"It turned out Villiers was a street. A narrow, dark passage that runs from Charing Cross to the Victoria Embankment Gardens, near the river. I'd been through it before, but I'd never stopped to look at its name. It's a street that doesn't allow cars but is full of foot traffic, flustered people rushing up and down from one Underground stop to another. You don't exactly need to be Watson to guess it, but Gordon's was a pub near Rudyard Kipling's house. That much I had noticed, because there was one of those round blue plaques so typical of London that said he lived there from who knows when until he died. From the street, Gordon's looks like nothing more than a wall completely painted black, an old-fashioned pub wall. The moment you get close, it smells like beer and dog piss. It's the kind of dive you and I would never walk into. But there I was at six o'clock, pint in hand.

"Mark walked in on my third sip. His hair wasn't black, his features weren't sharp, he wasn't toned. If I'd only had your description, I wouldn't have recognized him. Just so you know, Mark Granger has turned into a bald man with a double chin and sadness in his eyes. A quick glance at his fingers was enough to confirm I had the right man. He picked up his mug with one hand and a handful of almonds with the other.

"'Come on. You can't smoke in here.'

"I followed him outside. He walked with slumped shoulders. He led me to an open alley that looked more like a private path. Gordon's has a terrace on Watergate Walk, an even narrower damp and shadowy path. You can't even fit three people standing next to each other. Even less so, with the pub tables lining one side of the path. We sat at one, set our beers down, and your friend arranged the almonds in a single line. You can't imagine how filthy that tabletop was.

"'Did Paulina get married?'

"'No, no.'

"It took everything in me not to say, 'Actually, the person you were really with in Salou was Gina'—that is, you—'but she was pretending to be her mother because you'd showed up with Paulina's business card. To play along, to not break the spell, she never found the moment to tell you the truth.' But I didn't say it there at Gordon's. It was hard, though, not to slip up and talk about you using a name aside from Gina.

"'Does she have children?'

"'No. No, she doesn't.'

"'At eighteen she was a doll. A perfect body . . .'

"And forgive me, but I had to agree with him on that point. But Mark Granger isn't a playboy anymore, or a happy man, or funny like you say he was in Salou twenty years ago. Your seducer can't look up from his feet now. And I'm not surprised.

"'Is something wrong?' I asked him.

"'For me?'

"He was silent. We were surrounded only by office workers performing their daily after-work ritual.

"'Yes,' he finally said. And then, 'Did you come on behalf of Paulina to ask me how I'm doing?'

"'No. But I can tell you—'

"'Want me to tell you? You want to know what's wrong with me?' He took a long drink. 'Their names are Anthony, Jamie, Giles, Marie,

Miriam, Shahara, Neetu, Sam, Shyanuja, Anat, Philip, William, and Gladys—mean anything to you? They're my problems.'

"I lost track of the names. He recited them in a row from memory without hesitation. When he finished, he swallowed two whole almonds.

"'I saw all thirteen of them die, right in front of me. You don't know who they are, do you?'

"'Should I?'

"'On July 7, I was assigned Route 30. It runs from Hackney Wick to Marble Arch. What do you actually know about me?'

"'Honestly, very little.'

"'I'm guessing you know I'm a bus driver.'

"'Yes, yes. That's what Gi . . . what Paulina told me.'

"'Things got complicated after nine a.m. Passengers boarding the bus said there had been explosions in the Underground. There had been a bomb at Aldgate, Edgware Road, and another at Russell Square. People boarded and repeated things they'd heard on the radio or from others. Nobody knew anything for sure. The rush-hour confusion kept growing, minute by minute, and soon the police cut off streets, cordoned off others, and made us change our route. The 30 never goes up Upper Woburn Place, but they weren't letting anyone through King's Cross. The traffic jam was monumental. The buses trapped each other in a convoy. One 30 bus behind another, just inches apart. At Euston we picked up loads of disoriented and frightened people with no idea where we were going. They just wanted to get as far away from the Underground as possible.'

"'When we reached Tavistock Square, by the British Medical Association, I was stopped, and suddenly, hell opened up right in front of me. The bus ahead of mine, another 30 identical to the one I was driving, exploded. The blast tore the entire roof off in one go. Half the bus, the rear section, simply vanished. The bus, the people on it, the blue seats—everything. Everyone and everything went flying right in front of me. It shot up into the air in a single second and disintegrated.

You can't imagine what that's like. You can't grasp things, until you're inside the nightmare.'

"I didn't know what to say.

"'I promise you that since that day in 2005, there hasn't been a single day I haven't thought about it, not a single night I haven't woken with a jolt like everything was exploding again.'

"'I'm so sorry, Mark. I'm speechless.' I touched his forearm.

"'Tell Paulina that the Grangers always escape by the skin of our teeth. But this time I almost wish I'd . . . Anyone who's seen hell is trapped there. You can't get out.'

"'I'm so sorry. Now I understand why you retired early.'

"'I spent a few days hospitalized, in shock. Then they discharged me, but it wasn't long before I was declared permanently unfit for work. Post-traumatic stress disorder, they said. In plain terms: Your life is fucked forever.'

"'I'm truly sorry. Truly, Mark.'

"'They got on the bus to flee the Underground and died anyway. Life is so brutal. Chance is so cruel.'

"'It was al-Qaeda, if I remember correctly?'

"'The man who blew himself up with his backpack was eighteen. Between the four suicide bombers, fifty-two people were killed. In less than an hour, it was over. Anyone who's seen hell can't get out. No one can convince me otherwise.'

"Mark was a spent man. And there I was over a business card, a book, a question that, in that moment, almost seemed ridiculous . . . I felt like an idiot. But since I was there, having found him and gotten him to meet me, I tried to steer the conversation back. You know, Gina, I've always been a prudent man.

"'According to what Paulina says, you were a big reader.'

"'Yes, that's true. Good memory . . .' He smiled for the first time, with the pride of a seducer who still carries that inside him somewhere. 'I hope she remembers something else about me.'

"'Now, Mark, I don't know if you feel like picking up a book?'

"'Feel like it? *Pfft.* I don't feel like anything. What I do have now is time. Yes, I try. I read sometimes. I pick up a book thinking it'll distract me, but I get tired of it right away. I leave everything half unread. The reality I experienced was so brutal that no story can stand comparison. Everything slips through my fingers.'

"'You're not in the mood, I understand. Can I tell you what Paulina is asking to see if you remember?'

"'Go ahead.'

"'You came to Barcelona with one of Paulina's business cards . . .'

"'Correct.'

"'A card you found inside a book . . .'

"'And it said "Call me." on it in French.'

"'*Appelle-moi*, exactly. The question is actually twofold. Do you remember which bookshop you bought the book in?'

"'And what's the second?'

"'Do you remember which book you found the business card inside?'

"'I might still be useful to someone here for once. Back then I bought a lot of books, very close to here. Either I went to the second-hand booksellers in Covent Garden, or if I was looking for something new or a specific novel, I went farther up, to Charing Cross. Do you know the bookstore Foyles?'

"'I passed it on the way here.'

"'There's a basement downstairs with a few armchairs where you can sit and read. That's where I picked up a novel by John Fowles and sat down to read it. Sometimes I read the first chapter and if I liked it, I took it home. And either I was sitting there, or maybe I was already at home, and Paulina's business card fell out from somewhere between the pages. I took it as a sign.'

"'A novel by John Fowles?'

"'*The Collector*. Have you read it?'

"'No, no. Lawyers read denser books.' I felt the absurd need to apologize. 'Is it any good?'

"'It's really good. It's the one about a young guy from London, an introverted, ultra-shy boy who turns out to be a sex maniac who kidnaps a student. But when he has her locked up at his house, he treats her sweetly. It's what they call a psychological thriller, but it's very well written.'

"'And what does the protagonist collect?'

"'I didn't say? Butterflies. He collects butterflies.'"

Her ear glued to the phone, Gina let Biel tell her about the whole investigation and his meeting with that Mark who was reduced to wreckage, a collateral victim of the worst attack on British soil since World War II. She felt deep pity for that man who had appeared like an angel the second she was leaving home after a fight with her father. Suddenly, on hearing the magic word, she had to interrupt her friend's exaggerated lawyerly narration.

"Don't you see, Biel? Do you remember what Jean-Pierre said to my mother in the first letter? While at dinner, she asks him why he collected butterfly books. Jean-Pierre didn't collect butterflies. He collected books about butterflies."

"Why do you think I called you euphoric, Gina?"

"And where did my mother put the business card? Bravo, Biel. That really is a big clue. Do you think my mother went to Foyles in London and slipped her cards into the butterfly books?"

"Isn't that love? A kind of madness?"

"But what if it wasn't only in London? My father told me she traveled a lot in her last years."

"Can you imagine?"

Biel hung up, satisfied. *She owes me one,* he thought. And he was convinced that sooner or later he'd collect in the way he liked best. He dreamed of experiencing, if only once more, one of Gina's silent orgasms. She, on the other hand, exhilarated by the discovery, no longer thought about Biel or poor Mark Granger. From that moment on, she had only one goal. She had to meet him one way or another. She had to find Jean-Pierre.

16

The Man Who Walks

Paris, First Anniversary Without You

My dearest, most beloved Pauline,
I am writing to you, just like you asked in your first and only letter, through my good friend, your cousin.

(By the way, Julie, it makes me happy to hear you're pregnant, that it will be a girl named Fabienne. You've chosen well with the name too. Send my congratulations to Alain. I imagine you're both very excited. We'll have to quench our thirst to celebrate soon. I'll bring the champagne. You pick the day.)

Now, my beloved Pauline,

Over the course of this year, there have been many times I've wanted to talk to you. About painters I've met, mishaps in the house or at work, neighborhood trifles, butterfly colors that have surprised me, trips I've taken, bookshops I've seen, music I've listened to that's moved me while thinking of you. Or about foods I've tasted with new flavors, and how I would have liked us to comment on each flavor, each nuance.

As you may have seen, I've held back. Desire has never been lacking. Not a single day. Not to write to you, or see you, or touch you again. If I haven't dared, my love, it's because I understood that your silence was to be met with silence. I told you already that you would never have to complain about my behavior. I would not be a nuisance or a burden. I would not make you uncomfortable or pursue you, no matter how much I longed to. And that's how it's been until today. If you speak, I speak. If you are silent, I am silent. Without reproach.

But today, Pauline, something happened that I had to tell you about. That's why I filled my fountain pen, took out the finest paper I could find in the gallery, and sat myself down to write to you, certain that it wouldn't bother you, especially once you hear the story.

Today, almost like he knew that it had been a year since our last kiss, the man who walks came into the gallery and went straight to the Warhol lithograph, the only one I have in the very back.

I think I told you about the man who walks, although I'm not sure you ever saw him. The man who walks is a local neighborhood figure no one knows, where he sleeps, what he does, but for many years now, he walks up and down the rue de Seine, every day of the year, maybe twenty times a day. He goes up one sidewalk and comes back down the other, from the river to Saint-Germain-des-Prés. And back again. Always on foot. Summer and winter. As if he's counting his steps. No one knows for sure whether he's alive or dead. Whether he's a *clochard* or *boulevardier*. I'm inclined to think he's neither, though he looks more like a disoriented beggar than a spy. From what I've read, they don't want spies who are past the age of sixty anymore. The truth is, no one has ever seen the man who walks beg for money, and based on the way he dresses, he doesn't seem short on money, but I can't say for sure if he's ever had any. With all due respect, my thought is that he's a poor madman with some disorder or lingering wartime trauma.

The man who walks is always alone. He doesn't carry any packages and never takes his hands out of his pockets. During the winter, it's his coat pockets. During the summer, it's his pants pockets, which (it would drive you crazy) are inches too short. It's as if he hides his hands in an extreme gesture of shyness. He doesn't speak. He mutters, his mouth is twisted, and his Adam's apple is pronounced in a way I've seen only in certain Russian men.

Well then: Early this afternoon, while I was on the phone behind the front counter, the man who walks opened the gallery door for the first time ever. A historic moment, Pauline. He came in without wiping his feet on the mat and slipped his hand back into his pocket. Before I hung up, he was already inside, without a *bonjour* or a wave. Honestly I was startled. He didn't say anything. He nodded toward the back of the room, toward Andy Warhol's *Marilyn's Lips*. Do you remember the lithograph of the five colored lips that used to hang beside the office door? He approached it and said just one thing in an English that sounded Nordic to me: *"It's crooked."*

I didn't think so at all. But the man who walks, standing there, kept staring at Marilyn Monroe's lips. Then I asked him in English if he liked it. And do you know how he answered? *"It's crooked."* Without another word, he turned around and left just as he had come in—head down, feet dragging, and hands in his pockets. An hour later I saw him pass by again on the opposite sidewalk, as he does so many times every day, rain, snow, or scorching heat.

I didn't dare ask him what he's looking for, where he's from, or why he walks all day long. I would have liked to know why on earth he wanders up and down like a ghost, why he never speaks to anyone, why there's only one street in the world worth walking, what he finds so special about rue de Seine. Should I have asked him these things, my dear Pau? I honestly thought I had no right. I would have hated for the man who walks to feel that, rather than helping him, I was only curious about him for the sake of gossip. Poking my nose into his business might have put me in a position of superiority, don't you think? In the end, I thought, let everyone live their bitter comedy as best they can. Let them do as they please. No one is anyone to demand explanations. That's what a private life is, isn't it?

Once he was gone, I hurried to fetch the magnetic level and set it on the frame. At first glance it looked straight to me. I'd have bet my life on it. But, to my surprise, the bubble was slightly off. The picture did indeed slope on one side more than the other. The culprit, I saw immediately, was a nail at the back that had worked loose. How could that wandering Nordic see it from the street, when he seems like a gawker? I'd swear he never looks into shop windows.

Then, searching for an explanation, I thought about what day it was today, and perhaps you'll find it naive, but I connected the dots. Do you know the name of the original Warhol, my dear Pau? *I Love Your Kiss Forever Forever.* Seized by a thoroughly irrational spirit, I thought it was a sign meant for me, for us. The man who walks had come to deliver a message: Remember that today is a year since you gave Pauline your last kiss, and that it would be okay to write to her, to say hello, I'm here, I'm still here, for whatever you want, whenever you want, no rush, because life takes many turns, and in the moment we think this will be forever, in the moment we feel calm and settled here, but tomorrow we may be somewhere else. When that moment comes, I'll be by your side again, kissing your sweet lips be it four more days, or four months, or four years, or forty. You never know. I will be with you and for you, always.

Yes, time has passed. A year, and you see that nothing has fizzled in me. It's been the shortest year because I've felt you close, and the longest year because I haven't seen you. As we discussed while you ate onion soup in summer at Les Deux Magots, there's a "before" and an "after" to many things in life. There's a "before" and "after" coming of age, a "before" and "after" the death of parents, a "before" and "after" the first paycheck or the first time you make love, or the first time a friend lets you down. (All of this is hurtful and disappointing, but it happens to all of us.) But in my life there is no "before" and "after" you. There is only a "during." Four days of fire and magic, and time stopped there. Suspended in happiness with the discovery that love (with a capital *L*, like ours) is not possible without pain.

And welcome, dammit, to that nail in the heart.

There's something I don't know if I should tell you, because it is embarrassing even for me. But the intimacy of letters permits such things. So I'll say it, and that's that. I hope it won't trouble you.

Twenty days after you left, not even a month yet, I went to the perfume section at the Galeries Lafayette, and bought myself a small bottle of Chanel No. 5, which they insisted on wrapping as a gift. At home I removed the cellophane and the box and placed the bottle in the drawer where I keep emergency supplies: scissors, paper clips, a stapler, markers, envelopes, some tape, and now the little bottle of perfume. Sometimes, not every day, I open it, close my eyes, breathe it in, and I'm back with you. I smell your faint scent of flowers, bitter orange, and jasmine from the night of the wedding. You never wore it again. You saved it for that special occasion (more for Julie than for me). But each time I open the perfume, I feel the soft skin of your neck at my lips. And with your permission, I kiss it. Your eyes laugh and crinkle as they always do when you laugh, like the time I tried to teach you to dance a sirtaki while we walked along the Seine on the way to my place. Your back open in a dress that by now ought to be displayed in a museum of good taste. A sirtaki on wet cobblestones. What pretension on my part, what ridiculousness, singing and dancing in a Greek fashion without really knowing how. But you laughed so much, my dear.

Did you know Coco Chanel asked for a women's perfume that smelled like a woman, and they brought her No. 5? The miracle is that no two women smell the same. No two women react the same way to the same perfume. Your young, sweet skin is, I'd say, genuine Bourbon vanilla.

I'm doing well. I eat, I take care of myself, I hang and rehang pictures. As you can imagine, tourists still have the same tastes: The more color, the better it sells. No secret there. Lichtenstein comics, Jasper Johns flags, and now the collages of Gilbert and George, two young British artists everyone likes. Not long ago I sold the Le Corbusier that was in the window the first time you came to the gallery. Now, on the easel by the entrance, I've put up some political graffiti by Jacques Villeglé. The poster look always catches the summer passerby's eye. It's about time the heat arrived, by the way. This year I used the Paris cold to roam the world. Everything remains in place. I've searched for good weather, but above all I've searched for books. Butterflies, you know. I found one in a catalog I bought in Buenos Aires, almost as beautiful as you. Sometimes I look at it, so green and brilliant, and it almost smiles. Actually everything smiles at me since I met you. Is it the same for you, my dear Pauline, or am I too bold to imagine it to be the fact?

I'll say goodbye by speaking again of the man who walks. Have you ever listened to Schubert's songs of the wanderer? "Der Wanderer," songs for baritone. Look for the disc. Put it on in a moment of calm. Close your eyes and listen with your heart. Think of me. I'll be thinking of you. As always. Forever.

My dear Pauline, I can't say I miss you, because I have you.

We have each other.

You already know that.

Jean-Pierre

PS: In the first letter I sent you, I mentioned a phrase from someone famous. I didn't remember it in full, nor did I know who wrote it. It was Plato, the wisest of them all. Four hundred years before Jesus was born, he already knew how to say a truth as solid as a cathedral: "The greatest declaration of love is the one not made. The man who feels deeply speaks little."

He was right. Don't you think, my dear?

17

A World Within a World

The outskirts of the Torre dos Clérigos were more open and luminous than Paulina had imagined. From the moment the train had dumped the Castro–Homs couple out at São Bento station, Porto struck them as less dark and crowded than they had pictured during the long hours on the train from Barcelona. Before arriving somewhere for the first time, almost everyone imagines the light, the streets, the colors, and the smells awaiting them. Guidebooks, both the useful and less useful ones, tend to compress corners and synthesize them into postcard images in the traveler's mind. After a first walk, once streets have been trodden and buildings and lighting have been scrutinized, expectations evaporate, and the visitor begins to see reality in focus. Porto, they soon realized, was a watercolor city, especially along the waterfront. Paulina especially had a weakness for cities that had a river running through them. It meant they were cities of contrast with different sides. And maybe because they were reminiscent of Paris. She was also especially fascinated by cities with funiculars, because it meant there was somewhere to climb and see with a beautiful bird's-eye view. Porto offered both. And a Livraria was waiting for her on Rua das Carmelitas.

They walked from the station to the hotel on the banks of the Douro so they could stretch their legs and because they had packed a single suitcase with the bare essentials for the two nights in Portugal. As soon as Manuel stepped through the revolving door of a three-star hotel with high aspirations, he was already expected in the lobby. Two men in ties were to take him to an industrial estate in Rio Tinto to negotiate contracts rife with convoluted clauses. He checked in, and gave Paulina a quick kiss. He didn't even have time to go up to room 204 to wash his hands and rid himself of the rusty smell of the train that annoyed him so much. Paulina stayed upstairs only briefly. Just long enough to open the suitcase, put her clothes away in the wardrobe, and hide in her nightgown the box of new business cards. She had had two boxes of five hundred printed at Cromoherma, the Baldrich brothers' graphic arts firm on Carrer de l'Àngel, near Fontana station. The Baldrichs usually took on larger, more artistic, more showy orders. They had never done business cards before. But for Paulina, a batting of her eyes was enough for them not to say no.

She opened the box, took out a handful—maybe thirty—and filled the card holder she had bought just for the occasion. She slipped it into her handbag and, nervously, like someone about to commit a misdemeanor, went out to catch a taxi.

"To Livraria Lello, please."

"Livraria Lello e Irmão?" She had gotten the meticulous driver used to dealing with tourists. "On Das Carmelitas, *senhora*?"

"Yes, yes."

Paulina had never seen a bookshop facade as imposing as Lello's. A singular neo-Gothic building with pale stone and modernist finishes. It looked more like a church than a shop. But she came with an idea, and with her focus, she didn't have the patience to contemplate architectural filigree. Once inside, the first glance did take her breath away. At once, the grand wooden staircase dominating the space reminded her of the *Titanic*'s staircase she had seen in a picture in a book at home. It was stately, with the noble aging of dark wood. She was then entranced when she looked up and noticed the staircase's sinuous curve, like a giant centipede unwinding. She oriented herself easily with the

Portuguese signs. What she was looking for would be on the first floor. There she noticed the staircase bulged magically, like it was suspended midair. The ceiling, a colored stained-glass skylight spanning the length of the shop, was another work of art, bathing the entire Lello e Irmão in light. She walked through the corridor, which seemed to lead toward nature, and stopped in front of the animal books. She read the spines one by one. A shop assistant labeling prices offered to help.

"I'm looking for anything on butterflies."

She was quiet.

She had gotten a shop assistant who was also meticulous with languages.

"Mariposas. ¿Libros de mariposas?"

"Oh, *borboleta*, you mean."

The clerk pulled out three books, set them on a side table, and went back to sticking labels on books. Paulina leafed through them. They didn't strike her as very old or very new, particularly original or irresistibly beautiful. But you never know what's missing for a collector. She opened them, turned the pages, and in her nervousness saw nothing—no photos, no drawings, nothing. *Borboletas* everywhere, that much was true. The trick was to look interested, undecided, to buy time until the sales assistant left the area. When it seemed like no one was watching, she took the card holder out from her bag, pulled out three cards, slipped one into roughly the middle of each book, and closed them with a decisive gesture. Her heart was pounding like she had just strangled a pit bull, and she returned the books to the shelf. The message had been sent. The trip to Porto was now worth it. Like nothing had happened, she fled down the stairs without even taking note of the elegant bloodred carpeted steps. Once outside, she felt the need to put distance between herself and the scene of the crime.

Manuel had no choice but to fly to get to the United States. It would take too many days by ship, and there was no commercial route crossing the Atlantic. He made it to New York with the help of two whiskies and a pill. Paulina didn't need to sleep. The excitement of seeing skyscrapers for the first time kept her up. The thrill of knowing that the next morning she would be at Rizzoli on Fifth Avenue to leave a token for Jean-Pierre excited her even more. Once in Manhattan, an unexpected problem arose: Manuel, more protective than fearful, would not let Paulina walk out on her own.

"But . . ."

"I'd never forgive myself . . ."

"What do you think would—"

"You never know."

So they toured New York together, Manuel thoroughly unnerved. Arm in arm for two days. They didn't separate for anything. Not until the second evening, when Paulina, already anxious that time was slipping away, decided to take a risk. Without giving him a chance to object.

"I'm running down to the pharmacy to buy bandages. I saw there's one right below, next to the hotel." She already had her jacket and handbag in hand, so Manuel couldn't react. "I'll be right back."

She ran to 712 Fifth Avenue. Based on her calculations, it was between Fifty-Fifth and Fifty-Sixth. Just three blocks farther, and she'd be standing before a magnificent French-style building. The marble floors and bronze chandeliers gave Rizzoli the air of a select private club's library. But it was a bookshop with character, the kind Jean-Pierre loved. Photography and animal books were on the second floor. She was out of breath. To save on time, she asked directly whether they had interesting butterfly books. Eight different titles. Wow. At least two copies of each. She didn't even look at which ones. Using her body to shield her hands from the shop assistant's view, she took out the card holder and began distributing cards here and there so each book could hold at least one.

"Thank you."

"Already done? None of them interest you?"

"No, thank you. I changed my mind."

Once more she felt the strange urge to flee the bookshop at full speed. On the way back to the hotel, she found a pharmacy, bought bandages she didn't need, and rehearsed an excuse she'd give Manuel when—she'd bet her life on it—he asked her about the delay. When she entered the room, her husband was snoring with the TV on. He was leaning against the headboard. At least he'd taken off his shoes.

The next day they drove to Boston in a rental car. Manuel had been promised it was a calm city, the most European of American capitals. Some neighborhoods were reminiscent of Victorian London with so many exposed brick buildings. Others, like the downtown, leaned toward the impersonal financial districts common to so many of the Continent's cities. Paulina went to the Brattle Book Shop alone without excuses or subterfuges, and took her time to enjoy it. She thought it was a unique place, insolent, unlike anything she had seen. Most of the shop was outdoors, occupying a rectangular space that exposed the gray dividing walls of three worn buildings with very little charm. Everything was so urban, and the contrast with the old-book market left passersby surprised. The Brattle sat in a cul-de-sac—like the beloved rue du Trésor—but it had little else in common. There was no glamour there, and there never had been. At the back stood a black iron fire escape, zigzagging down like in the movies, descending from one building toward a steep drop. The books, all old, filled shelves bolted to the walls and bookcases on wheels that were as tall as she was, all set out in the open. A sign proclaimed it the oldest secondhand bookshop in the United States. If Jean-Pierre ever came to Boston, he would certainly dive into that sea of books. She was told sales only stopped when it rained. Despite the cold or wind, both of which Massachusetts had plenty of, the shop never closed. Paulina watched how people in gloves clutched steaming cups of coffee to warm their hands as they wandered among piles of used books. She rummaged for a long time before finding what she was looking for. The organizing method was disorder, and chaos was an added difficulty. Not until she found an old guide to butterflies—she checked to make sure that was all there was—did she finish the task, catching two colds along the way. She glanced left and right, and in a flash, she was done. She was beginning to take pleasure in the risk. The game was reminiscent of love.

She went to London alone. Manuel had heavy workdays—closing fiscal years, convening boards, drafting minutes for all the companies he advised. Paulina left Gina at home with Isabel, knowing her daughter loved being with the maid, who spoiled her and anticipated her wishes. It was like staying with a grandmother. On her first afternoon in London, Paulina traced a bookshop route on a map. She left the Westbury in Mayfair, walked down Old Bond Street, lingered at the Burlington Arcade windows, and emerged on Piccadilly, facing Hatchards, a bookshop founded in 1797. She'd been told that shops bearing that crest above the door were places the queen frequented. She also felt like royalty, walking beneath the flags above the black small-paned door. Inside, order and silence reigned. In her search for butterfly books, she noticed the shelves were subtly tilted to make searching easier—the books at Hatchards greeted you face-to-face. No need for finger-along-the-spines guesswork. She found what she thought might be a rarity. *La Mariposa y el Tanque*, four illustrated Hemingway stories about the Spanish Civil War, published in Spanish by Bruguera, a Barcelona publisher. She'd seen books in every language in Jean-Pierre's apartment, even in those he didn't understand. The ritual was now well practiced. Each time she acted more decisively, more confident no one would see her slip her business cards into books in Britain's oldest bookshop.

The next stop, according to the map route, was supposed to be London's largest bookstore, and depending on the guidebook, the world's most extensive by square meters and titles. If it had the most books, surely it would have the most kinds of books he would choose and rummage through. She let herself hope. Her Mastroianni went to London every year for the antiques fair. She headed toward Piccadilly Circus, crossed Soho with her bag slung tight, marveled at the streetlights of old theaters on St. Martin's Lane, and reached her destination: Foyles, at 119 Charing Cross Road. It was a world within a world. If she found too many butterfly books, she might run out of cards. She left six in the antiquarian section. She was recommended a novel about a butterfly collector in the literature section. It had been adapted into a movie in the sixties, she was told, starring Terence Stamp. He played a lonely young man obsessed with an art student, who buys a cottage with gambling winnings. Jean-Pierre, a movie lover, must have seen it. She took out a card and, in a fit of longing, wrote two words: *"Appelle-moi."* She closed the book and, as she returned it to the shelf, felt a twinge, maybe an intuition that the message would travel far.

She woke up at the Westbury. It was raining. The concierge with the top hat lent her a hotel umbrella and opened the taxi door. He said it was the best way to reach King's Cross so she wouldn't miss the train to Glasgow. Four and a half hours later she arrived. It was worth it just to see how the place looked almost clandestine in the bleak street and vulgar building. You had to purposefully go to Voltaire & Rousseau, a hub for students and intellectuals. Paulina could hardly believe that in such a renowned secondhand bookstore, three cats roamed happily atop mountains of books strewn across the floor. There were piles upon piles of volumes that no longer fit on dust-filled shelves. There were places that had gone untouched for decades. Amid so much old paper, amid the brownish, sad atmosphere, stood a green wooden staircase, paint flaking, used to climb to higher shelves. After two hours searching for a needle in a haystack, she managed to leave only two cards, with little hope Jean-Pierre would ever find them if he reached that remote corner of Glasgow.

That same afternoon, a trip to Inverness, another river city, restored her spirits. Only two years earlier, Leakey's had converted an old church into a bookshop. From outside, with its eighteenth-century bell tower, it maintained the austerity of a place of worship. Inside, the transformation gave off a magic and mystique. Paulina had never imagined a place like it could exist, and felt happy there, surrounded by paper and order. The journey north had been worth it. She searched for books and smiled. She couldn't help it. She thought of Jean-Pierre in Scotland's largest secondhand bookshop, feeling close to him. When she returned to London the next day, her card holder was empty.

Someone had once told her you couldn't go to Venice alone. Nostalgia will eat you up. If you're in love, it will devour you. Whoever had given that advice was right. Paulina invited Júlia to spend three days with her in Italy. Gina would stay home with Isabel, who was surely happy to be in charge. The cousins flew to Milan, and while Júlia visited the Duomo, Paulina escaped to Bocca, the old bookshop in the Galleria Vittorio Emanuele II, to hide business cards in books. Six hours later they were gliding by gondola through the canals of Sestiere Castello. They were narrow, impossible channels. Sometimes their turns were so sharp no taxi or motorboat could pass. Only experienced gondoliers knew where to plant a foot on the wall and counter with the oar to round the corner. Campo San Lorenzo, Palazzo Cappello, Palazzo Cavagnis. It felt like Venice belonged to them alone. Seen from below, they felt they had entered a tunnel through time, with moss embedded on crumbling walls revealed by the water's small waves. The gondolier pointed out a broken green wooden door. It was the delivery entrance to Acqua Alta, a bookshop they had to visit at all costs. Why else come to Venice? Paulina entered from the back. Since Voltaire & Rousseau she'd not seen anything as chaotic, with secondhand books everywhere. There were some that filled a gondola in the center. Another gondola hung upside down from the ceiling. Books filled two white bathtubs that Júlia found endearingly naive. It was impossible to know what lay inside. On the walls, there hung a wooden helm here and there. There was a skull with a pirate hat that they each wanted to pose with, first one cousin, then the other. The ceiling was low and irregular, and instead of steps to the first floor, there was a staircase made of books you had to climb on top of. Never had they seen anything so unique. There, with an atlas of butterflies in hand, Paulina didn't hide the ritual from her cousin.

"Do you really think Jean-Pierre will come to Venice? To this musty bookshop?"

"He does. He travels. He thinks he collects butterfly books. In truth, he collects bookshops."

"And if he ever finds the card, what do you expect him to do? If you want to see him, write to him. Call him. Do you want me to tell him?"

"Honestly?" She grabbed her cousin by the shoulders shyly. "Don't. Neither he nor I will allow the feeling of victory we had in Paris to be spoiled."

"But then," Júlia murmured, "why do it?"

"I like leaving clues to my love. He'll find them or he won't. He'll know or he won't. It doesn't matter. What we lived deserves a try. Why do I do it?" She thought for a few seconds, then answered without hesitation. "Because this is the trail of love."

Neither of them could imagine, in that intimate moment of happiness and confession, of having found an answer and spoken it aloud, that Venice would be Paulina's last trip.

18

Suddenly, the Cliff

Paris, May 18, 1984
Black Friday

My dear and heartbroken Julie,

You called to tell me two days ago at this time. And I'm writing first of all to thank you for thinking of me immediately. I'm grateful for the call, but I still can't accept it. I simply don't believe it. It's too much. I don't believe it or want to believe it. Pauline. It can't be. Thirty-one. She was fine, you told me. You were crying so hard, and I was in so much shock—and I still am—that I'm not sure I understood you. She woke up with a headache? She asked her husband to take the little girl to school, because she was going back to bed. Is that what you told me? And it was already too late by the time the maid arrived? Either way, the details aside . . . A cerebral hemorrhage. At thirty-one? I've never heard of a case like that. It's hard to believe and, more than anything, hard to swallow. The grief is enormous, the pain insatiable, and the rage infinite. The sorrow, as you can imagine, isn't for me—no doubt it's the same for you—but for her. A life cut short, so young, all at once, without the chance to see Gina grow up. Suddenly everything goes to hell.

Life begins, life ends. We all know that, but the injustice makes me feel rebellious. Right now, furious and crushed, I would grab fate by the throat. Even though I'd have everything to lose and it would serve no purpose, I'd confront it and insult it until I lose my voice, my strength, and my dignity.

I walk, Julie, back and forth, from here to there, and I don't know what to do or think during these black days and in the ones to come. It's hard to think, and even harder to order the thoughts and the memories that rush out of me, like tears. And I have a headache from crying so much. Is it the same for you?

Sometimes, when I manage to calm myself down, I think that I have loved only one woman and that I lost her twice. It's too late for reproaches. I know. But at the airport, when she was returning home from your wedding, maybe if I had insisted that . . . When there is no cure, what good is it to poison your own blood? And now I have lost her for good, without being able to tell her: "You know what, Pauline, every day since I met you, I've seen your smile at my side when I close my eyes." I have so many things to say . . . Why do we always wait so long to say them? Why do we live holding back words and feelings? Why do we never realize it's getting late?

In one of the letters, I wrote that I didn't miss her because I had her. That's how I felt. Maybe because I knew that at any moment we could see each other, or communicate with each other, one way or another.

I learned to live far from her because I felt her near, always with me. You know those fire hose cabinets in theaters and hotels that say "Break the glass only in case of emergency"? In that same metaphor, that is not very poetic, I admit, I convinced myself on more than one occasion that maybe one day, she or I would smash that emergency glass with a hammer to meet each other again and experience our love at leisure. So I confess, after the fact, that deep down I also didn't say I missed her because I maintained a secret hope that we would be together again. Physically together. Forever. And suddenly, the cliff. In a single minute, my dreams and hopes have been swept out to sea.

Now that death has cruelly shattered all those possibilities, I have to confess to you, with tears flooding the table from where I write, that I missed her, I miss her, and I will miss her hopelessly. No matter how I remember every hour of our four splendid days together, no matter how I venerate her with a lover's pride, no matter how much I love her like I have never loved anyone, the only truth is that yes: I will miss her. So much. Every day. Until the gentle foam comes to collect me too.

Do you know what seems to me the cruelest and most unbelievable thing of all? To accept that Pau is no longer part of this world, that she will know nothing of what will happen tomorrow and the day after that, and the next year, to her family or on the other side of the world. I remember that, at our first dinner at Les Deux Magots, we argued—no, we didn't argue, we discussed—when history began. *Before Christ is prehistory. After Christ, and up to a second ago, is history,* she told me, sure of her theory. *The counter of history restarts at zero with the birth of writing,* I insisted. And that would be with cuneiform in Mesopotamia thirty-five hundred years before Christ. And Julie, honestly, what nonsense it was. Sticking the label a little more in this direction or that direction doesn't matter, not one bit. What I mean is that your cousin, like all of us, knew what happened in the Stone Age. She distinguished between the Paleolithic era and the Neolithic era. She was aware of how we evolved from caveman to *Homo sapiens*. She didn't confuse the Bronze Age with the Iron Age. She studied how the pyramids were built in ancient Egypt, what people ate in the Middle Ages, how far the Byzantine Empire extended. And of the Renaissance—the era in which I'd pay everything I have to spend a week in—we studied what Michelangelo meant throughout every square inch of the Sistine Chapel ceiling. We know by heart whose head was chopped in the French Revolution, why the railroad was key to the development of the United States, and how Hitler's last hours went—or Marilyn Monroe's.

Pauline knew it all about everything before her, her contemporaries, and her family. She will know nothing about everything after her. To me, that is the most brutal thing about death: period. Before here, everything. Back from here, nothing. Absolute.

"So then, when do we live?" That's how our conversation continued at Les Deux Magots. We exist while we are here, and while we are remembered. And I can see it as if it were now. We came up with three additional examples. Einstein, Flaubert, Kandinsky remain. They are immortal because their work makes them eternal, we concluded. But people like that are few. Out of the more than one hundred billion people estimated to have been born on earth in all of human history, we chose four, Christ included. How many names do we know? A thousand? Two thousand privileged people everyone knows and knows what they did? Fine. And all the rest? We are here while we exist, or while our children and friends remember us, and then our grandchildren. By the next generation practically no one mentions us, no one remembers us for anything, no one even knows we existed. The whirlpool of time swallows the drops to return them to the ocean. And in no time, we stop existing.

That's why, Julie, in these bitter hours—between sobs and curses—an idea has begun to roll around in my head. It's absurd, maybe. Maybe it's only a fixation, but I'm so blinded right now that I can't tell what is and isn't worth it. I won't be the one to do it, but I've thought that someone—who, I'm not sure—should know your cousin's story and tell it. Only that way can Pauline be immortal, and only that way can our love, hidden until now, endure forever. One day, in my apartment on rue du Trésor, she said: *"I ask only one thing: Don't turn our story into a novel. It has to be for the two of us."* But now I think, what harm would there be in revealing it? On the contrary. Perhaps a long time from now, when I'm gone too, someone will be drawn to the spine of a book, pick it up, and find a modest story inside that tells them what kind of woman Pauline was. How she felt, how she lived, how she loved . . . And afterward, the reader might place a hand on the cover and exclaim, "Friends, love exists. Love is the answer."

Because that is the answer, isn't it?

I realized it in Girona, one morning. Did Pauline ever tell you about our meeting? Did she tell you anything about the most intense moment of our lives? Almost two years ago, I had to go down to Perpignan to buy a series by Villeglé owned by a political graffiti collector in the south. I remember it was a Friday. I closed the deal. I was in the hotel room, ready to take a shower, and after turning it over and over in my head, I decided to do what for months and months I hadn't dared. I called Pauline's home in Barcelona. Just as you heard, I did it. I still don't know how I dared do it. As I keyed in the numbers, the adrenaline, the pulse, the tension . . . everything came out of me. And despite the regret, my fingers were faster than I was, and the tones of an international call sounded at once.

Once the number had been dialed, I came up with a plan. If someone other than Pauline answered, I would hang up immediately. If it was her, I had a short and quick proposal. Of course, I wanted to say a thousand things, but I had to resist temptation and let her, when she set the receiver down, say: I don't know who it is. Wrong number.

I would have liked to tell her: "Nothing new, my love, I love you madly. Nothing new. You already know." I would have liked to tell her I was fine, not to worry about me, that hearing her voice for ten seconds was enough to live on for ten more years. I would have liked to tell her: "Don't worry if what happened in Paris made you feel guilty. Don't punish yourself, my love. Infidelity to another is often a return to fidelity to oneself. There is nothing wrong in finding your own feelings again." I would have liked to tell her so many things, Julie, but I knew I couldn't play her like that. I couldn't make her weak. I couldn't allow that, when she hung up and returned to her family life, someone might notice that she was shaken by the call.

It was her. Thankfully, it was her. Her *Hello?* opened my heart. *It's me, Pauline. Don't say anything.* "But—" *Don't say anything.* "Who are you looking for?" We were silent for a few seconds, listening to each other breathe, the receiver pressed into our ears. And then I said what I had to say, quickly: *Tomorrow, I'll be in Girona before lunch. I'll go to Llibreria 22. Butterflies, you know the drill. The 22 in Girona. It's a new bookshop. I heard about it, and I want to see it. I'm doing well.* "I think you have the wrong number," she answered, in her language. And she hung up. And I hung up. I didn't even say goodbye. I didn't want to weaken her. I couldn't make her emotional. I couldn't tell her how much I loved her.

You can imagine, Julie, the kind of night I had before getting up at dawn and catching the first train to Girona.

And Girona, what a city, what a discovery. My memories of that day are blurry, like a dream, but it felt like it was like Florence, with houses hanging over the river, and a singular bridge—Eiffel too—and right there, on a quiet bend, was the bookshop where I'd arranged to meet your cousin. I had no delusions she would show up. But the spark of the "perhaps," of the "maybe," that it would be a sign if she appeared, kept me in a restless state I couldn't control. If I had put my pipe to my mouth, my teeth would have chattered with nerves.

I'd already had two coffees in the square in front of the bookshop before noon. By one I had walked all of Llibreria 22, shelf by shelf, from *A* to *Z*. The owner knew his trade—he had ambition. He was a young man with shiny black hair, a center part, and a proud mustache. I liked how he treated customers. He spoke as readily about movies as he did about poetry, always with passion, a cigarette between his fingers. Guillem was his name. Like my father's, I thought. It sounded nice in Catalan, *Guillem*, better than in French, which sounds more pretentious. He showed me, patiently, everything he had on butterflies, an interesting rare book about American monarchs that I paid for and they put in a bag I still keep. Then I went on waiting, pretending to browse a novel here and an essay there. Never had time on my watch run so fast. I looked at it constantly, and as the minutes passed, my hopes slipped away.

I distracted myself by leafing through an enormous volume on Salvador Dalí. On every page, a reproduction of Gala, his wife and muse. The book was called something like that. As I held it, it sounded like someone was whistling the first notes of a sirtaki inside the shop. Was it real or a dream? It was Zorba's song that she and I had danced to one night in Paris by the river. In that moment I heard it with perfect clarity. I turned, fully moved, and there was Pauline, standing there, breathtakingly beautiful, more radiant than ever, eyes surrendered, smile nervous. Like mine, I suppose. After so long, after wanting it so much, she was only four steps away, and she had put on the perfume from the day of your wedding, the Chanel she saved for unique occasions.

Everything happened in tenths of a second, and as I went to embrace her, a child appeared behind her, holding her hand and her skirt. She had come to Girona. Pauline had managed it and come to see me. But she had come with Gina. Our eyes met. I said her name. She said mine. Gina asked, *"Mama, who is that?"* And Pauline answered that I was a friend of Aunt Júlia's. And we stood looking at each other in silence, in a lovers' agitation, the passion of those who, in a cruel instant, want to embrace and cannot. I stepped closer. We didn't even exchange three kisses. Not two. I took her hand. She didn't pull away. And when both our eyes filled with tears—whether from joy or frustration—we spoke. Little, in French, so the child wouldn't understand.

"You came," I said.

"Yes. I was dying to see you."

"Me too."

"Are you well? You look very well."

"You too. Beautiful as always."

"I needed to see you."

"Me too."

"Know that what I feel for you has never diminished. Never."

"I'm glad to hear it."

After what felt like a long pause, Pauline continued, *"I'm always with you too, on rue du Trésor, on rue de Seine."* The girl had discovered the children's books and was going toward a giant Babar the Elephant book. *"How's the gallery?"*

"It's going."

"I came in to buy Gina a book."

I sensed the conversation was ending, that I could afford only a brushstroke or two. *"Can we grab a coffee, even just one?"* She said yes. We left the 22 and went back to the bar in the square. Across from me sat Pauline and Gina, who began drawing with paper and pencils the bar gave her. As you can imagine, we continued speaking in French. In fact, she spoke. Softly, rapidly, as if she were being chased. She told me my call had moved her, that she had had to come up with a convoluted story to come up to Girona, and she admitted she'd spent the night shaking, unable to sleep. She had sensed it was our last chance, and she knew at the same time that our meeting carried enormous danger. The moment she heard my voice on the phone, her emotions had been stirred in every direction. She felt that in a single night she had to gamble her life on a heads or tails. And she wavered between anxiety and desire, between temptation and continuing as before.

"Manuel is a good man," she told me. Those were her words. And the two of them, with Gina, the three together, were a family. At times she was sure she shouldn't come to Girona at all. But then she realized how much she needed me, how much she wanted to see me, and the fervor with which she loved me. She imagined—again, her words—that she could take out two changes of clothes, pack a suitcase, come find me, run away, begin a new life.

She confessed she had thought it over endlessly, and that what mattered most of all was that she had come. Everything flew by, Julie. When I was about to ask if she had the suitcase in the car, if I had any chance of . . . Gina tugged at her arm to show her mother the drawing: a little figure sketched in a couple of scribbles. Pauline said, "*Very nice, Gina,*" to brush it off, but the child insisted, demanding attention, and then

Pauline asked, *"Who is it?"* and her daughter, almost like she was connecting dots, like she understood what we were talking about, like she knew French, bright as she was, answered: *"Daddy. It's Daddy."*

Pauline bit her lip to hold back tears. Seeing her so moved, frankly, broke my heart. Neither of us could contain the agitation, the passion of that moment. Never had silence said so much. I understood at once what our future was, what Pauline had decided. I saw it in her eyes. I read there too that time was slipping away, that she wanted to leave. I asked her only one more thing.

"Are you happy, Pauline?"

And do you know what she answered?

"Now, very happy."

"Are you happy?"

"Now, very happy."

That's all. And before her daughter could see me cry, before she could notice the makeup running down her mother's eyes, Pauline said au revoir, stood up, put her hand on my shoulder, and walked out of the bar with Gina clinging close. I followed her through the window with my eyes, watching her disappear across the square. What a distinguished way of walking, how elegant. What sadness.

I never heard from Pauline. Her coffee remained in the cup, and a waiter cleared away the drawing and the jar of pencils to entertain a child at another table. And me? I took a while to leave the bar, ecstatic to have seen her, elated to have reaffirmed our feelings, and crushed, too, for having lost her again right before my eyes. I ordered a malt and remember little else. I know I wandered the city without finding the way or the right time to return to the station. *"Now, very happy,"* I repeated with every step, lost in a meadow turned forest. *"Now, very happy."*

Sometimes intention counts more than the words. And I was convinced, the moment her answer left her mouth, that that "now" referred to the fleeting instant of finding each other again, to the precise scene of being together, even if it was just five minutes that felt like five hours, or five seconds. Everything happened fast but in slow motion. Do you know what I mean? In the weeks afterward, I turned that "now" over and over, hearing a dozen possible intonations—questioning, affirming. I even thought it might refer more generally to her life in Barcelona, with her family. That idea frightened me, but then I realized I was mistaken. What mattered wasn't whether it meant "now that we're together" or "now with my way of living," but that wherever she was, with whoever she was, she was happy. And if Pauline was happy, I could not wish her anything more. Anything else would have been selfish on my part.

"Now, very happy." Her last words. Today, with her terrible death that will take me months to accept, I know I will live the rest of my days with those three words. Tell me, isn't this something we have to tell? *Are you happy? Now, very happy.* Isn't that the essence of love?

I write to you, Julie, while Schubert's songs play, the ones Pauline and I listened to at my apartment, and listening to them today is unbearable. Schubert wanted to compose love songs and what came out was sad. Now I understand. How long will it take before I can hear our music—Bulgarian love songs—and not want to smash my head against the past? I write with her pipe in front of me, the pipe she smoked. Yes, you read that right: the pipe that one day, suddenly, she wanted to try. You know how alive Pauline was, how open to new experiences. Looking back now, it's as if she knew she had to gather all these experiences, because her body maybe sensed it was in a rush. And time is never wasted.

Life begins, life ends, as I said before. But we are children of what we've loved. And I will carry Pauline with me always. I want nothing more.

Let me speak of Gina. Only a few lines to say that I think about her a lot, though I do not know her. I saw her only in that brief meeting in Girona. As you can imagine, I watched her mother more than I watched her, though the child did seem quick and bright. She really was so wise, the little one, that she did not let go of her mother's hand for a second. I would have done the same. I wouldn't have let her go either. You say her uncle went to fetch her from school to give her the news. What a moment. What an ordeal. In all of this, she's the one that fills me with the most pity. To lose her mother like that, so young, will mark her forever. Sooner or later these things surface. You can't predict how, but they end up breaking through. Even though she doesn't know me at all and has never even heard of me, and it must stay that way, when you see her again, give her the kiss I didn't give her in the bookshop.

You told me you were going down to Barcelona for the funeral and that you'd be there for a few days. So you will read this letter when you have returned to Croissy with your grief. Call me when you and Alain are back home. You, at least, with Alain, your philosopher, you have your questions and answers at hand. In this deep disorientation, I too would need someone to stitch together the few certainties of life. I would like, then, to come and hug you. In days of cold and loneliness, I feel that a tight embrace from you, who loved her like a sister, will do me good. And I would like to ask you what Pauline said exactly when you called her to read my letters. How did she react? What words did she use? I have always wanted to know what effect my written words from the heart had on Pauline. At one point, seeing that she stopped responding, I even began to doubt you had read her my second letter. Now that everything is over, I must ask for your forgiveness, Julie, for having thought badly of you in a moment of blindness. Forgive me for doubting you.

And forgive, too, the length of this letter. It has helped me, I suppose, to vent, to remember, and to cry. I haven't known how to do anything else in the last few hours. I will not apologize for that. I want to believe it is normal. Those of us left behind to turn off the light must harden our hearts, I suppose. Life begins, life ends, *n'est-ce pas*?

With as much shock as affection . . .

With fury and infinite sadness.

Jean-Pierre Zanardi

19

We Have the Words We Deserve

The Vueling plane landed punctually at Orly. The moment Gina set foot in the airport terminal, a little after nine in the morning, she felt a strange pang. Her mother had arrived there in the spring of 1981 for her cousin's wedding, weighed down by two suitcases. Gina was arriving in the autumn, thirty-some years later, with a small carry-on suitcase she hadn't had to check and a cross-body satchel that weighed a ton. Pauline had landed in Paris without knowing that four days awaited her that would change her life. Gina—leather jacket, jeans, boots—arrived with a single mission: to find, meet, and talk to Jean-Pierre Zanardi, gallery owner and author of the three most suffocating love letters she had ever read.

For fifty euros including tip, a taxi took Gina where she asked. Number 44, rue de Seine, on the Rive Gauche. When she got out of the car, she remembered that the early-morning dew near the river in Paris seeps into your bones.

"Are you sure it's here? Rue de Seine?"

"Yes, yes," the driver replied, rolling his window back up before pulling away.

Number 44 on rue de Seine was not the Galerie Anouk. Gina couldn't believe what she was seeing. Jean-Pierre had changed the gallery's name. It now read "Galerie Pauline." It wasn't a mirage. She rubbed her eyes and realized that it was true. If only her mother had known. She slung the bag over her shoulder, grabbed her suitcase, and, performing a gesture she had imagined many times, rang the bell. The lights were on inside, though no one was visible. The sign on the door said they opened Tuesdays at ten, and it was already five past. She rang again, holding her finger there until, from the back of the shop, a woman appeared.

Maybe Jean-Pierre was inside. Maybe the woman approaching the door, dressed head to toe in flamboyant prints, was his new partner. She didn't want to think about it, though he would have had every right. Why name the gallery after her mother?

The woman—around fifty, a colorful sculpture in her own right—turned the key and opened.

"*Bonjour.* Come in."

"Good morning."

"We keep it locked, for security . . ."

"Oh—good morning." Gina stepped inside with her suitcase. "I'm looking for Monsieur Jean-Pierre Zanardi."

"On behalf of?"

Damn. What a question. Gina decided to tell the truth and go straight for it.

"I'm the daughter of a friend of his, from Barcelona, and I've brought him something."

"I'm very sorry, then. Monsieur Jean-Pierre retired a few years ago."

"Oh . . ."

"He transferred the gallery. We had always been drawn to this space, and we were lucky to be the first to make an offer. Would you like to look around? I'm sure you'll like it."

"No need, thank you. Everything's beautiful. The place, the paintings, I can see that. But forgive me, would you know where I might be able to find him?"

"Oh . . . Not in Paris anymore. He went to . . . He said he would retire to . . . Just a moment, please."

She called out to the back. *"Marcel, où est-ce que Monsieur Zanardi est parti vivre?"*

Marcel, dressed like a circus performer to match his wife, emerged from the storeroom and handed her a scrap of paper with Jean-Pierre's new address. Gina left so quickly that she never heard the new owners explain that the only contractual condition Jean-Pierre had imposed on them when selling the gallery was that the name Galerie Pauline be kept forever. Gina rented a car with a full tank, put the suitcase and satchel in the back seat, and headed south. With the help of a Coke and two vending-machine coffees, she reached Capbreton. The seaside town, long emptied of summer visitors, had taken on a ghostly air that didn't trouble her in her distracted state. At five thirty, she climbed a hill at full throttle, curve after curve, toward a lookout with views over the bay and, not far from there, toward Jean-Pierre's address. She parked right in front. She stowed the suitcase out of sight, grabbed her satchel, and entered the grounds. The door was open. No dog came out. It seemed deserted. Only birdsong, from magnolias and cypresses, muffled the sound of the sea, and its heroic crashing against the rocks. The freestanding house had a ground floor and two stories. The windows must have looked out the back, over the water. The main facade was peeling here and there from the damp. *Houses age at the pace of their owners,* Gina thought. The threshold sat one step above the doormat. She stood there decisively, fingers crossed that luck wouldn't pass her by. After so many miles and detours, she was about to come face-to-face with her mother's lover. A black iron hedgehog used for scraping mud off shoes caught her eye. Life hadn't been all flights of fancy for the Frenchman. She took a deep breath and rang the bell. Inside, Jean-Pierre was dozing off with the television on, an episode of *The Sopranos* playing in the background.

"J'arrive!"

He set his pipe down in the ashtray and stood up with some difficulty, leaning his body to the side, pushing with his left hand off the armrest while almost dropping one knee to the floor in a practiced contortion. Once upright, steady thanks to a balance honed by repetition, he took up a cane with a silver handle. He walked toward the door in short steps but with as much momentum as he could muster, deftly nudging aside a few photography books that had collapsed into the hallway.

"I'm coming!" he called again, hoping whoever it was hadn't grown tired of waiting and left. "Who could it be at this hour?"

On the other side of the doorway, Gina pulled her T-shirt down with both hands and adjusted the strap of her oversized satchel. She hated the way it pinched across her chest, a breast on each side. She rang again and, to pass the time, ran her foot over the worn spikes of the hedgehog.

"I'm coming, dammit," he muttered. "Patience."

She heard him right behind the door. She breathed out again. When the door opened, a blade of sunlight shot straight into the hall. They were momentarily dazzled. Before her stood a silver-haired man with healthy skin, standing elegantly with the aid of a cane.

"Jean-Pierre?"

She asked with hope on her lips, certain she had found him. He looked her up and down, narrowed his eyes, and exhaled, as if shedding three decades at once.

"No need to tell me who you are." He smiled. "No need. You're the spitting image of your mother."

"Really?" She couldn't hide her emotion. No one had ever said that to her before, and she felt it at the precise moment she needed it most.

"Come in. *Avanti.* You're Gina . . ."

"Yes. Gina Homs. Pleased to meet you."

She stepped inside, exchanged three kisses with him, and rested her head gently against his chest. He steadied himself and wrapped an arm around her shoulders in a paternal embrace. She felt that he was strong at nearly eighty. He must once have been very handsome. In truth, he still was. She remembered that her cousins had shown her a picture from her Aunt Júlia and Alain's wedding album in which Jean-Pierre appeared. They said, *"Look, this is him."* She, who couldn't quite wrap her head around the idea that the man could have been her mother's lover, had thought him an odd figure, wearing what looked like a baseball-style blazer, with visible seams crudely re-stitched in red thread. According to the calculations she had made on the flight from Barcelona to Paris, he couldn't have been older than in his seventies.

"Come in, please. I don't have much to offer. But we can talk as long as you like. Come in and sit. I'd like to know about you." Flustered by the unexpected visit, he added, "We'll be better back there. What brings you here?"

"Curiosity, I suppose. I don't really know. The desire to meet you." She slipped off the satchel, which was heavy as a mountain, and sat on a chesterfield sofa in the glass-walled room, a huge window over the Atlantic. She understood at once that the tall motorized chair, the one whose back rose and fell and whose footrest slid out, was Jean-Pierre's. "Are you sorry I came?"

"On the contrary. I'm only sorry you're calling me *vous*, as if I were an old man. *Tu*, please . . . *Tu*, please." He let himself drop into the chair as if everything hurt, and set the cane on the floor. "*Tu*, please."

"All right. *Tu*, Jean-Pierre."

"You've come from Barcelona, I imagine? Do you still live there?"

Gina was surprised that Jean-Pierre remembered her name, that he knew where—

"I still live there, yes. But I've just come from Paris. Let's say the clues led me to the wrong place."

"You went to Paris?" He turned off the television with a remote attached to the chair. Tony Soprano had just strangled Ralph Cifaretto on the kitchen floor.

"What do you think? I looked for you. I went to rue de Seine 44, to the Galerie Anouk, and, my first surprise, I see it's called something else now."

"Touché. So I've been caught."

"And now . . ."

"Does it bother you?"

"What? That your gallery has my mother's name? Galerie Pauline. Please."

"It isn't mine anymore."

"They told me."

"I sold it. They kept the name. A sign of good taste." He didn't feel like talking about a closed chapter. "Really, what would you like to drink?"

He pointed her toward the kitchen. Gina went to the fridge for a pitcher of water and brought it back with two glasses. She was parched from the drive. She told him she'd rented a Renault on boulevard Raspail and, hypnotized by the GPS, had reached Capbreton in six hours. She spoke while looking around, left and right, taking in Jean-Pierre's house. Jean-Pierre, on alert, unsure where his visitor might be going with all this, took refuge in his pipe. It appeared that he lived alone. There were no traces of family. It was the house of a sage, or a widower, or someone with taste who lived there year-round. It was not, in any case, a summer house. Neither the house nor the man had been abandoned. They had simply grown old together. There were books everywhere. Gina had never seen so many in one place. The shelves ran from baseboard to ceiling. There were also books of every size and subject piled on tables, and even stacks on the floor, so lopsided they survived only because of the lack of movement. One thing didn't fit. The walls were empty. She did not see a single painting in the whole house. Nowhere. Not one frame. What a surprise. From the chesterfield she still couldn't spot a single one—figurative or abstract—as if all the art had stayed behind in Paris. In front of her, beyond the magnificent bay window, only the autumn blue of the ocean was painted.

"Here. I brought you this." Gina, decided, placed three letters on his knees. "Do you recognize them?"

"You have them?"

"Aunt Julie kept them, in a box. We found them when . . ."

"Oh. Then I'm glad *you* have them. Did you read them?"

"Thirty, forty times."

"Are you joking?"

"It's perfect. I put together the whole story from your three letters. I don't know if there are more."

"Your mother only replied to the first. I have it upstairs. I've read it fifty or sixty times . . ."

"You win," Gina said. They laughed. "I wasn't trying to compete . . ."

"We agreed we'd write as long as she wanted. Do you want to know?"

"Of course." *Why do you think I came?* she thought.

"I sent the letter through Julie, your aunt. She read it to her, I suppose by phone, and if Pauline wanted, she replied directly to me. That was the arrangement. The first letter, she answered, in the heat of the moment. After that, she didn't answer anymore. When a year had passed since we'd met, I wrote again, but there were no more signs of life, and I thought that, for whatever reason, she no longer wanted to continue."

"Can I tell you something?" Gina chose her words carefully. "The second letter, the one that was also in Aunt Julie's box, Julie never even opened it. The envelope was perfectly sealed. It's not that my mother didn't read it. It's that Aunt Julie didn't even open it."

"I understand . . ." He forced himself to be steady. "Pauline must have asked her not to open it, not to read it to her . . ."

"Then why didn't she tear it up or throw it away?"

"I don't know. Maybe because one day, who knows, with time, Pauline would want to read it. But she didn't have time. Or perhaps in case you, later, might want to read it."

"You think?"

"I don't know. But that's how it happened. In the end, we all have the words we deserve."

"Do you want them?" Gina glanced at the letters. "They're yours."

"Thank you, Gina. I know perfectly well what they say. You can keep them . . . I have enough with your mother's."

"The letter you sent Aunt Julie when my mother died is honestly the most tender thing I've ever read, Jean-Pierre."

"It's easy to write passionately when someone you love dies."

He handed the letters back with a polite gesture and took a sip of water. He could have recited word for word the two letters he'd sent Pauline. He remembered nothing of the letter about her death addressed to Julie. He had no desire to. It had been a long time since he'd gulped down an entire glass.

"You know, you asked me earlier what brought me here." Gina got up and continued, her eyes on the horizon. "Deep down, I think it's . . . I don't know . . . the need to know my mother. I don't know who she was, I don't know what she was like. Everyone has their own tragedy. And maybe this is mine. From the letters Aunt Julie kept, I know my mother loved you above everything, and I need you to tell me how she lived, how she felt, how she thought . . ."

"I only knew her for one long weekend." The pipe gave him time to think twice before saying it. "Have you asked your father?"

"Yes."

"And?"

Gina turned so she wouldn't be speaking with her back to him. Some things must be said looking someone in the eye.

"It feels like those four days with you contained more life than ten years with my father."

"I wouldn't get ahead of myself." He bought time, pressing down the tobacco with his little finger. "Your mother loved me, yes. Very much. As much as I loved her. But how do I say this without it sounding like a reproach, because it isn't. Look . . . We never spoke of it, your mother and I, but I've often wondered why we didn't take the step to be together. Why we didn't, if we were dying to."

Now it was Gina's turn to be left with her mouth agape. She began to sense what Jean-Pierre was about to say.

"I had only things to gain. She had things to gain and things to lose."

"But . . ."

"I was single, I lived alone, and I had nothing to lose. She had you. If your mother didn't take that step, let me phrase it this way, it was because of you. I'm sure of it."

"I don't want that burden on my conscience."

"It's not a reproach. Not to you or to Pauline, not at all. I don't want you to misunderstand me. I loved and love Pauline as if we'd lived together from the night we met. But if you wanted to know what your mother was like, the woman who died when you were nine, here is your answer. This was your mother. And you can be very proud."

Jean-Pierre didn't expect Gina not to react after saying that. No cold, no heat. He was surprised to see her bend down silently, take the enormous satchel from beside the chair, and pull out a parcel. The day's surprises weren't over.

"This is for you . . ."

A gift. A book wrapped in marbled paper. For what?

"You shouldn't have," he said, careful not to tear the sticker from a Venetian bookshop.

"I knew you wouldn't have this one . . ." She settled back into the chesterfield. "Though it's not as if you lack any books here . . ."

"Everyone has a hobby. Someone said we are what we've lived, but we are also the books we've read. And sometimes the ones we've only leafed through, because you can't read everything. We would need three lives to read it all. I claim the right to skip pages."

He unwrapped it with clumsy hands, trying not to rip the glossy paper.

"Ah. *Atlas di Farfalle del Mondo.* Wonderful. Thank you very much."

"You'll immediately say you already have it, or you have it in another language . . ."

"No, no, not at all," he lied, the way only the French and salesmen can lie.

"I'm sure you have it," Gina said. "But I don't care. I'm sure you don't have exactly"—she emphasized the next words—"*this copy.* There's a mystery hidden in it, and you have to give me two minutes to explain."

"Whatever you like. We're in no hurry, are we?"

"Do you know what my mother did in the last year before she died?"

Jean-Pierre stopped looking through the book and looked up to listen. For decades he'd asked himself that same question.

"My mother dedicated herself to traveling. More than a year. With my father or without him, she'd get on a plane to go and visit bookshops. If my father went for work, fine. If not, she went straight ahead alone, because my father never liked flying. I was very small, so I stayed home with Isabel, the maid, the caregiver, I don't know what you call her here. My mother went, as if taking inventory, to what she believed were the ten best bookshops in the world. We know she was in Glasgow, Buenos Aires, Boston, London, Venice, and who knows where else. She collected bookshops, but she came back without books. How is that possible? Why did she go? Why did she come back with her hands in her pockets?" Jean-Pierre listened, his eyes wide as saucers, as Gina continued, carried away. "It took me a long time to figure it out. I had to travel too, and I spoke to a contact in London, to find out, and in the end I did. This is not just any book. It's not just another butterfly book. I found it at Acqua Alta in Venice, a secondhand bookshop. Do you know it?"

"Yes, yes . . ." He was transfixed by the story.

"My mother went to all those bookshops with a single objective. She looked for butterfly books and, inside, secretly, without anyone seeing her, she left one of her business cards. A personal calling card. From our home."

He was silent. His eyes teared up.

"In some places she wrote 'Call me' in her handwriting. In others she wrote nothing, just the card with her name, address, and telephone. And so, one by one, book by book, shop by shop, she placed her cards in the butterfly books of the world's great bookshops. Why did my mother do that?"

"I can't believe it . . ."

"To send you signs. To say to you: 'Hello, my love, I'm here and I'm thinking of you.' To surprise you. To prove her love."

"My God . . ." He wiped his eyes with both hands. "My God, Pauline."

"Did you never find one?"

He shook his head like a child furious about a punctured ball.

"Even today, surely, there are books out in the world with my mother's cards inside. She knew you traveled everywhere to find and buy rare butterfly books, and she had the secret hope that one day, in some secondhand bookshop, in some corner of the world, you would open a book to any page at all and discover that she had performed magic."

"That is . . ." He was astonished, stunned, shaken. ". . . Magnificent."

"I bought this one for you in Venice. You can't imagine how my heart jumped when I picked up the book, ran my fingers through it like this, and the proof of my mother's love fell out. If it made *me* that happy . . ."

Jean-Pierre hurried to turn the atlas upside down so the message from his beloved Pauline would drop into his lap. A proof of love. He cried and laughed at the same time. He would have felt ridiculous with anyone else there, but not with Gina, Pauline's daughter. Not in that moment, which justified an entire life.

"I thought I had to buy it and bring it to you."

"Look." The card fell from the atlas and fluttered in a zigzag, like a butterfly, onto his lap. He couldn't stop laughing, his cheeks still wet with tears. "How did you ever think of such a thing? How did you ever think of it, my dearest, most beloved Pauline?"

Silence arrived all at once in Capbreton. Biting her lip, her eyes blurred with emotion, Gina respected Jean-Pierre's nostalgia. With the book open on his lap and Pauline's card in his hands, he seemed transported back to those four spring days that had made all his barriers collapse. *You saved my life,* he wrote in one letter. Gina began to understand how her mother could have fallen in love with this sensitive and cultured man, who still carried charm in every wrinkle.

Twenty minutes later—facing each other without a word, understanding everything—Jean-Pierre closed the atlas and slipped the card inside with exquisite care, as if it were a sacred marker. He set it on the small table and picked up a black leather pouch with a zipper.

"Will you stay a few days?" he asked, already beginning to tease the tobacco loose with his fingers.

"Tomorrow I have to return the car at Bordeaux airport."

"Stay and talk. Until next week. I have tickets to go to Inverness before the real cold begins. You can stay here. Or do you have family waiting for you?"

"Me? No. And now . . . who would I be with? I haven't had the luck to find someone like you."

"Of course you have. Don't fool yourself."

"No, no . . . I'm telling you, I haven't. You only have to read the letters to know my mother knew true love. It's magnificent. Hats off to her, hats off to you two. Me, on the other hand, I feel like I'll reach forty and, yes, I've had a great time, I've laughed a lot, I've gone here and there, but it's all been, how do I put it . . . light?"

"Banal?"

"Yes. Maybe. There's never any commitment, I think. All of us, for me just as much as them, I mean everyone, it's nobody's fault. We've always kept the barriers down so the train could pass and we wouldn't get hurt. Light, banal. Skeptical about love, I'd say, as if love were an old-fashioned coat. And you, on the other hand, you knew a woman for four or five days and you've lived more than thirty years without her but with an intensity I envy."

Jean-Pierre had the sense that for the first time since she'd walked through the door, that confident, decisive Gina was about to fall apart. He decided to shake her awake.

"You came here, you say, to know more about your mother. And I tell you she was happy because she loved. You yourself have brought me proof. So I wonder: What about you? Are *you* happy? Are you feeling it? Why don't you allow it? You're not even forty, Gina. What are you waiting for? Go out and let go. Love, love for real. Love even if it ends, even if it isn't forever. So what? How many people have you met who have never suffered because they have never loved?"

"People of my generation? Many. I don't know how many, but many. I'm not the only one. We wear armor because we don't want to suffer, and we settle for crumbs. Sex is fun, yes, very. It's pleasurable, it's exciting, it's everything for an hour, or fifteen minutes, but maybe it isn't the point. Maybe it isn't enough. Maybe it's fear. Maybe it's selfishness. I don't know what it is, but when I think about it and I realize it, I think: What the hell am I doing?"

"Then don't stop at the anecdote. Make use of the era you've been given. You have the luck, the immense fortune, of living in a time when society doesn't judge you, when there are no rules, when everyone lives with whoever they want, when you don't have to tolerate the other person if you don't like them enough. You have the gift of history. You have conditions that should make it easier. And yet, when anyone tells you you have it better than at any other point in human history, it seems precisely that lack of limits that holds you back, that slows you down."

"Yes, yes, maybe." She hadn't expected Jean-Pierre to speak with such vehemence. She defended herself: "But all that, the clarity you have now, you see it when you're older, when you have whole days to take stock of how your story turned out."

"It has nothing to do with age, Gina. I'm talking about commitment. You've confused love with American romantic comedies. Love isn't a Meg Ryan movie. Movies, fairy tales, they've done you a lot of harm. I don't know what you're looking for. If you want to be loved, love. Love exists. Love exists, but you have to go all in. All in!"

Gina nodded, up and down, more out of reflex than agreement. Jean-Pierre realized he'd gone too far in tone and took a breath to come down.

"Forgive me, Gina. I don't know anything about your life. I wish everyone could have a story like ours, mine and your mother's. Of course I do. However it may have ended. I do. When it comes to you, you'll know it. Don't be afraid, dive in. But you have to want happiness, and you have to work for it. Give yourself a chance to love. Let love shake you. Do you hear me?"

She closed her eyes to agree. He wondered if it was even appropriate to speak that way to someone he had just met.

"And that's enough. I won't say anything else. And forgive me for preaching, for putting my nose where I—"

"Not at all, Jean-Pierre. I liked hearing it. I liked slipping into my mother's skin and hearing you."

"I'm not used to speaking to anyone, and the one day I have an audience . . ."

"Can I ask you something?"

"I'm not sure I'm in a position to say no . . ."

"I'd really like you to tell me, everything that you can tell, of course, what happened in Paris between you, from Aunt Julie's wedding until you took her to the airport. What happened in those four days to make a bond so strong, forever."

He didn't dislike the idea. To remember was to relive. But—

"One day I promised your mother I wouldn't make a book of it."

"The statute of limitations has run out, Jean-Pierre."

Having Gina in front of him felt like hearing Pauline. They knew how to get what they wanted. Seduction, it was called.

"There's no crime. Love is never punishment, never a sentence. And now you'll think this old man has lost his mind, but sometimes I've wondered whether all this should be written down and known. You could write it, the book. A novel about happiness."

"And?" She was confident, already certain she'd get her way.

"We'll have dinner and I'll tell you. In the basement downstairs I have a truffled Brie de Meaux, and we'll find some wine, I suppose, that you will like. We'll eat, and I'll tell you everything, yes. I'll be delighted."

"Perfect!"

"First, I ask you one favor . . ."

Gina nodded, *bien sûr*, he could count on her. She agreed without conditions.

"Come with me."

Jean-Pierre rose from the chair with practiced mechanics, as if nothing hurt. He bravely refused to take the cane. He needed to appear in good form before Pauline's daughter, as if the visit had miraculously invigorated him. In the end it was vanity, the pride of coquetry.

Slow as an ox, with Gina watching wide-eyed, they crossed the corridor, passed the front door, and reached his bedroom. The bed was made, the coverlet smooth, clothes hung in the wardrobe arranged by color, the whole room neat as a hotel rented by the hour.

"I don't have a gift for you. I didn't expect you . . ." He pointed at the dresser. "But I'd like you to keep something."

On top of an English antique secretary were three black-and-white landscape photos, each mounted and framed. In all three she recognized at a glance Pauline and Jean-Pierre at their best.

"You've never seen this. A first time."

"Never!" Enthralled, she bent her knees to get closer. "My mother was radiant!"

"She was beautiful. This one was taken by a waiter at Brasserie Lipp after dinner." He spoke with the manners of a dignified man. "Your mother never got to see them. I had them developed the very day she left. I couldn't send them to her, of course."

"And this?" The lovers were laughing face-to-face, coffees on the table, in a leafy terrace.

"Below my place. One afternoon, on rue du Trésor. I lived two doors down. At ground zero." He surprised himself with the sarcasm. "The dangers of love."

"She looks so happy." Gina thought that yes, now that she was older than her mother had been, she resembled her a great deal. "I love seeing these photos, Jean-Pierre, but when I have her right in front of me, it makes me furious not to remember my mother with a laugh like that. Do you know what I mean? It makes me angry not to remember her. Not knowing what her voice sounded like—"

"Exactly like yours. The voice. You have it exactly. I assure you. And this one"—he picked up the third photo. "You know where it's from. No need to say anything, right?"

A group of laughing friends, perhaps twenty of them, with the newlyweds, Aunt Julie and Alain, in the middle, and Pauline, elegant as an actress, at one end in her blue dress. And four heads away, Jean-Pierre, seductive, proud in his white artist's blazer, pipe attached, the night they met. Gina adored old photographs. The more people, the better. She studied faces, imagined lives, and always thought the same thing. They're all dead. In that photo, not all. Her mother and Aunt Julie were, yes. Someone else surely too. Jean-Pierre himself looked like a resurrected man.

"Take them into the living room. We can't see them here very well." He turned off the light. "I have to put in stronger bulbs."

They shut the bedroom door, retraced their steps, and sat again with the Atlantic at their feet, with an irrepressible desire to talk and listen. The Brie waited in the basement at room temperature. Jean-Pierre, attentive to detail, began his account with the wedding night. Gina discovered not only that her mother was a graceful rock-and-roll dancer, that she was fascinated by mentalism, that she could guess exactly how many steps lay between two Parisian churches. She also understood why Pauline had fallen for that gallery owner who, from certain angles, seemed to resemble Marcello Mastroianni to her in his final years.

Darkness fell. Little by little the sun set over the glass room. It was the artwork Jean-Pierre contemplated each evening. That sunset, however, he didn't notice the ocean fading or the final setting of light. Absorbed in the story, they missed every reddish stroke of dusk. So long as fate allowed him, he was grateful that nature framed, day after day, the last drops of honey in the bay window of his life.

About the Author

Photo © Umami Brands

Xavier Bosch is a celebrated Catalan-Spanish writer born in Barcelona. The author of ten novels and two short-story collections, Bosch has been honored with bestselling book of the year six separate times in his home country of Spain. He's also won two of the most prestigious prizes in Catalan literature: the Sant Jordi Award (2009) and the Ramon Llull Award (2015). His novel *Algú com tu* has been translated into seven languages.

In addition to his creative writing work, Bosch is a respected journalist with a long and storied career. He has starred on radio and television, created several successful audiovisual formats, and worked as a newspaper editor. A sports specialist, Bosch is one of the most influential writers on FC Barcelona. The author has also directed two documentaries on classical music and serves as a full member of the Acadèmia de la Llengua Catalana. For more information, please visit http://www.xavierbosch.com.

About the Author

About the Translator

Samantha Mateo is a translator from Chicago. She holds an MA in humanities from the University of Chicago, where she specialized in Catalan and translation studies, and a BA in linguistics from Columbia University. She currently works in academic publishing. In 2022, Samantha was an American Literary Translators Association (ALTA) Emerging Translator mentee for Catalan. Her translations have appeared in the *Denver Quarterly* literary journal and *Granta* magazine.